Praise for Zane and Addicted

"Snatched me up from the first page and didn't let me go until the end. A great read!"

—Margaret Johnson-Hodge, author of *Butterscotch Blues*

"Hot! Sensational! This is one you won't be able to put down!"

—Franklin White, author of *Fed Up with the Fanny* and *Cup of Love*

"Erotic and well-written, *Addicted* sizzles and satisfies. Zane has managed to pen a novel that expertly portrays both romantic and earthly love and does more than simple justice to each."

—Karen E. Quinones Miller, author of *Satin Doll*

Praise for Zane and Shame on It All

"At a time when much of African-American fiction has fallen into formulas and mediocrity, Zane has lifted the bar of literary standards again with this insightful, often hilarious work, which showcases her talent for satire, irony, penetrating analysis and downright hijinks. The sista can write! This book is a complete departure from her earlier efforts and one that should bring her the notoriety she so deserves. If you loved *Addicted,* then *Shame on It All* will give you a whole different view of this woman's immense talent."

—Robert Fleming, author of *Wisdom of the Elders* and *The African American Writer's Handbook*

"Zane has done it again. *Shame on It All* is well-crafted and fast paced with just enough drama to keep you talking to yourself."

—Carl Weber, author of *Lookin' for Luv* and *Married Men*

Books by Zane

Addicted
Shame on It All
The Heat Seekers
The Sex Chronicles: Shattering the Myth
Gettin' Buck Wild: Sex Chronicles II
The Sisters of APF: The Indoctrination of Soror Ride Dick
Nervous
Skyscraper
Afterburn

Edited by Zane

Chocolate Flava: The Eroticanoir.com Anthology

The
Sex Chronicles

Shattering the Myth

Zane

ATRIA BOOKS

New York London Toronto Sydney

ATRIA BOOKS

1230 Avenue of the Americas
New York, NY 10020

Originally published by Strebor Books International LLC

ISBN: 0-7434-6270-X

First Atria Books trade paperback printing February 2003

20 19 18 17 16 15 14 13 12

ATRIA BOOKS is a trademark of Simon & Schuster, Inc.

Manufactured in the United States of America

For information regarding special discounts for bulk purchases, please contact Simon & Schuster Special Sales at 1-800-456-6798 or business@simonandschuster.com

Dedicated to all of the
sexually uninhibited women in the world
that are sick of being judged.
People always lash out at that which
they don't understand. Do not allow their
fears to dictate the choices you make in your life.
If we can free our bodies, then we can
also free our minds.

Caution!!:

If you are sexually repressed, sexually oppressed,
or have any other sexual hang-ups, please put my
book down now and walk away from it because
The Sex Chronicles
is just too damn *hot* for your ass.

Disclaimer:

Because I know the drama is going to come, let me say this
now. I am in no way trying to promote promiscuity, the
spreading of disease, or extramarital affairs. However, I am
trying to promote healthy, uninhibited, satisfying sexual experiences for those women that are tired of disappointing sex.
Sex was here for thousands of years before I started writing
erotica, and it will be here for thousands of years after I am
gone. This book is a work of fiction and should be treated as
such. With that said, I hope you enjoy the book.

Peace,
Zane

Contents

Acknowledgments   xi

Wild

First Night   3
Sock It to Me   10
Be My Valentine   19
The Interstate   26
The Godfather   32
The Barbershop   39
If You Were Here Right Now   48
The Airport   53
The Diary   59
The Seduction   69

Wilder

Nervous   77
Wrong Number   84
A Flash Fantasy   91
A Time for Change   99

Get Well Soon   106
Dinner at Eight   111
Animal Farm   116
Harlem Blues   122
Lust in a Bus Depot   127
The Bachelorette Party   135
Sweet Revenge   144
Blind Date   149
Vacation of a Lifetime   158
Mailman   166
Body Chemistry 101   174

Off Da Damn Hook

Alpha Phi Fuckem   180
Room 69   188
The Cat Burglar   198
My Knight in Shining Armor   207
Valley of the Freaks   219
Stakeout   226
Masquerade   236
Wanna Watch?   246
Nymph   251
Kissin' Cousins   261
The Voyeur   268
Sex Me Down Village   275
Dream Merchant   283
The Pussy Bandit   289
Alpha Phi Fuckem—The Convention   296

A Personal Reflection from Zane   305

Acknowledgments

I wrote my first erotic story in November 1997 and never intended for more than two or three people to ever read it. The exact opposite happened. *Everybody read it!* Before I knew it, I began to receive numerous e-mails from people wondering if I had written anything else. Within a few days, I completed three other stories and placed them all on the Web. Within three weeks after that, my site had accumulated more than eight thousand hits. Needless to say, I was shocked.

While writing runs in my family and over the years people have always encouraged me to put my creativity to use, I had never once thought about writing erotica. I had never even read any erotica. All of a sudden, I had a long mailing list followed by a monthly newsletter.

People e-mailed me and said, "Why don't you write a book?" I said to myself, "Why not?" Three months later, I had written more than fifty erotic tales. Thus, *The Sex Chronicles*. The reasons I chose *Shattering the Myth* as the subtitle are too numerous to mention, but I'm sure you can figure it out. I have faith in you. I never knew that so many people had sexual hang-ups, that so many people would try to tell adults what they should and should not read, what they should and should not write, what they should and should not do in the privacy of their own homes. Once a person becomes an adult, she should be able to do whatever she wants as long as it is not illegal and does not harm or infringe on the rights of someone else.

Even though you would think the above statement would be common sense, you would be surprised at the e-mails I get from people, saying things like, "Why are you wasting your talent on this filth?" "You must sit around doing nothing but having sex!" and "People would never buy this kind of work. You need to conform and write a black romance novel or one of those sistahgurl books."

All I can say is this: If you don't like my work, then why are you reading it?

Basically, I let the one or two negative e-mails out of three thousand get to me at first but not anymore. Forget them! I write erotica for the thousands of people that do want to read it. Is erotica the only thing I will ever write? Absolutely not! I have already completed three novels and have four others in progress. I just love to write, period. I will be the first to admit that none of my novels are what one would consider mainstream. They are controversial. I intentionally made them that way. I want people to finish one of my novels, put it down, and say "Dammmmmmmn!"

Addicted is a murder mystery, *Shame on It All* is a sistahgurl novel, and *The Heat Seekers* is indeed a black romance, but they all have chutzpah! Bottom line, as long as people will read my work, I will continue to write it. For those of you that tried to stop this and yet are sitting here reading every word I write as usual, please don't step to me with your judgments. I would appreciate you not wasting your time or mine. For my loyal readers, I love each and every one of you, no matter what your race, no matter what your sexual persuasion. Making love is universal.

While I cannot even begin to acknowledge every single person that has continuously encouraged me and shown undying support, there are a few people that I must recognize. First and foremost, I would like to thank my children for coming into this world through my body, for loving me unconditionally, for inspiring me to make something out of my life, and for always making me laugh when I am feeling down. I would like to thank my parents for being understanding and supportive when I still wasn't quite sure what I wanted to do with my life. Without them, I would not be here on this earth. I am just thankful that they gave me emotional and financial support and stood by me no matter what. I would like to thank my two sisters for giving me a shoulder to cry on, an ear to talk into, and examples to follow since I am the youngest. I am very lucky to come from an extremely close-knit family and to have a huge extended family that sticks together even through the darkest of times.

I would definitely like to thank Shonda Cheekes, my publicist, and Pamela Crockett and Michelle Askew, my entertainment attorneys, for giving me that extra little push I needed when I was in the trenches, for letting me vent my frustrations in their direction when the negativity started from those people who *claim* they never judge people. Yet they decided to not only judge me but to crucify me as well.

A special thank-you to all the people on the Black Erotica message boards, to all the people in the Net Noir and Black Voices book chat rooms, and to all the people that have spread my work around and forwarded my newsletters and links to all three or four hundred people at their jobs.

Last but definitely not least, I would like to express my heartfelt thanks and appreciation to the thousands of people on my mailing list. I cannot tell you how much all of it means to me. Signing on at night and finding anywhere from fifty to three hundred e-mails in my in box from just one day provides me with the strength I need to carry on. This book is for all of you. I hope that everyone enjoys this book, but you have to be able to open up your mind before you can. I must caution you that I have an *extremely* vivid and sometimes even sick imagination. If you think you can hang, then turn the page. You can't say I didn't warn you.

With that said . . .

Welcome to

The Sex Chronicles

Shattering the Myth

Peace and much love,

Zane

First Night

We ride up the coast to Maine on your brand-new motorcycle and stop for the night at a cozy, secluded bed and breakfast inn. They show us to our room. It is very romantic, with a fireplace and antique Victorian furniture. Beside the sofa is a round little table with a white linen tablecloth and burning white candles. Our room also has a huge, king-size bed on a riser with two steps leading up to it. The bed has large fluffy pillows, crisp white sheets, and a huge down comforter.

As they deliver our dinner to our room, we can see that it is beginning to rain through the large, picturesque windows. The room has a balcony. We open the French doors so we can hear the raindrops and feel the cool breeze as it enters the room. We sit down at the dinner table and begin to sip on the Dom Perignon while we eat the tender steak, baked potatoes, carrots, and oven-fresh rolls we ordered for dinner.

After dinner, we take the throw blanket that is sprawled across the sofa and lay it out on the floor by the fireplace. We continue to drink the champagne and toast each other as we watch the embers glisten in the fire and listen to the rain.

We feed each other fresh strawberries dipped in chocolate and discuss the drive up. Then you take my hand and lead me out onto the covered balcony. We can feel raindrops trickle across our skin. You kiss me, and our tongues intertwine as we begin to kiss deep and passionately. You go back inside the room for a moment, returning with an empty bottle that previously contained the Perrier springwater we drank on the bike on the way up. You set it on the edge of the balcony, with the lid off, and little raindrops begin to fall into it. You look me in my eyes and tell me you are going to collect the raindrops in the bottle and save them as a remembrance of the night we first made love.

I run my fingers across your cheeks and then take your hand and begin to suck your fingers, putting each one entirely into my mouth and sucking it gently. You pick me up. I wrap my legs around your waist, and you hold me up against the wall on the rear of the balcony. We begin to kiss again, but deeper this time, as I caress the back of your head and run my fingernails down the center of your back, tickling your spine through your shirt.

The black skintight dress that I changed into for dinner and your white shirt and black trousers begin to get damp from the rain. You can see my hard nipples protruding from the top of my revealing dress. You pull the shoulder straps of my dress down and begin to suck on my left nipple and palm my right breast in your hand, rubbing your thumb across my nipple. You begin to grind your hips between my legs, and I can feel your hard dick applying pressure to my pussy. I begin to gyrate my hips on top of your dick through your pants.

You let me down gently back onto the balcony and turn me around with my face against the wall. You reach around me and grab my nipples, pinching them, and I begin to moan. I turn my head to the side to meet your tongue. We kiss again as your left hand reaches down between my thighs and begins to finger my pussy, pushing my panties to the side. I hold one of my hands up over my shoulder and grab the back of your neck, pulling your tongue closer into my mouth as I grind my pussy onto your fingers. You now have two of them inside of me.

You pull away from me and then kneel down, push the bottom of my dress up over my hips to my waist, and then rip my hunter green satin thong bikinis off. You grab my ass cheeks firmly and bite each one of them softly. You suckle on them hard until I have hickey marks on each one of them. I squirm a little from the pain as you bury your face in between my legs from behind. I arch my back, pushing my ass farther toward you. You begin to suck on my clit from behind, my ass all in your face. You begin finger-fucking my ass while I grind my pussy and ass all onto your face and tongue. I begin to moan uncontrollably, and you say "Ummmm" as you devour my pussy juices and finger my ass.

After a few more minutes of this, you stand back up, and I turn around. You pick me up, and I straddle my legs around your waist again. We begin to kiss as you carry me inside, walk up the two steps on the riser, and lay me softly on the comfortable bed.

I watch as the lightning from the storm seems to track on all the high round parts of your body. I cannot ever remember feeling more desire than at this moment. I lean toward you and gently feel your lips touch mine. Oh, how soft they feel. I could never dream of a more sensual moment.

With fire in my soul, I seemingly lick the honey from your lips as our kiss begins. Deeper and deeper, I am drawn into you as I continue to lick the sweetness from your lips. I begin to softly suckle on your bottom lip for the life-giving energy of your soul. My desire grows even more intense as your hand caresses my back and the nape of my neck.

You kneel over me on the bed and slowly take your shirt off, letting it fall silently to the floor. You reach through the darkness to feel the smooth surface of my skin. Gently, you massage my shoulders as you lower the straps of my dress. Soon the wonder of my exposed, hardened nipples and firm breasts fills your eyes.

I pull my arms from the straps and knowingly touch you where you need to be touched the most, caressing your dick through the pants you are still wearing.

I kiss you again with a passion full of fire. You cannot hold yourself back any longer as you grab my breasts and massage my tender nipples under your thumbs. How soft they feel under your touch! With each stroke, I can feel my desire rising. You reach with an open mouth to take my breast in. You lick the tip of my left nipple just to taste the sweetness of me. Slowly, you close your lips to encompass my sweet dark pearl. You suck for moments that seem to last an eternity. Then you bite gently into my tender fruit, pulling a little more with each increasing bite.

You stop for a moment, lifting your lips from my nipple. You watch as my nipple shivers in the air. You blow a gentle puff of air to dry the moisture from me and watch as my hardened nipple grows even more impressive.

You lick a soft trail down to my belly button, kissing my skin gently with each pause. You pull the rest of my dress off to reveal all of my smooth, flawless body.

You take my right foot into your hand and begin to suckle on my pretty, polished toes as I take the toes on my left foot and caress your dick with them. I cannot control my desire any longer. I sit up on the edge of the bed where you are standing, anxiously undo your belt buckle, and unzip your pants. You help me slide your pants and satin boxer shorts completely off, and you kick them aside.

I take in your beautiful, scrumptious-looking dick with my eyes, biting on my bottom lip in anticipation of the tremendous amount of delight it will bring me. Gently, I take it into my hands and massage it up and down the shaft with one hand and caress your balls lightly with the other.

I want so badly to partake of your splendid nectar. I take the tip of my tongue and lick the head of your dick straight down the middle, immediately tasting your delicious precum. I want some more, lots more, so I take the head of your dick into my mouth and suckle on it, contracting my cheek muscles in and out as I attempt to draw every single drop of precum that exists onto my awaiting taste buds.

The intensity grows as you begin to feed me your dick, gliding more and more of it into my mouth each time you direct it in and out. I moan with delight as your dick fills my throat. My own saliva begins to trickle out the sides of my mouth onto my erect nipples. I arch my neck so that I can deep-throat your entire dick. I can feel the head of it hitting up against my tonsils while your balls slam up against my chin. You taste so delicious, it's almost scary. I never knew a man's dick could be so delectable.

We are lost in time as you stand there feeding me your dick for moments on end. Even though I begin to gag on it at times, I gladly continue to suckle on it without hesitation. You tell me you don't want to cum yet, and you glide it slowly out of my mouth. I still want to partake of it, so I lick around the shaft with the tip of my tongue in long, circular strokes. Then I go underneath your dick and tickle your balls with the tip of my tongue. You moan a little and run your fingers through my hair while I take your ball sack gently into my mouth and bounce it around on my tongue. I am like a kid in a candy store, wanting to taste a little of everything.

I start to flicker my tongue at your belly button as you stand in front of me. I move my tongue up the center of your stomach as I get on my knees on the bed so that I can bite

gently on your nipples. Then, you lift my chin up so I am looking deeply into your soft bedroom eyes, and you begin to
tongue-kiss me with an intensity I have never known. My pussy
is so wet! I can feel drops of my own juice running down the
center of my thighs as the rain continues outside and the cool
breeze invades our private haven through the open patio doors.

You take me by the hand and lead me over to the table with
the linen cloth where we had shared our romantic meal. You
tell me to lie down on the table as you sit in a chair directly in
between my legs. I oblige and you anxiously begin to suck on
my throbbing clit. It is covered with my juices by this point.
You hold my thighs open with your hands and use your fingers
to hold the lips of my pussy open so that you can partake of my
sweet pearl. I moan as I lose control of my body, surrendering
myself to you completely. I feel your tongue direct its way into
my throbbing pussy walls. You stick a finger into my ass and
begin to finger-fuck it while you tongue-fuck my pussy. I grind
my pussy up into your face and begin to cum. I can feel you
sucking all of it out of my pussy. After a few more moments of
concentrating solely on my pussy, I can feel you lapping up all
the juices that have trickled down my thighs earlier, as if to
make sure you let not one drop of my sweetness go to waste.

You stand up between my legs and ask me if I am ready to
feel you inside of me. I tell you I want nothing more. You stick
the fingers of one hand into my mouth. I begin to suck on
them as your other hand is still busy fingering my ass. As I lay
there looking up at you, suckling on your fingertips, I see you
lean forward and feel the head of your dick opening my pussy.
You glide it in, and I arch my back, pushing my pussy farther
onto the edge of the table and onto your dick. You glide your
dick in and out of my hot, contracting pussy, making me take a
little more of it each time it invades my sugar walls. Our

moans are in unison now as we both take pleasure in our bodies melting together.

You fuck me harder and harder until I can feel your balls slamming up against my ass. I can feel myself climax again, and I let out a low scream. I caress my nipples with one hand and grab you by the back of your neck with the other, making you bring your dick deeper into me.

You lift me up gently, your dick still buried deep inside me, and carry me back over to the bed. You press my legs over my shoulders, using your chest to hold them in place, and begin to fuck me with no mercy. I cannot take it. I grab onto the headboard trying to pull away as you pound your dick deeper and deeper into me. I can feel the head of your dick inside my stomach. It is a confusing mixture of pain and pleasure, but I want it all. I want you to tear my pussy up, fuck me like I have never imagined, so I take it and I cum over and over again. Orgasm on top of orgasm.

Time loses all meaning. We continue to fuck for what seems like hours on end. Long after the rain has stopped and our Perrier bottle is filled with memories of our first night together, as the sun begins to fight its way over the horizon, you are still fucking me.

I bury my head sideways into a pillow while you hold onto my ass cheeks, one in each hand, and pump your dick in and out of my pussy from behind. As cum trickles down the inside of my thighs onto the sheets below, I silently hope to myself that it never ends.

Sock It to Me

Have you ever seen a man whose body just looked like the words F-U-C-K M-E spelled out? If not, then you've never been inside Lou's Gym in Washington, D.C., and laid eyes on Geren Stevenson, also known to me alone, as Mr. All That. What can I say, ladies, except he is all the things any red-blooded woman's dreams are made of rolled up into one. When you look at him, you can't help but want to lick him all over like a lollipop.

My uncle Lou owns the gym. I worked there in the evenings, doing mostly nothing. I did close up nights because my aunt Geraldine liked Uncle Lou to be home in time for dinner. She's one of those old-fashioned, big-boned women who believes she needs to cook soul food every night. Thus, Uncle Lou rushed out of there no later than six every evening to go chow down on his fried chicken, collard greens, and sweet potatoes or whatever his woman had slaved over the hot stove preparing all day.

Geren came in five nights a week, Monday through Friday, like clockwork. He came in straight after work and arrived about seven. I didn't close the gym up until ten, so that gave me plenty of time to watch him work his ass. He was about six feet tall, around 200 pounds of solid muscle, as deep chocolate as it gets. Like the old adage says, The darker the berry, the sweeter the juice. He had a bald head, a beautiful smile, and dark bed-room eyes. His skin was as smooth as a baby's ass all over. Simply put, I was hopelessly head-over-heels in love with him.

Geren was an accountant by day and an amateur boxer by night, a heavyweight. He would come in to work out with his trainer, Willy, and his sparring partner. I loved to watch him. The way he pounced around the ring, the way the muscles in his arms contracted as he swung them back and forth, the way he bobbed his head from side to side so he wouldn't get knocked the hell out. I even loved the way he smelled. He always smelled like heaven to me. Most men have that au naturel smell after working out, but not Geren. I would have licked his ass dry, sweat and all.

Unfortunately, I was not the type of woman Geren was attracted to. He had all these tall, beautiful, sexy, big-tit women in nice clothes and lots of makeup coming in there looking for him all the time. The kind of women who wouldn't even walk to the corner store until the hair, nails, and face were done. They were all in their early to mid-twenties.

On the other hand, there was me. Only eighteen, five years younger than him, flat-chested, and barely pushing 100 pounds soaking wet. I was taking some courses at the local community college after barely making it through high school academically. My uncle Lou was kind enough to kick me some money for working for him, but he wasn't paying me much of anything. My future was looking pretty dismal at the time, and my love life wasn't looking any better. I was a big-time tomboy, always in sweats or baggy jeans, but after all, who needs to dress up to work behind the front desk at a gym and hand out towels? My hair was cut real short, and my nails were stubs since I used to bite them all the time because of nervous energy.

I had only been with two men, the boy I lost my virginity to in the ninth grade and my high school sweetheart. He ended up going away to another state for college. Geren was my dream lover, but there was no way he would wanna get freaky with the likes of me.

Then, the big snowstorm of '92 changed my life. It was one of the worst snowstorms in Washington, D.C., history. The cars were covered completely with snow and ice, people were ice-skating down the street in front of the White House, and even the entire federal government was shut down. Even though it was a horrible day weatherwise, it turned out to be the luckiest day of my life.

Why? For the first time, Geren and I were completely alone in the gym. I told Uncle Lou I would stay and keep the gym open because I walked home anyway. The small, cozy flat I shared with my mother was only about three blocks away, but Uncle Lou and Aunt Geraldine lived on the other side of town. They did the Jefferson thing, you know? Started a successful business and did the *moving on up* scenario.

Geren was working out on a punching bag. He also lived within walking distance, so it was all good. He was alone. His trainer couldn't make it in because of the snow. There had been a few other stragglers, but they all left about 8 P.M., an hour earlier. I was pretending to watch an old rerun of *Sanford and Son* on the time-weathered, black-and-white television Uncle Lou picked up at a pawnshop. The picture was barely visible, and there was a clothes hanger where the broken-off antenna used to be. I was not really watching it anyway. I was too busy watching Geren out the corner of my eye.

He was beating the hell out of that punching bag. I remember thinking how sorry I would feel for a man who pissed him off in a dark alley. He finished up his workout by jumping some rope. I could envision his dick bouncing up and down in his jock strap and trunks. My pussy was so wet.

Then, he asked me what was up and I freaked. I said the typical D.C. answer of the '90s, "Just chillin'." I freaked, because that was the first time he had ever said anything to me. In all the time he had been coming in there, he never said a word to me. He would walk up to the front desk from time to time, I would hand him a towel, he would smile, and that was it. I guess he felt he should say something to me, since we were the only two people there that night. Little did he realize, he had just made my fucking decade.

I almost creamed on myself when he started wiping the sweat off his body with a towel and then started guzzling down a bottle of ice-cold Gatorade. He reminded me of one of those Diet Coke commercials where all the women in this office are waiting anxiously for the soda delivery man to come in and guzzle down a soda so they can cum all over themselves. I wondered how many panties would get wet if those same women were there at that very moment watching Geren guzzle. I seriously doubted there would have been a pair of dry panties in the house.

He started walking toward me, with his boxing gloves tied together by the strings and hanging around his neck, bouncing around on his six-pack stomach. I panicked. Why, I'm not sure, but I just did. I started to hand him a fresh towel, figuring he would get the towel and hit the showers as usual. He didn't. Instead, he leaned on the counter and started a conversation with me. He was so fucking fine, I wanted to just reach over, grab him by the neck, and bury my tongue in his mouth. Somehow, I managed to control myself. I was too shy to ever do anything that provocative anyway.

Quite to my surprise, we had one hell of a conversation. We found out we had a lot of the same interests, such as music, sports, movies, and even baseball cards. I have been collecting them since early childhood, and it was the same with him. He told me how most of the women he dated didn't know a thing about sports and how cool it was to find a woman who actually liked them. I was shook because for the first time he was talking to me like there was some interest there. I figured it must have been my imagination, 'cause no freakin' way would he get with the likes of me.

The snow was coming down like crazy. It was nearing ten, so I told him I needed to lock up soon. He asked me to hold off long enough for him to take a quick shower, and I told him it was no problem. He took a fresh towel and headed toward the locker room. When he got there, he turned around and said, "Wanna join me?"

I was *tooooooo* through and couldn't manage any words at all. I figured I must have misunderstood him until he extended the invitation again. He looked me dead in the eyes and said, "If you wanna join me in the shower, I would love that!" He noticed my hesitation and added, "If you change your mind, come on in!" Then he disappeared into the locker room. A couple of minutes later, I heard one of the showers go on.

I was frozen, didn't know what the hell to do. I thought about how long I had wanted him and how this chance may never come again. I thought about how my mother would always tell me, when I was a little girl, that the only thing to fear is fear itself. I thought about how his strong hands would feel all over my body and how much I wanted to caress his silky, soft skin. I thought about how much I used to want a man to fuck the hell out of me. My high school sweetheart had been a huge disappointment in the area of lovemaking. Bottom line, why the hell not?

I locked the front door of the gym and went into the men's locker room. I walked down the row of lockers until I got to the end, where the shower stalls were lined up against the wall. I could see Geren's sexy silhouette through the frosted glass of the one he was occupying. I opened the door to the stall, and before I could utter a word, he reached out, grabbed me through the steam, and pulled me inside with him, clothes on and all.

Geren lifted me up against the wall. I put my legs around his waist as he buried his tongue into my mouth. He was not the best kisser in the world, but as much as I craved him, he could have sucked both my lips clear off and I wouldn't have cared. What I loved about him, straight off the bat, was how powerful he was. I could feel his dick, hardened, in between my legs. I couldn't wait to feel it deep inside me.

He pulled my red sweatshirt over my head and off. Then Geren removed the bra that was covering my itty-bitty titties. My breasts may not be big, but I still derived much pleasure from having him suck all over them. My nipples could have cut Sheetrock. I took the tip of my tongue and licked straight down the center of his bald head while he bit gently on my nipples. I had always wanted to fuck a bald-headed man. It meant I would have two heads to lick instead of just one.

Geren let me down just long enough to finish taking off my clothes, which he did with a quickness. Within the next two minutes, everything from my sneakers to my panties was soaking up water on the floor. He picked me back up against the wall, with the water cascading down both of our bodies, and I could feel the head of his dick rubbing up against my baby-fine pussy hairs. His big body felt so good up against my tiny frame. The other two men I had been with were small men, but Geren outweighed me two to one, and his dick was so huge.

I felt the head of his dick invade my pussy walls, and then

his entire dick was inside me. It was so big that I almost felt paralyzed at first. I had to get used to it before I could try to maneuver my pelvic muscles on it. I started kissing him deeply and palmed the back of his head like a basketball. His dick was the bomb. We fucked for a good half hour in the shower, and then he came. I could feel his hot cum shoot up inside me. I have no idea how many times I came during that time period, but it was at least five. Geren dick-whipped me something good.

We got out of the shower, and I thought we would just get dressed and leave. I always kept some extra clothes in the ladies' locker room, but his ass wasn't hardly finished with me. He laid me down on one of the benches in the locker room and then straddled the bench himself, lifting my legs all the way up in the air and wrapping them around his neck until just my shoulders and head were still on the bench. He bent over slightly, bringing his mouth to meet my elevated pussy, and began a tongue expedition. He tore my little pussy up. I came again and again. Then, he let my back rest back on the bench and pushed my legs back over my head like I was a gymnast doing a routine on a balance beam and ate my ass out. I was so in love, in lust, and several other things I can't even think of the correct terminology for.

He put his dick inside me and picked me up, carrying me into the main part of the gym, bouncing me up and down on his dick along the way. Somehow, he managed to get us both into one of the boxing rings with his dick still inside me. I have yet to figure that one out. There, in the middle of the ring, he fucked me even harder than he did the first time. There was cum everywhere.

We got into the sixty-nine position and devoured each other. Simply put, it was divine. Until that very moment, I had never taken an interest in sucking dick, but I tore Geren's dick the hell up. I put my lips to the shit and went to town on it. He came in my throat, and I savored every last drop of it. It was downright delectable.

We fucked and fucked all night. We fucked some more in the ring. We fucked on a weight bench. We fucked on top of the front desk. We fucked on the beaten-up leather couch in the back office. That's where we were when the loud rattle of the snowplow scraping the street in front of the gym awoke us. The sun was streaming through the mini-blinds.

I jumped up immediately when I realized the sun was up and told Geren we had to get the hell out of there fast. He agreed, and we got dressed with a quickness. Geren knew my uncle Lou would come after him with a shotgun if he caught us ass out like that. I threw my wet clothes in a gym bag, kissed him good-bye at the door, locked up, and hurried home before my mother noticed I hadn't slept in my bed. I was legal, sure, but you know how mothers can get. I didn't feel like playing twenty questions.

I managed to make it home without falling on the ice and busting my ass. I crept into my bedroom and laid there with my stuffed teddy bear, Casanova Brown. I have had him since second grade. I fell asleep dreaming about Geren.

I figured things would just go back to normal after our night of unbridled passion. I would go back to lusting after Geren while I sat behind the front desk. He would go back to having all sorts of luscious women meet him there. I was content with it, though. Just one night with him was enough to satisfy all my sexual needs for the rest of my life. I didn't care if I never saw a dick again.

Funny how things turned out. Things didn't go back to normal. Geren brought me a dozen roses to the gym the very next evening and asked me out on a date. I was overwhelmed and blushed like all hell. We went to a Bullets basketball game and enjoyed it. Both of us were yelling and screaming at the refs and throwing popcorn and all the other normal things the fellas do at a b-ball game.

Apparently, Geren was sick of all the fancy women that weren't interested in the same things he was and found me to be his ideal soul mate. It was a whirlwind romance. When Christmas rolled around a mere two months later, Geren gave me a jar full of peppermint candy with a small red box hidden in the middle. Inside the box was an engagement ring. I was so stunned with delight, I barely got the word "Yes" out to accept his proposal.

We were married the following spring, I quit community college and went to Howard University, graduated with honors, and I'm now in law school. Geren gave up boxing and started his own accounting firm. My boo is still built like all hell, though. We're doing very well and moved into the house we had built from the ground up six months ago. We have a set of three-year-old twins, and life has never been better.

Sometimes dreams do really come true. I got my future in check, and I got my Mr. All That. By the way, my uncle Lou still has his gym open, and Geren's younger brother, Geoffrey, works out there now on a daily basis. He is the spitting image of my boo. I often wonder what lucky girl will snap his ass up. One of you younger sisters want the directions?

Be My Valentine

It was twelve on the dot when I pranced into your office as instructed by the agency. I was dressed in white tights and black mid-high tap shoes with red ribbons in my hair. What was most striking about me was the huge red heart, about twice the size of my body, made out of quilted material.

I had only been working with the singing telegram agency for a little over a week, hoping to cut down on a little bit of the financial stress attending the School of Music at the city college was putting on me, when I was overwhelmed with assignments for Valentine's Day. You were my fifth one, and the day was only halfway over. My feet were sore, my head was hurting, and the heart was making my skin itch. Somehow, I still managed to smile as I entered your office.

I almost tripped over an extension cord. I couldn't see my feet, the costume was so big. You caught me just in time before I toppled to the floor. It was then our eyes first met. You had the most sensitive, beautiful eyes I had ever seen on a man. The warmth emitting from your hands made my heart skip a beat.

You let go of my arm, and the trance was broken. I

regained my balance and then told you my name was Yardley. I explained I was from the Songs R Us Singing Telegram Agency. I informed you that you were the lucky recipient of a singing telegram from a woman named Shannon and asked you to confirm that you were indeed Clarence.

Once you assured me your name was Clarence, I handed you the card from her and started tap-dancing my little heart out, sore feet and all. You found the song I sang, about Cupid shooting you with his arrow, very amusing. Our eyes met again, and I realized how sexy you truly were.

I finished my little song-and-dance routine and reached into my bag so I could get the box of chocolate candy included in the package deal. Graciously, you accepted it from me, and I was on my way out the door, after telling you to have a nice day, when you asked me to hold up a minute.

You reached into your pocket and withdrew a ten-dollar bill. I refused it, making you aware that all tips were already taken care of. Once again, I said good-bye and headed toward the door. Once again, you asked me to wait a moment.

At that point, I began to get a bit confused. My next assignment was clear across town. I was pressed for time, so I told you I really had to go. That's when you started talking real fast, trying to fill me in on the whole sordid story before I disappeared out of your life for good.

You explained how Shannon, the woman who sent the telegram, was your ex-girlfriend whom you recently discovered cheating with a close friend, how you had made no bones about telling her it was over and done with, and yet she was being persistent in trying to get you back.

As interesting as the whole thing was, I was wondering what any of it had to do with me, so I asked. "What does that have to do with me?" That's when you told me how cute you thought I was, asked me was I involved with anyone, and when I replied with "No one special," you asked me out on a Valentine's date later in the evening.

I started making up excuses on top of excuses at first, telling you how much studying I needed to do, how tired I would probably be after working all day, and so on. It turned out Shannon was not the only persistent one. You kept on me until I committed myself to the date.

I wrote down my address and phone number and hurried out. You yelled behind me, letting me know you would be there to pick me up about eight. As I got in the elevator, I had the biggest blush on my face. You were so sexy, and I was so excited. I had been depressed about spending Valentine's Day alone. In the span of a few minutes, all that had changed.

The rest of the afternoon passed by swiftly. Time always flies when you're running around like a chicken with your head cut off. I was beat after spending the whole day hopping on and off subway trains. It was the fastest way to get from place to place and not have to worry about parking. People on the subway trains had gotten a big kick out of seeing me dressed up like a heart, with the exception of this one little bratty kid who kicked me in my leg and then ran away before I could stuff a tap shoe up his ass.

I got back to my dormitory room, totally exhausted, but I had no intention of breaking the date with your sexy ass. I took a long, hot shower that helped refresh my aching bones, took the red ribbons out of my hair, and transformed myself into a sexual diva by the time you arrived to pick me up.

When you pulled up in your black Jag, I was anxiously waiting for you in the community room of the dorm. It took every inch of willpower in my body to keep myself from bum-rushing you at the door. Instead, I let one of my dorm sisters answer the door when you rang the bell and pretended like I wasn't pressed. She showed you to the community room, where you handed me a dozen long-stemmed red roses, a box of candy, and a teddy bear holding a little red pillow that had *Be My Valentine* embroidered on it.

I was extremely impressed you would shower me with so many gifts, having just met me that afternoon. I told you how much I appreciated the gifts. I asked my dorm sister to put the roses in a vase for me and take them, along with the other items, up to my room. The look on your face told me how pleased you were at the *new* me. Instead of being cute, as you described in your office, I was a hottie in a red spandex above-the-knee dress and red high-heeled pumps.

We drove downtown, and you surprised me with a horse-and-buggy carriage ride through Central Park. It was so romantic. I can't ever remember a man treating me with such a special evening. Little did I realize, the night was far from over.

We spent the entire carriage ride getting to know each other better. I told you all about growing up on a farm down South, while you shared your NYC upbringing with me. It was obvious we came from completely different backgrounds, but we got along like old military buddies.

After the carriage ride, we got back in your car and headed to a restaurant/jazz club in Jersey. I had heard the place was very nice, but had never been there. We had a lovely steak dinner, with champagne, while listening to the band play some awesome jazz music.

It was then you took me totally off guard, got up from the table, and went up on the stage to sit in with the band. You shook hands with a couple of the fellows in the band whom you obviously knew. One of them handed you a saxophone.

You announced to the whole audience that you were dedicating your sax solo to me. I couldn't help but blush. You played the saxophone with such grace and perfection, it made my heart skip a beat like it did when you touched me in your office.

I was so happy to find out we shared a love of music. It made my interest and admiration grow for you. When you finished your solo, the audience gave you a standing ovation. I stood up and clapped louder than any of the rest. I even stuck my pinkies in the corners of my mouth, trying to get off a whistle or two.

We kicked it way into the late-night hours, sipping more champagne, listening to the band, and delving deep into each other's minds. Halfway into the second bottle of champagne, I knew I wanted to make love to you before the night was over.

It was getting near closing time, and I was quite tipsy, which made me bold enough to talk freaky to you. I told you, "I want you to take me someplace and fuck me in all three holes till I pass the hell out!" Astonishment came over your face.

You recovered quickly and expeditiously paid the check. But instead of leaving the club like I thought we would, you led me through the kitchen and up a stairwell. The club was on the street level of a large building. We walked up a good four flights. I had no idea where you were taking me.

I thought you were nuts when you stopped at the top of one of the flights of stairs and started unlatching a window. You pushed the window up, and the February air started breezing in. You helped me out on to the fire escape. It was a little difficult because my dress was so tight.

I told you about my tremendous fear of heights, and you reassured me nothing would happen to me. Once you kissed me, all of my fear disappeared, and I became lost in your touch. Your kisses were so tender, your hands were so gentle, and my pussy was so incredibly wet.

I started to unbuckle your belt while you began to work on

my dress, pulling it up and exposing first my thighs and then my red satin panties. I got your pants unzipped and whipped out your dick. I told you to sit down on the steps of the fire escape. I sat on the step directly below you.

I started sucking your dick, immediately getting to partake of some delicious precum. That only made me want to suck it all in. That's exactly what I did. I deep-throated your dick until I could feel your balls slamming up against my chin as I took it in and out my warm mouth.

You leaned back on your elbows and enjoyed being my late-night dessert. I pulled your pants down farther around your knees and spread your legs, biting gently on your kneecaps as I worked my way up to your balls. I carefully took your ball sack into my mouth and then suckled on it, contracting my cheek muscles around it.

I sucked you long and hard. I had never sucked a man's dick so fervently before, and that, mixed with the excitement of being on a fire escape, turned my ass out. I sucked you royally, like the Nubian king that you are, until you gave me the succulent treasure I was hunting for and came in my mouth. I sucked you soft and then worked at it until it was hard again. After all, we still had some unfinished pleasure to attend to.

Once you were hard again, you got up and told me to get on my knees on one of the steps and spread my legs. I complied and pushed my booty out to meet you as you rubbed the head of your thick, juicy dick up and down the crack of my ass.

I was craving for you to take my ass, but you moved your dick farther down and aimed for my pussy instead. Your dick entered me, and I was dazed. So many nights, I had dreamed of a dick completely filling my pussy to the brim like yours.

You started fucking me hard, just the way I love it, and spread open my ass cheeks so you could finger-fuck my ass at the same time. Before you pushed your finger all the way in my ass, I was cumming like all hell.

You used your free hand to reach around and caress my hard nipples, managing to pop one out of my cleavage-showing dress and bra with little effort. We could hear all the horns and tires hitting potholes on the street below. For a few moments, I had forgotten we were so high up. I looked down and saw all the people and cars and almost freaked.

Being the intelligent man you are, you sensed my fear and told me to enjoy it and give you all my pussy. I started grinding on your dick hard, trying to grip onto it like a vise every time it tapped the bottom of my pussy.

I'm not sure exactly how long we stayed up on that fire escape fucking, but by the time we went back downstairs, the place was practically deserted except for the band members getting their things together and the manager.

You took me up on the stage, grabbed the sax again, and played me a private solo. I grabbed a microphone and sang a romantic ballad to you I wrote for one of my music classes.

You took a Valentine's Day that otherwise would have been spent in my dorm room feeling lonely and depressed, and turned it into the best one I ever had. Instead of taking me back to my dorm, you did what I requested in the restaurant. You took me home to your penthouse apartment and fucked me in all three holes until I passed the hell out.

Now, I live in your penthouse with you, and every day is Valentine's Day, because every day you give me your heart and I give you mine.

The Interstate

You pick me up from my office around 6 P.M. It is cold and damp, and the sun has been replaced with gray clouds. There is a light drizzle as I push my way through the faceless people on the crowded downtown street, holding a newspaper over my head to shelter me from the rain.

I make it to the curb, where you have reached over and pushed open the passenger-side door for me. I get into your black sports car. You help speed up the process by taking my leather briefcase and tossing it in the backseat.

You glance into your side-view mirror as I buckle my seat belt, hoping for a break in the traffic so you can pull out and join the slow-moving parade of cars headed toward the interstate. When you realize it will be a few seconds before you can maneuver the car into the street, you turn toward me, lean over, and give me a kiss on my painted, full lips. They are a little damp.

There is a break in the traffic. I take off my high heels to rest my aching feet as you proceed slowly in the direction of the on ramp to the interstate. You have some jazz playing softly on the stereo system. The only other noise in the car comes from the wipers clearing the droplets of rain off the windshield.

The rhythm of the wipers moving back and forth in slow motion makes me fantasize about the way your dick moves in and out of my pussy when you fuck me slowly in our king-size waterbed. I can feel my white silk panties beginning to get moist because I have been dreaming of having you inside me all day at work.

I gaze at you, the outline of your profile as you patiently make your way through the four city blocks of traffic to the interstate. Once we get on the highway, the traffic is moving slowly. You relax a bit and start asking me about my day. We exchange standing-around-the-water-cooler stories, but my eyes are concentrating on the bulge in your pants. I lick my lips, admiring the fact that you always fill out your pants so well, even when you aren't hard. I want you to be hard, though. I want you to knock the bottom out my pussy.

I begin to run my fingers up and down the inside of your right thigh. You look at me, and I give you the look you know all too well in return. The look that tells you how much my body is yearning for your touch. The highway is crowded with thousands of people in cars, trucks, but we are in our own little world. The rain begins to come down heavier, and you turn the wipers up to a higher speed. The faster rhythm of the wipers only makes me hornier. I hate the fact we won't make it home for at least another half hour. I need you with a quickness.

The traffic has come almost to a standstill. There is an accident up ahead. That makes me even more perturbed. By this time, I am feenin for you big-time. I take off my seat belt, lean over, and start suckling on your earlobe. The scent of your cologne arouses me even more.

I continue to suck on your ear and flick my tongue in and out of the canal as I caress your dick through your pants. You bring the car to a complete halt long enough to bury your tongue in my awaiting mouth. Your kisses always bring me so much joy. The car behind us blows the horn. The traffic has started moving again, and we are holding up the flow of cars in our lane.

I pull away from you so we can move on, but my pussy is on fire. I sit in the passenger seat with my left knee on the leather and my other leg over by the door so you can see my panties while I move them to the side and begin to finger my pussy. I suck my own juice off my fingers as you watch intently, darting your eyes back and forth between the road and my pulsating clit.

I continue to finger myself and then let you have a turn of tasting the sweetness. I put my fingers up to your mouth so you can suck them. I kiss you again, this time both of us tasting my pussy on our tongues as they intertwine. I unbuckle your trousers and dig for the treasure until I have it safely removed and easily accessible.

I place my head between your stomach and the steering wheel and take the head of your dick in my mouth, contracting my cheek muscles on it and drawing some of the precum out of it. As always, it is delightful. I waste no time deep-throating your dick. You begin to shiver as you lose control of the steering wheel a little. I suck harder. I don't care if we wreck or not as long as I get my freak on.

We are in the far left lane, and you see a small dirt road coming up in the median, one of the ones that is covered by trees and has a sign stating "Authorized Vehicles Only." You pull off the highway onto the road and park up among the trees so the car is practically invisible to those passing by.

You push your seat all the way back so I can get to your dick better. The rain starts to come down in heavy spurts, as if all the angels in heaven are crying tears of joy at the same time. I deep-throat your entire dick and gag a little on it because of its mass. You begin to moan and caress the back of my neck with your fingertips and run fingers through my hair.

I suck you for endless moments, caressing your balls gently in one of my small, delicate hands and holding the base of your dick in the other. You tell me you are cumming seconds before you shoot a hot load of cum into my mouth. I lap up every drop that escapes from the sides of my mouth until I get it all.

I lower my head farther so I can suckle on your balls. You reach over and pull up my skirt, reach your hands under my panties, and begin to finger my ass. I squirm as cum starts to trickle down between my thighs onto the seat of the car.

Even though the rain is coming down hard and beating up the roof of the car, you tell me to get out. You know making love in the rain has been a longtime fantasy of mine. I slip my shoes back on as you get out and walk around to my side and open the door for me. I join you in the rain. You pick me up and carry me to the hood of the car. I lie back on the hood while you pull my panties off.

The traffic is picking up now. The accident has been cleared. I marvel at how fast the cars seem to be passing by the spaces in the trees as you begin to suck on my moistened clit. The rain is pouring down, and we are both instantly drenched. My hard nipples are prominent through the sheer material of my blouse. I look up to the clouds as the rain falls all over us.

You eat my pussy with the passion that is ever present with us and put your hands under the small of my back, making me arch it just enough for you to reach the top button of my blouse. I help you out by undoing the rest of the buttons for you.

You suck on my pussy until I cum all over your face, glazing it like a freshly baked doughnut. I rub my own breasts and push them up toward my mouth, one at a time, flicking my tongue over each nipple. Once you get done licking up the cum off my inner thighs, you join me in my breast-sucking endeavors. You take over like a man on a mission, taking each breast completely in your mouth in turn and sucking on them with more horsepower than a vacuum cleaner. I run my fingertips up and down your muscular back and wrap my legs around your waist, letting you know what I really crave.

We hear a horn blow from a passing car and realize we must be more visible than we thought. I can feel your dick spread my pussy lips apart, switching the imaginary sign on my clitoral door from vacant to occupied. You put it all in and then pick me up and carry me deeper into the trees. The rain is still coming down. Cars and trucks fly by even faster on the interstate as the work traffic begins to die down for the evening.

You place my back up against a tree and begin to fuck the hell out of me just the way I like it. I reach above my head and grab onto a tree branch to get more leverage so I can ride your dick better, and ride it I do. You push my breasts together and suckle on both of my nipples in unison. I shake the tree branch so hard when you cum inside me that the water on the leaves splashes down on us like a high-pressure showerhead.

We are headed back to the car, about to get in and head home, when a state trooper pulls onto the access road. We scramble to fix our clothes real quick while he gets out of his cruiser. As I explain to him why we are there, making up a lie and telling him I am pregnant and had to pull over because I was nauseous, you kick a pile of leaves around in an effort to bury my panties, which are exposed on the ground.

He asks us for identification along with our car registration and then lets us go when everything checks out. He informs us that the access roads are for official vehicles only, such as police, fire trucks, ambulances, and such. He releases us with a warning. He probably suspects the real deal, but can't prove it since he didn't catch us in the act.

We get in the car and head home, stopping by a Chinese carryout on the way in. It is too late to cook dinner. After dinner, we take a long, hot shower together and make love for the rest of the night in our waterbed. The sounds of the water in the bed as you work my pussy over reminds me of the raindrops. I revel in the fact that you have made yet another one of my fantasies come true.

The Godfather

Out of all the men in the world, Norman was the last one I needed to get freaky with. He was the best man at my wedding to Tyler, and he is the godfather of our two kids. However, he is also too damn sexy for words.

In a way, I feel guilty about what I did, and in a way I don't. Tyler has been ignoring me a lot these past six months or so. I have come to the conclusion his behavior is attributed to one of two things. Either he doesn't feel as strongly about me as he did when we took our wedding vows, or he is fucking around his damn self. I tend to think it is a lack of feelings, because if he were cheating, he would be accusing me of cheating also. That's how men do it. They accuse you of doing the same shit they are in an effort to throw you off the track.

Don't get me wrong. I love my husband. I'm not even going to try to fake the funk about that. I fell in love with Tyler the first time I laid eyes on him, even though I had a slight concussion. I met Tyler when he hit me over the head with a hard-ass baseball at a college game. I was a cheerleader, and he was playing first base. I don't know what the hell happened. The game was going smoothly, and we were winning 4–1. Next thing I knew, I saw the damn thing headed toward me, and before I could duck, I was ass out.

When I woke up, he was looking me dead in the eyes with a look of concern all over his face. "Are you okay?"

"Hell, no, I'm not okay! You hit me with a damn baseball!"

That was it! The rest is history. We started dating, started fucking, and ended up falling so madly in love that one day we went to the justice of the peace and got married. Norman, who has been Tyler's best friend since kindergarten, was his best man, and Mavis, my ace boon coon, was my maid of honor. We got hitched and then went out and took a hell of a lot of tequila shots to celebrate.

In fact, our wedding night almost turned into a foursome until Tyler kicked Norman and Mavis out of our motel room. They've always denied it, but I bet the two of them went somewhere and sexed each other down. After they left, Tyler and I kept on hitting the tequila, but it became a bit more interesting.

We got butt-naked, and Tyler told me to lie flat on my back on the bed. Then he took the salt shaker, one of those cheap ones that comes in a set with pepper for about a buck at the grocery store, and got creative on my ass. He licked my left breast all over and then covered it with salt. Then he squeezed the juice from a lemon slice from the center of my breastbone all the way down to my fine pubic hair. He licked up some of the salt, took a shot of tequila and then lapped up the lemon juice, tracking it with his tongue until he reached the grand prize.

He would eat my pussy for a few moments and then do it all over again. It drove me crazy. By the time he finally fucked me, I had cum about six or seven times already. The sex between Tyler and me was always the bomb. Until recently, anyway.

Both Tyler and Norman are sexy in their own individual

ways. Tyler is light-skinned with deep brown eyes. He's five-foot-eleven and about 190 pounds. Norman's about six-two, deep chocolate with light eyes and about 210 pounds. They're both built like all hell, and to this day, they work out together three nights a week at the gym.

Fucking around with Norman was totally unintentional. I'm not going to try that old line and say he tripped and fell in. You wouldn't believe that one anyway. But, on the real tip, I never meant to fuck him. I just wanted to help him through some rough times.

To make a long story short, Norman had been shacking up with this girl named Tracie, and it was all good between them. That is, until he picked up the phone one day and heard her making plans to bump coochies with another woman. When he confronted her and asked her was she gay, she took it to the bridge and replied, "Shit, I'll be gay 'cause I'm happy as a faggot in dickland when a woman is eating my pussy!"

Needless to say, that threw him for a fucking loop, and he didn't know how to deal with it, poor baby. He really cared for Tracie, and while it may not have been true love, his feelings were real, and he was extremely hurt. The hurt turned to devastation when she picked up less than a week after he caught her on the phone and moved in with her other lover.

Tyler wasn't home the night Norman called to break the news that Tracie was gone. He had taken our two sons, Aaron and Courtney, to a college basketball game. Norman seemed so upset that I decided I better go over and check on him in person. On the way over there, getting sexed by him never crossed my mind.

Within five minutes after I got there, however, I knew my ass was in trouble. There was something different about Norman that night. He seemed so sensitive, so vulnerable, and so damn sexy. To me, nothing is sexier than a man expressing his true feelings, and that's what Norman did that night. He laid it all on the line.

When he started talking about how he planned on asking Tracie to marry him and have his kid, we both started crying. He laid his head in my lap while I cradled him in my arms like a baby. I began to wipe away his tears with my fingertips, but he took my hand and started sucking on my fingers. I was too through. Damn shame he did that. He started to try to go for a nipple through my blouse, and I pushed his head off my lap, proclaiming, "I have to go!"

I jumped up from his leather sofa and headed toward the front door of his apartment. He was on my tail, literally. When I reached the door, unlocked it, and tried to open it, he pushed it back shut. He pressed me into the door, and I could feel his dick piercing the small of my back. It was hard, and it was very, very big. I know I should have insisted on leaving. In fact, I told him, "I should leave. This isn't right."

"No, this is very right." He started sucking on my earlobe, drawing my hoop earring into his mouth along with the rest of it. When he stuck his thick, juicy tongue inside my ear canal, fucking was a done deal. He had found one of my spots. "Turn around, Janel."

I turned around to face him, and before I made it all the way, he got down on his knees and started pulling my taupe gabardine skirt up over my thighs, exposing my off-white, thigh-high stockings with lace around the top and my off-white silk panties. All I could say at that point was, "Damn!"

He pulled my panties down. I lifted up my legs, one at a time, so he could get them over my taupe pumps and completely off. He pushed my left leg up and placed it gently on his right shoulder and began to lick my pussy lips with his thick tongue. I was trembling all over, halfway because I felt guilty and halfway because I was feenin to see what was coming next.

I didn't have to wait long to find out. Norman carried me back into his living room with my legs straddled around his waist. He sat me down in his leather armchair, spread my legs open, and placed one over each arm of the chair. He lifted my hips up, scooting them forward a little so that my pussy was on the edge of the chair. After that, boyfriend dug into his meal, and all I could keep repeating was, "Damn! Damn! Damn!"

I guess you're wondering how I could let the godfather of my children suck on my pussy like that. Right? The answer is simple. It felt damn good. When he whipped his long, thick dick out, I didn't fret about that either. I just put my lips to the shit and went to work on that bad boy. Tyler's not hung like Norman, and I thought I was going to have problems taking it deep, but after a few moments of gagging and exerting much effort, I worked it like a master.

His dick was like a chocolate eclair. Chocolate on the outside and creamy on the inside. I contracted my cheek muscles around his dick, and all the blood rushed into it, causing the veins to bulge. I caught a good rhythm, and he started trembling, caressing the back of my neck with his fingertips and running his fingers through my hair. About fifteen minutes later, after almost developing lockjaw, he finally came. It was worth all the trouble because his cum was delectable.

I started taking my legs down, getting ready to get up and go home before Tyler and the boys beat me back. Norman stopped me. "No, wait, Janel. I'm not done with you yet."

"This isn't right, Norman." I was putting my legs down while he was steady holding them open. "We can't do this shit to Tyler."

"Shit, we've already done it. No matter what happens from this point on, the dirty deed has already begun." With my legs still spread out over the arms of the chair, he pushed my back onto the chair and started unbuttoning my blouse. "I'm a breast man."

That was all he had to say. My breasts are another one of my *spots*. "Is that right?"

"Damn skippy!" He got my blouse all the way open and unfastened the clasp in the front of my bra. He started palming both my tits at the same time. I was a helpless victim, so I put my hands behind my head and enjoyed the ride.

Norman suckled on my nipples for a couple of minutes and then did some deep-throating of his own. He pressed them together and sucked on them both simultaneously. I was so mesmerized by the way he was giving my tits the once-over, I never even saw the dick coming until it parted the lips of my pussy and directed itself all the way in. Norman helped a little, but his dick had a mind of its own.

With my hips still hanging over the edge of the chair and legs spread-eagled, he grabbed my ankles and pushed them as far apart as possible so he could tear my little ass up. I had never been fucked like that before. My inner thighs were shaking more than they did both times I gave birth. Having his huge dick inside me was like having labor pains all over again.

Norman started fucking me so fast and hard, I could feel and hear his balls slamming up against my buttocks. I started screaming, *literally*, because I couldn't handle the sex he was giving me. He had to let go of one of my ankles so he could cover my mouth before his neighbors called the police, or alerted building security. That's how much he made me lose it. I was a fucking maniac and started biting on his hand to muffle my own screams. He didn't stop, nor did I want him to. He didn't stop until I came about three times. Then, he exploded inside me like a Mack truck hitting a brick wall at 100 mph.

He lay there on top of me with his knees still on the floor and his dick pulsating inside me for a few more minutes before I whispered, "I have to go, Norman."

He didn't say another word while I got up and fixed my bra and blouse. I stopped near the front door to slip my panties back on, and as I headed out the front door, I looked back to see him sitting there in the armchair with his head buried in between his hands. For him, the guilt trip had already begun.

We have never mentioned it, nor do I plan to. I feel it's for the best. Norman has yet to get in another serious relationship since Tracie, and I see the way he looks at me whenever he comes over. I'm just grateful Tyler hasn't noticed it. As for me, I do have some guilt, but I just got caught up in the heat of the moment. With Tyler ignoring me half of the time, I look at it this way. If it had to be someone, I'm glad it was Norman.

Would I ever do it again? Absolutely not! Well, *probably* not. A girl has to have some scruples, you know?

The Barbershop

Enough was enough! I had tried everything imaginable to get the brotha's attention short of hanging a *Take Me, I'm Yours* sign on my back. I first met Keanu when I took my little brother, Darwin, to the Cutting Edge Barbershop to get a fade one Saturday morning.

I sat there pretending to be enthralled in an issue of *Sports Illustrated* while all the men cackled on and on about this honie or that honie. Movie stars mostly who wouldn't give any of them nuccas the time of day. I would gladly invest in a vibrator before giving it up to any of their busted asses.

This one snaggletooth brotha was sitting in the corner, waiting his turn and bragging about how he could turn Halle Berry out. I started to interject my two cents and tell his ass to get real. There he was in his plaid shorts, white sleeveless undershirt, black penny loafers, and white tube socks with red stripes, bragging and boasting about how he could fuck a sista so hard that she would beg for mercy. I started to tell him, "A sista will simply look at your ugly ass and beg for mercy."

By the time Darwin finally got into a barber's chair, I

couldn't take snaggletooth's bama ass anymore, so I told him, "Negro, please! No one wants your skank ass!"

That did it! I had managed to be incognito up until then, hiding behind the pages of the magazine. Once I spoke some words, it was like every nucca in the place suddenly noticed there was pussy present. All of them except for Keanu. His fine ass didn't even look my way. He was too busy shaping up this knucklehead who kept winking at me and doing that *I-want-to-lick-the-lining-out-your-pussy* motion with his tongue.

I don't know whether the pygmy in Keanu's chair drew my attention to him or the fact he didn't so much as give me a sideways glance, but I knew right then and there I had to have it.

I'm not sure how many of you sistas can relate, but there are times when you see something you simply must have, and you know from jump that you will move heaven, earth, and any hoes lurking around out the way to get it. That's how I felt when I first spotted Keanu.

About six-foot-two, café au lait, enough muscles to lend three other brothas some and still be the bomb-diggity, cinematic smile, neatly shaven, and bald as a baby's ass. Not the kind of bald where the nucca's head is shaped like a peanut or a gigantic, elephantine football, but the sexy kind of bald.

Before I could really get my erotic daydream going about his ass, Darwin's head was cut and the barber who cut it was in my face, holding his hand out for his ten bucks. The one who cut Darwin's hair, Randy, was not fine. In fact, his ass was not hitting on anything at all. His foul, au naturel breath made me want to shove a clove of garlic down his throat to improve the aroma.

When we walked by Keanu's chair on the way out, I tried to give him the eye. You know, the eye that tells a man you want to give him a candlelight bubble bath and then lick his ass dry? He didn't even glance my way. Now granted, I'm not the finest sista on the planet, but I was accustomed to getting mad play, and frankly, I was offended by the fact he didn't even blink in my direction.

It was all good though, because by the time we walked the three blocks home, I knew Keanu's ass was in for it. I was going to get that dick if I had to camp outside of that barbershop and kick tramps to the curb to get to it.

The next day I waited for the shop to close. I was standing outside under a dim streetlight, with the hoochie dress of all hoochie dresses on, smiling and profiling for his benefit alone. He grinned at me and then walked in the other direction. I was about to follow him when this damn wino came up to me and offered to trade a half-empty bottle of Thunderbird for a blow job. I missed my opportunity that night because I was too busy telling the drunken bastard to get the hell out of my face while Keanu was pulling out of the lot in his silver BMW Z3.

Okay, so maybe the all-out fuck-me-like-you-hate-me approach was a bit overkill. I decided to try the subtle approach next. I found out he attended Bethel Baptist Church and followed his ass there. I sat beside him in the pew, nonchalantly rubbed my thigh up against his, and even shared a hymnal with him while the congregation sang "Amazing Grace." I thought I saw a glimmer of hope, but as soon as church service ended, he was ghost.

That's when I began to wonder if my honie was funny, but I quickly decided even if he was a homie-sexual, I was going to bring his ass on back to the nana. He was mine, all mine. He just didn't know it yet.

I masturbated day in and day out, thinking about Keanu. Something had to give. There are only two ways to deal with any type of frustration. You either have to accomplish your goal or give up on the idea completely. The same rules apply to sexual frustration. I was not about to give up, so . . .

One Tuesday night, I waited until he was in the shop alone. In fact, he had already locked up for the night. At first, I tapped on the door lightly, like a cat scratching to get in, which was not that far off base because my kitty was damn sure purring. When he didn't answer the door, I banged the shit out of it until he raised the shade a little and peeked out.

He pointed to the sign on the door stating the hours of business, but I told him, "Please, I need to get a quickie!" I meant that shit literally, too.

Keanu unlocked the door and countered, "Miss, we're closed for the evening."

"My name's Tammy, not Miss, and this won't take long. I just want a quick shape-up."

We stood there staring in each other's eyes for a brief moment. I noticed his were a dark gray. My punnany heater meter went up ten degrees.

"Okay, I guess I can shape you up real quick." He grinned at me and stepped aside to let me in.

Now ordinarily it would seem strange for a woman to go to a barbershop for a shape-up, but my do is short. Any shorter, and it wouldn't be a do but a don't, so I wasn't too obvious. My real hairdresser did use clippers on it.

He motioned for me to get into his chair and went to get a smock for me. I waved it off and told him, "I won't be needing that."

He looked at me, dumbfounded. "You should really wear this so your clothes won't get messed up."

"Don't worry. My clothes won't get messed up." With that, I let down the straps of my black sundress and let the bad boy fall to the floor, revealing my naked-as-a-Butterball-turkey ass.

That's when something came over him. Maybe he realized freaks really do come out at night. He giggled and blushed nervously. "What are you doing?"

I bit my bottom lip and grabbed him by the chin so he would look me in the face. "Getting ready for my shape-up."

Then I sat in his chair and spread my legs, letting each one dangle over the sides. My pussy was so exposed, you could have taken pictures of my fallopian tubes from thirty feet away.

"Have you ever had a woman do something totally freaky to you?" I ran the fingers of my right hand through my baby-fine pubic hair and then played with my clit, gliding my middle finger in and out of my pussy walls. "I was wondering if you could shape this up for me?"

He hesitated, then gleamed like a lighthouse beacon. "I'm a professional barber. There's nothing I can't shape up."

"Kewl! Then get some shaving cream and a razor and get to work."

He silently obeyed my wishes. I couldn't help but notice the sudden pep in his step as he gathered all his shaving equipment. He stepped on the bottom of the chair, pumping it a few times to make it go higher on the riser, and then pulled up a wooden chair. He sat down, positioning himself between my calves, and then grabbed the heels of my black pumps, the only things I had on, and spread my legs open even wider.

"UMMMMMM, you like this, huh?" I asked him, still playing with myself with my right hand and lifting up one of my breasts with my left one so I could flick my tongue seductively over my hard nipple.

"No damn doubt about it," he responded and then removed my hand from my pussy, holding it by the wrist and licking the juice off my middle finger. He drew the entire thing into his mouth and then let it out slowly.

"UMMMMM, that's what I'm talking about," I moaned. "Let's get jiggy with it."

He laughed. "Yeah, let's!"

He mixed up some shaving cream and then gently spread it on my pussy, commenting as he went along. "You know, I've never shaved a woman's pussy before, but I have often dreamed about it. I think it's *sooooooo* sexy."

"Well, I'm living proof that sometimes dreams do indeed come true." I reached out and started rubbing his sexy-ass bald head while he gently and methodically started to shed my vagina of its fur. "I wanna see it. Hand me a mirror."

He complied, and then I held the mirror at an angle where I could watch him go to work. Five minutes later, my coochie was officially free like a runaway slave, and I was ready to get to the good part.

"You did an excellent job. Thank you!"

"No, thank you. The pleasure was all mine."

"Would you like me to take my legs down now, or did you want to do a closer inspection of your work?"

He knew the dilly. "No, don't take them down yet. Hang on a sec while I get a towel."

I knew it was coming. The dick I had been helplessly craving. He came back with the towel, wiped the remaining shaving cream off, and then positioned the towel beneath my ass cheeks.

Brotha man must have had the munchies, because he wasted no time eating his late-night dinner. I think I came about five times in twenty minutes. He spread my pussy lips open with his long fingers and then gave me one hell of a tongue-lashing with his thick, juicy tongue. He was so starved, eating me up like Pac-Man devours dots, I pondered whether he might have smoked a dime bag of weed before I got there.

"Rub your head in it," I instructed him and when he placed

that shiny, café au lait, bald head deep in between my cum-drenched thighs and rubbed it around, it looked like a glazed doughnut that put Dunkin' to shame.

I grabbed the back of his head and pushed his tongue deep into my pussy. I'm surprised I don't have his facial features branded into my vaginal lips to this very day.

This went on and on, the only sounds in the shop being my moans, his moans, his sucking, and the irritating second hand on the wall clock. By the time he was done, the towel beneath my ass was drenched.

"Fuck me," I requested.

"I fully intend to. I'm going to fuck the living daylights out of you."

He stood up, and I helped him whip his dick out faster than a ninja whips out his sword. It was just like I love them too. I have a predilection for big-dick men, and Keanu definitely fit the bill.

He pulled me by the heels of my shoes again, like they were the joysticks on an arcade game, repositioning my ass closer to the edge of the chair so he could get to the good stuff easier. I grabbed the head of his dick and directed it where I wanted it to go. My vagina burned a little at first. Minute particles of the shaving cream probably went in with his dick, but I didn't care. After all, that's why they make Monistat 7. I wanted it all. I got it all.

He pushed it completely in and lifted my legs up in the air, working the hell out them joysticks and fucking me without mercy. He leaned over and grabbed a hold of one of my nipples with his teeth and worked me all over. No, this was not a homie-sexual. This was a superhero. A man's man. A hoochie's delight.

"Aw yeah, take this pussy, baby!"

"Where do you want me to take it?"

"To the bridge." We both laughed, realizing how corny we were being, but the sex was the bomb.

He took his dick out and told me to stand up and turn around. I bent over the chair so he could hit it from the back. Boy, did I get into that shit then. I put one knee up on the worn leather of the chair, grabbed a hold of the neckrest, and worked my pussy on his ass.

He grabbed me by the shoulder, taking it deeper, and I started howling like a damn dog. At first, I was wondering what or who was making those noises. Then I realized it was me, and Cujo wasn't waiting outside the door after all.

Keanu started babbling. "Oh shit! Oh damn! This is some good-ass pussy! Oh shit!"

That's when I knew he was about to shoot the mother load. Damn, did he! He pulled it out and came all over my ass so much, I needed about four other sistas' asses for backup purposes.

We rested up for a good fifteen minutes. Okay, make it two minutes, and then I went to town on his dick. It was amazing. It was spectacular. It was a fucking miracle, the way I sucked his damn dick. I wish we had a camcorder rolling, because I could have sold that shit on the Internet and clocked some serious dollars. I never knew I had it like that. *Sheit!* I would have made my girl Kandi, a part-time college student and part-time call girl, jealous as a mug.

Keanu started babbling again as I sucked the life out of his loins. I caught a rhythm, relaxed my throat, and let the head of his dick bang up against my tonsils until he exploded, lining my stomach with some Negropectate.

We fell asleep that night, right there in his barber chair, with me sitting on his lap with my legs hung over an armrest. When the sun came up, Keanu fucked me royally again on the rinky-dink table covered with sports and skin mags. We had to end up throwing all those back issues away. A foreign substance was sticking the pages together, if you get my drift.

Keanu and I have been dating seriously for nine months now, and I'm not letting his ass go anywhere. I don't have to pay for haircuts anymore, my pussy stays smooth as silk, and my sex life is all that plus a buck fifty. I may have stretched it a bit when I called him a superhero, since he can't fly and he can't shoot spiderwebs from his wrist. He may not be a superhero, but he's damn sure a superman.

If You Were Here Right Now

If you were here right now, we would lie in my bed, butt-naked, slow music on the radio, maybe some Maxwell. Just talking and chillin' out at first, talking about life in general, caressing each other's bodies, sipping some wine. We would have a few scented candles burning while we applied scented oils to our bodies.

Then I would prop myself up on a pillow and dip my nipple into a glass of wine and hold my breast, letting you suckle the wine off it. I would do the same thing with my other nipple, feed it to you. I would use my other hand to rub up and down the shaft of your dick, rub my thumb over the head, get some of your precum and suck it off my fingers.

I would lie down on the pillow and tell you to dip your dick in the wine and then feed it to me. Tell you to fuck me in my mouth as you swirl your middle finger around the opening of my hot pussy. You would straddle my head and slide your dick in my mouth. I would grab onto your buttocks, pushing your dick deeper and deeper into my mouth. You would feel my throat squeeze the head of your dick as I arch my neck so I could deep-throat it, sucking my cheek muscles in and out, feeling your balls on my chin as you fuck my throat.

I would moan and gag a little but keep sucking it with pure delight as you finger my pussy into a creamy forth. We would begin to sixty-nine, with you on top lowering your dick into my mouth. As you lower your head to taste my sweet pussy, you would suck my cum off your finger. I would squeeze your buttocks tightly while I sucked your dick deeper and deeper, telling you that you taste so good and to fuck my mouth harder, baby. You would open my clit and slide your tongue inside me as you pumped your dick in and out my mouth.

I would feel your tongue flicker inside my pussy walls as I fed off your dick. You would slowly start to finger my asshole while you hummed on my clit. We would lie there devouring each other, the only noises being the sounds of Maxwell and us sucking each other's juices.

You would pull back on the hood of my clit and clench my love button between your teeth, gently biting on it. I would feel your balls slamming up against my nose as you slide two more fingers into my pussy and pinch my nipples as I arch my neck up more so I can gently suckle on your balls. You would suck the cum out of my pussy as though it were life itself while you continue to finger my asshole. I would suck you harder and deeper and then begin to taste your hot cum going down my throat, shooting deep in my belly. "MMMMMMMMMM-MMM!! You taste so delicious, boo!!!"

It would run out the side of my lips, down my cheek. I would tell you I want you to take this ass, baby, and take it now. You would tell me to turn over on my stomach and I would comply. You would slowly slide a greased finger into my asshole. I would grab onto the railings of the headboard, ass muscles tense with anticipation as you play with my pussy with a dildo. You would insert another finger in and start to pump my asshole. You would add a third finger, moving them in and out to prepare me for your thick dick.

As you position yourself behind me, you would use your other hand to rub my ass cheeks, priming them for action. Continuing to fuck my pussy with the dildo and with pussy juice all over your hands, you would bend over and bite my ass cheeks. Left then right, and then smack me on the ass. My pussy would cream and my asshole would loosen as you grease up your dick. You would hold my ass cheeks open and put the head of your dick into my ass, slowly sliding it in as you remove your fingers. Then you would move it in and out, pushing another inch into my ass each time until you get it all the way in, and then we would just freeze, dick all up in my ass, letting my ass muscles relax around it.

I would tell you to fuck this ass, baby. The initial thrust would be fantastic as you pump deeper and deeper into my sweet asshole. I would want it so bad as you stretch my ass to the limit. You would begin to slide it out and thrust it back in slowly, grinding it in deep. You would reach under me and I would hold on tighter to the bed rails, moaning beyond control as you put the dildo back in my pussy, working it in and out my pussy walls. I would begin to scream as you fuck me into oblivion, balls swinging back and forth against my ass. Banging my clit with the dildo, you would feel it through the walls of my asshole. The sounds of your thighs slapping my ass would echo throughout the room.

I would tell you to cum in my ass, baby. You would slap my ass and reach and grab my hair, pulling my head back. You would tell me to lick my pussy off the dildo. I would take it out and suck my own juices off of it. Dayum, I would taste so good. Your dick would glisten as you fuck my asshole deep and hard. You would reach under and pinch my nipples and twist them gently. Then, you would reach back and pinch my clit as I lick all around the dildo, sucking my juices off of it like I am sucking your dick.

You would lay me on my side, without pulling your dick out, and continue to fuck me up the ass. I would throw my leg over your thigh and rub my clit as you finger my pussy with three fingers. You would bite my shoulders, then my neck, and make me scream as you slam into my asshole. I would squeeze my ass muscles around your dick, rubbing my clit and sucking my pussy juices off the dildo. You would feel your balls tighten as my ass clenches at your dick. You would wanna cum but you wouldn't. Instead, you would pull out and lay me on my back, placing my legs in the air wide open.

You would drop your dick deep into my pussy, and I would wrap my legs around your neck, grinding my pussy up toward your dick. You would start to frantically but deliberately pound my pussy, fucking me hard and deep. I would feel it in my stomach as I grab the back of your head with one hand. Your balls would tickle my asshole. I would grab one of your buttocks with the other hand, pushing you deep into my pussy walls. I would pull your head down and lick the top of your freshly shaven head. You would suck my tongue deep into your mouth as you push my legs back farther. .

I would kiss you passionately as you put my ankles over my head, shoving your dick deeper into my pussy. You would fuck me faster, and the bed would start to rattle. A bead of sweat would fall from your head and would land on my lips. You would start moving your dick into my pussy from side to side as I lick your sweat off my lips. You would put one of my legs down and straddle it while you hold the other straight in the air and turn me on my side. You would ride my thigh and fuck me sideways, watching your dick go in and out, glistening with my juices. My cum would be all over your dick and balls and trickling down onto the bedsheets. You would catch some of the cum running down my thigh, wipe up some with your finger, and put it in my mouth.

My orgasm would start to build as you fucked me harder. I would start to gasp for air as cum exploded out of my pussy and squirted all over the bed. You would ride me like there is no end to this pussy. I would beg you to stop, but I really wouldn't want you to, so you wouldn't. You would pull your dick out and suck on my pussy, taking me beyond the limit of any ecstasy I could ever handle. You would lie here, nibbling gently on my pussy, as we both passed out from exhaustion, both knowing that once we woke up, we would be ready to go at it all over again.

That's what we would do if you were here right now!

The Airport

You meet me at the airport right on time after my return flight from Jamaica. Even though I had a great time vacationing with my friends, I can hardly wait to see you. My eyes light up as I see you walking toward the gate to meet me. You look so sexy in the khaki slacks, black jacket, and white button-down cotton shirt. I can feel my panties begin to get damp underneath the red spaghetti-strap sundress that I have on.

I look into your eyes and see the same sparkle that is in my own as you put your arms around me. Just then, a female customs agent approaches me and says she needs to search my bags. She is very pretty in her regulation uniform and has long dark brown hair, hazel eyes, and smooth caramel skin just like mine. She searches my bags and then tells me she needs me to follow her to a room.

I grow concerned because I have no idea what she thinks I am guilty of. I follow her to a nearby room while you wait for me by the gate. She takes me in the room and tells me she needs me to disrobe so that she can strip-search me. I ask why, and she says it is common procedure, with women traveling alone from the islands, to ensure I am not smuggling drugs in as a mule.

I obey and take off my dress. I am braless, and all that remains on are my red silk panties and my black high-heeled shoes. She instructs me to take my panties off as well. She approaches me and lifts up each of my breasts, examining them, and I begin to realize what it is she really wants. She tells me to turn around and bend over the single table in the room, and I comply. I feel her spread my ass cheeks open, and then, without warning, she sticks a finger up my ass. I immediately get nervous because I have never been with a woman before. Yet her hands on me, and now her finger in my ass, are making me very aroused.

I can see her take a seat in a chair at the end of the table out the corner of my eye. Then she sticks her tongue into my asshole, and I shiver. While I know that you are waiting patiently for me to come back out to the gate, I begin to wonder how far she is going to take this.

I don't have to wonder long, because she tells me to turn around and face her. As soon as I do, she cups one of my breasts in her hand and begins suckling on my nipple, more gently but with more intensity than any man ever has.

Suddenly I hear the door creak open, and you are standing there. You have a look of shock mixed with excitement on your face as you close the door, asking, "What the hell is going on?" She looks at you and tells you, "Just watch and see!"

My ass is resting on the edge of the table as she lifts one of my legs up over her shoulder and begins sucking on my clit with a hunger I have never known. You can feel your dick come to attention because this has always been a fantasy of yours we have talked about but I swore I would never do. She sucks on my pussy for what seems like an eternity until you decide you cannot take it anymore. You are about to bust.

You tell her to move out the way so you can taste my sweet pussy too, now dripping wet from all of the attention it has been given. She gets up from the chair so you can sit down, and you push me all the way onto the table, forcing me to cross my legs behind your shoulders as you begin to devour my clit.

She watches for a few seconds and decides she will not be left out, so she bends over and begins sucking on my breasts again. I caress the back of your neck and run my fingers through her hair with my hands. Her ass is protruding up in the air, and you reach underneath the skirt of her uniform and start finger-fucking her while she continues to suckle on my nipples. I can feel your tongue deep inside my throbbing pussy.

I tell you to get undressed, you do, and then I let you take my place on the table, lying you down on your back with only your feet hanging over the edge. I sit on your face while she begins to suck your dick, deep-throating it without any hesitation. I am facing her, hands caressing your chest, watching her partake of your dick as you partake of my pussy and finger-fuck my ass.

She comes up for air, and I bend over to take over, sucking the head of your dick to get some of the precum out because I remember how delicious you taste. I contract my cheek muscles tightly around the head, trying to get every possible drop I can. She is licking up and down the shaft of your dick and sucking on your balls while I continue to work on the head.

We both begin sucking and licking your dick. We are so hungry for you. I can feel cum trickling out of my pussy as you lap it all up off my thighs. Saliva starts to escape the sides of our mouths as we take turns deep-throating your dick.

We can hear planes landing and taking off and people walking by in the hall, but none of us gives a damn, 'cause this is just too good to let go. Other than that, there are just a bunch of sucking noises and the delightful smell of sex in the air. The aroma is breathtaking.

As you suck on my clit even harder now, fingering my ass with one hand and palming an ass cheek with the other, I take my tongue and lick your belly button, then blow on it to make it dry before I wet it again with my tongue. I know how much that turns you on. I continue to do this for a couple of minutes while she deep-throats your dick.

I slowly take my pussy off your face and slide my wet pussy down over your chest, then your belly button. I tell her to let go of your dick so I can straddle it. I sit on your dick, facing away from you so she can suck on my breasts while I ride your dick. I can feel the head of your dick begin to part my pussy lips as you pump your hips up to meet my downstrokes. You are still finger-fucking my ass, but with two fingers now.

I move up and down on the shaft of your dick while she flickers her tongue at my nipples. You marvel at how tight my pussy is. I take a little bit more of it in each time I go up and down until it is all in. As I begin to grind my pussy onto your dick, she pushes both my tits together and suckles on both nipples at the same time.

Your back is arched off the table, meeting my every thrust as I start to ride your dick faster. I take my long tongue and flicker it over one of my nipples while she sucks furiously on the other one. My pussy is so hot and tight, and you try to pump and reach the bottom of it harder and faster. I put my hands on your thighs so I can get better leverage, and I begin to go up and down on your dick faster each time. You admire my ass, with your fingers in it, as it goes up and down. It looks so juicy.

Contracting my pussy muscles on your dick, I squeeze it hard as she gets the chair and sits down in front of us and begins to suck on my pussy and lick your dick while I am riding it, tasting us both at the same time. She reaches up and rubs my nipples while she is sucking on us both. I continue to fuck you hard, and I can feel my cum trickling down the inside of my thighs, down between your thighs, and onto the tabletop.

You take your other hand and pull me back by my hair so that I am lying with my back on top of your chest, still riding your dick. You start palming my breasts while she continues to get her eat on, and we are all moaning. My pussy juice is everywhere. I want you to shoot your hot cum all down my throat, and I ask you, "Will you cum for me?" and she says, "I want some of it too!" You tell me, "Whatever you want, I will do." So I get off your dick, and she and I both wait anxiously for you to give it to us. Your dick is throbbing, and veins are popping out of it everywhere. You look so yummy.

We both get on our knees as you stand up. We begin licking and sucking all over your dick. You stand, your knees feeling a little wobbly, and hang on to the side of the table. I take the base of your dick in my hand and begin to squeeze it gently. You grab both of our heads and begin pumping your dick into our mouths fast and furiously. As I take your balls into my mouth and bounce them on my tongue, you tell us, "I'm about to cum!" We can hardly wait. It starts to shoot out, and we both take some of it with our tongues and place some on our fingertips, rubbing it all over each other's breasts and faces, both of us smiling with delight. I whisper, "Hmmm, you taste so good, boo."

I get greedy, and I take your whole dick into my mouth, trying to get every last drop and contracting my cheek muscles around your dick, making all of it come out into my mouth as I arch my neck so your dick can hit my tonsils. You tremble as the last of it goes down my throat, but I continue to suck 'cause I want to get you hard again so you can fuck me in the ass before we leave. I tell you, "I want you to take all this ass right here!" She interjects and says, "We have to finish up before someone gets suspicious."

We all laugh as we get dressed. She finishes first and gives us both a smooch on the lips before she leaves, saying, "Thanks for the afternoon snack!" We leave and go to the baggage claim, where my bags have been spinning around on the belt for the last half hour or so. We go out to the car and you seat me in it while you put my baggage into the trunk. I sit in the car, waiting for you patiently, fingering my own pussy and then sucking my juices off my fingers. My pussy is so wet. After you get in and proceed to the exit gate, I take my free hand and rub it up and down your thigh, then to your crotch, and start to undo your zipper.

You reach in the backseat and hand me the card and box of chocolate-covered cherries you bought for me because you missed me so much. After we clear the exit gate, I continue to caress your dick and balls with one hand as you finger my pussy. I put one of my feet up on the dashboard so that my leg is up in the air and you can get to my pussy better. I roll down the window so that the cool breeze can blow through my hair and hit up against my legs and pussy as we hit the highway.

I want you to fuck me again, but I know I have to wait until we get home, or at least until we get off the highway, because I know how you like to make sudden stops. I decide to open the box of cherries instead, and one at a time, I put them in my pussy, drowning them with my juices, and then begin feeding them to you with my fingers. Needless to say, we pull off at the first rest area we come to. And there, on the hood of your car, you give me what I crave and fuck me in my ass just the way I love it.

The Diary

It had been a long time since I visited my grandparents, and I was excited about spending a couple of days with them for Thanksgiving. When I got off the plane, both of them were waiting for me. With the exception of a few added wrinkles on their faces, they looked exactly like they did when I was a child.

They drove me back to the big country manor where my mother and her three sisters grew up. Once I threw my bags in the bedroom where I would be staying, the one that belonged to my mother as a child, I went down to the kitchen to help Grandma stuff the turkey and bake pies for dinner the next day.

Thanksgiving dinner was going to be great because I would get to see my aunts, their husbands, and all of my cousins. My parents were traveling in Europe, so they were going to have to miss it.

After we finished preparing everything, my grandparents and I sat in the living room by the fire and talked about the good old days. Grandpa surprised me by having a pizza delivered. I had never even pictured my grandparents eating something that wasn't homemade, much less pizza. Times had really, really changed. There was no denying that.

One thing had remained the same, however, and that was how early they went to bed every night. By 9 P.M., they were both calling the hogs, since they got up around 5 A.M. every morning. They had retired years before but still rose early by force of habit.

I flipped through the channels of the old floor-model television in the living room, the only television in the entire house. They didn't have cable. There were a few sitcoms on, but none of them interested me. I looked through the bookcase in my grandpa's study, hoping to find something interesting to read. All his books were about carpentry, farming, fly-fishing, landscaping, home repair, and things of that nature, so I quickly gave up on the idea.

I quietly went upstairs to my mother's bedroom, undressed, put on a white cotton nightgown, and tried to go ahead and fall asleep. There was no freaking way that was happening, because it was way too early for me.

I was going to hang my garment bag up in her closet, but the closet was packed to the brim with clothing that belonged to her as a teenager. I slipped on my bedroom shoes and went to check and see if there was some space for it in the hallway closet.

I opened the walk-in closet in the hall and found some space for my bag. The closet had a door in the rear of it that led to the attic. I was mad bored, and since there was nothing to watch on television and nothing to read, I elected to explore the attic instead.

I nudged open the door to the attic stairs, which was hard to open and squeaky, being that no one had been up there in years. After ascending the stairs and finding the pull string for the lightbulb, I was surprised to see there were very few spi-

derwebs around. However, there was a lot of dust, and I almost
turned around in fear my allergies would start acting up.

I was reaching for the string to turn off the light when I
noticed an old hope chest in a corner by the window seat.
Normally, I am not a nosy person, but something drew me to
the chest like a magnet. Besides, my whole point in going up
there in the first place was to meddle through family heir-
looms and mementos anyway.

I tried to open the chest, but there was a lock on it and the
key was nowhere in sight. I shifted through a couple of boxes
filled with clothing, cheerleader pom-poms and batons, year-
books belonging to my mother and her sisters, and all the
usual things until I found an old rusty screwdriver.

I used the flat head of the screwdriver to bust the lock on
the chest. It didn't take much effort, since the lock was flimsy
after so much time. I sat down on the window seat and started
pulling things out. There were several photographs of my
grandparents when they were younger, pictures of their wedding, pictures of my mother and aunts as children and
teenagers, pictures of my great-grandparents and other family
members. There were some old lace handkerchiefs, a couple
of hand-knitted cardigans, and even a poodle skirt.

Looking at all the old things made me crack up laughing. I
couldn't even relate to times like those. For me, growing up
had been so different than the way my mother grew up. I guess
one day my daughter, if I have one, will be saying the same
thing about me.

After beginning to replace everything back in the trunk
neatly, I noticed something stuck at the bottom I hadn't
noticed the first time around. I yanked on it and got it free. It
turned out to be an old book of some sort with no visible
name on the cover. The underside of it was sticky, as if some-

thing, maybe water, had seeped through the trunk over the years and made it adhere to the lining of the trunk.

I was hoping it was some famous classic novel I could take back down to the bedroom and read until I got sleepy. It wasn't until I opened it up that I realized it was a diary.

The first page said, "This Diary Belongs To," but the name had been smudged, and I couldn't make it out.

I started flipping through it, looking to see if the keeper of the diary signed the pages, but none of them were signed. In fact, only the month and day were at the heading of each page. There was no year written down. I thought that was strange, but since I am not a sleuth or anything, I didn't ponder the fact for very long.

The handwriting was unfamiliar to me, but I knew for sure it wasn't my mother's. I wondered which one of my aunts the diary belonged to. Since I knew it would be inappropriate to read the diary, no matter whose it was, I began to close it so I could put it back. But there was a bookmark in it, and I wanted to see what it said, so I opened it to that particular page.

The bookmark turned out to have a friendship poem imprinted on it, along with a bouquet of flowers. That was not the interesting part, though. Some words caught my eye, and I was shocked.

I sucked his dick, Fingering me, and *I came so hard* seemed to jump right up off the page at me. I was like "DAYUMMMMM-MMMMM!"

I couldn't prevent myself from reading the whole page.

July 4th

I saw my Pookie earlier in the day at the Independence Day Parade. He looked so fine in his football uniform. He marched down Main Street with the football team and we, the cheerleaders, followed behind them with the marching band.

Momma wouldn't let me go to the lake with him and the other kids directly after the parade. She made me come home and do all my regular Saturday chores instead. I hurried through them, making sure I would have them all done so she would let me go to see the fireworks.

I managed to get everything done and she told me I could go. I took a long, hot bath and put on some rosewater so I would smell sweet for my Pookie. I put on a blue dress, a white sweater, some white bobby socks, along with my new pair of saddle shoes, and headed down to the lake where the fireworks show was going to be.

When I got there, Pookie and his friends had already been there for hours. They were kind of drunk from drinking the moonshine Pookie's Uncle Willy makes in his homemade still.

I rushed into his arms and he kissed me on my lips, slipping his tongue in my mouth for a brief second. He didn't dare kiss me any more than that in public. He knew if news of it got back to my daddy, we would both be in for a serious whupping.

The fireworks show began at dusk and all the vibrant lights, mixed with the loud bangs as they went off, were breathtaking. We were sitting on blankets by the lake that was surrounded by all the townspeople.

About halfway through the show, Pookie took my hand, rolled a blanket up and stuck it under his arm, and told me to come with him. I let him lead the way and we disappeared deep into the trees where no one could possibly see us.

We found a clearing about 200 yards from the lake and Pookie spread out the blanket on the ground. We could still see the fireworks in the distance yet we had all the privacy we needed.

I told him my mother told me to come straight home after the fireworks ended and he assured me I would be home early enough that I wouldn't get grounded.

Then we started doing the things we couldn't do in public. It wasn't our first time making love because we did it in his daddy's car about a month ago. When I lost my virginity, it hurt at first but then I realized how much I enjoyed it.

Tonight was even better since I was so much more relaxed. We both were. We started out by French kissing. His tongue was a tad bitter from all the moonshine but I loved it just the same. I have always loved kissing him. He is so passionate and domineering.

He unbuttoned my sweater and slowly slid it off me. Then he laid me back on the blanket, undid the top part of my dress, reached behind my back, and unclasped my bra.

After getting my breasts within his grasp, he started sucking on my hard nipples and I was taken aback. My nipples are so sensitive and whenever he sucks them, I can't help but moan from all the pleasure.

I could look up at the sky and see the fireworks bursting in the air as he pushed my dress up, pushed my panties to the side and started fingering me. It hurt a little since my pussy is still somewhat tight. At one point, I almost shrieked out in pain because he tried to stick three fingers inside me at once.

Pookie realized how uncomfortable it was making me and took his fingers out of me. I felt bad about it and told him I wanted to try that thing we have been discussing lately; me giving him a blow job.

He asked me was I sure I was ready to try it and I said yes but that was only partially true. I was nervous but anxious to return the pleasure he gave me when he performed oral sex on me that night in his daddy's car.

I told him to lie down on his back and I unzipped his pants and took out his hard dick. I just stared at it for a few moments at first because I had never taken a really good look at it.

After I built up some confidence, I sucked his dick right there in the woods and I would be lying if I said I didn't relish it. I have the feeling sucking Pookie's dick is going to become a favorite pastime of mine.

I moved my mouth up and down on his dick, taking more and more of it in until I got the whole thing in. Not bad for my first time. He must have found delight in it because he discharged the contents of his balls in my mouth. His hot cum trickled down my throat and while it was not the best tasting thing in the world, I found it to be quite savory.

He was so out of breath when it was over, I thought we weren't going to be able to do the actual sex act tonight, but he came back strong in a matter of minutes.

I could tell the fireworks show was about over because they seemed to be sending up the big combination ones they always do in the grand finale. I told Pookie maybe we should just go, but he told me how much he wanted to be inside me and I melted.

I laid down again and got in the missionary position so he could stick it in. It went in pretty smoothly; not like the first time when he had to force it in. He started pumping his dick in and out my pussy and lifted up my left leg, holding it up with his shoulder. He took me much harder tonight than before. I guess he figured it was time to take it to the bridge.

The grand finale of the fireworks was amazing, just like the love Pookie and I were making. He kept going and going at it and I was overcome by how long he lasted. One of my girlfriends told me that boys last longer after they cum the first time. I guess she was right.

I came so hard that it scared me. I didn't cum at all the first time we did it and so tonight, I experienced my first orgasm. It was amazing. While Pookie was walking me home, I kept replaying my orgasm over and over again in my mind.

When we got back to the house, he kissed me on my cheek because he knew Daddy was looking out on the front porch through the curtains. I told him I would see him at church tomorrow morning. I can hardly wait. As Pookie walked off, he turned around and said one day he was going to marry me. This might sound crazy, but you know what? I believe him!

After I finished reading the diary entry, I repeated the word, "DAYUMMMMMMMMMMM!"

I couldn't believe one of my aunts had written it. I guess

it's always hard to picture people older than me being young and having such experiences.

As I replaced the diary and put all the·other things back on top of it, I realized reading it had made my pussy start throbbing. I was so horny and had not a clue what to do. I didn't bring my vibrator or dildo with me on my trip for two reasons. First of all, because I didn't want them to show up on the X-ray machines at the airport and secondly, because who in the hell plans on masturbating while on vacation at their grandparents' house.

I had to do something, so I closed up the trunk and pushed it back in the corner, grabbed a baton from one of the boxes, pulled the string on the light, and then sat back on the window seat. The only light left in the attic came from the moonlight streaming in through the small square window by the seat and the faint light at the bottom of the stairs emitting from the hallway downstairs.

I pulled my nightgown up, pushed my panties out the way, and started fucking myself with one end of the baton. The rubber end and cold metal created a strange sensation, one that turned me on even more.

I pushed more and more of the baton inside me until no more would fit comfortably. I spread my legs open wider and starting grinding my hips on to it like it was a big, juicy dick.

I used my free hand to undo the top two buttons of my gown so I could caress my breasts. I pushed my right one up as far as I could and swiped my tongue back and forth across my erect nipple.

This continued on for a good fifteen minutes. The whole time I was imagining the couple in the story who were faceless to me. Yet the woman was obviously one of my mother's sisters. I was dying to know which one.

After playing the whole excerpt from the diary out in my

mind and fucking myself royally with the baton, I came like a clap of thunder. I sat there for a couple minutes to regain my normal breathing pattern, which had become shallow. It always does after I cum.

I made sure everything was just like it was before and then tiptoed back down the steps through the closet, shutting the door behind me, and went back to my mother's bedroom.

My grandparents were still sleeping soundly. By that time, it was getting pretty late. I may not have been tired before going up the attic but after masturbating like that, falling asleep came easily.

I woke up the next day still wondering whom the diary belonged to. I devised a plan in my mind to find out.

Thanksgiving dinner went off beautifully, and I had a great time catching up with my aunts and their families. While we sat around reminiscing about the past, I looked at all of them and couldn't picture any of them being the woman from the story. They all seemed so demure.

When they were all putting on their coats and such to leave, I put my plan into action. I told them I had lost my address book and wanted to make sure I had their correct information so I could write to them and call from time to time.

I went from one to the other, asking that all three of them write down their home address and phone number. Later that evening, while I was munching on a slice of Grandma's peach pie that I am totally and undeniably addicted to, I looked at the paper.

All the handwritings were similar. If not for the fact that their names were there, I wouldn't have known who wrote what. Unfortunately, none of the writing samples looked like the writing from the diary.

I figured a person's handwriting does change over the

years, and trying to figure the owner of the diary was a lost cause. I was just so amazed by it, but you win some and you lose some.

My grandparents took me to the airport the next day to catch my plane back home. I kissed them good-bye at the gate and told them how much I love them. I promised it wouldn't take me nearly as long to visit again as it did in the past. Grandma surprised me by handing me an index card, telling me she had written down the recipe for her peach pie.

I told her thanks and shoved it in my pocket. They were having final boarding, and I had to rush. I made it onto the plane and found my seat seconds before the pilot put on the Fasten Seatbelt sign.

I flipped through the airline magazine stuffed into the pocket on the back of the seat in front of me but found it dull at best. I had meant to pick up a novel or magazine in the gift shop but got to the terminal too late to risk it.

Once again, I was stuck with nothing to read. Halfway through the flight, I started thinking about my grandma's peach pie. I took the recipe out my pocket to look over the ingredients and directions.

I thought my eyes were playing tricks on me, but I instantly knew they weren't. The handwriting on the index card was identical to the one from the diary, and I was in shock. The woman in the diary, the one whose sexual experience had driven me to the point of masturbation, and ultimately orgasm, was my own grandmother.

It wasn't until a week later, when my mother called from Europe, that I found out Grandma's pet name for Grandpa used to be Pookie. *Dayum, who would have thought it!*

The Seduction

The first time I laid eyes on you, I knew that I wanted to feel you inside me. The first time you kissed me, I thought that I would die. Yet and still, two months and several dates later, we had yet to make love. Partly because you respected me enough to wait and partly because we both wanted the first time to be special.

I decided it was time, since I knew that my body could not settle down for another night's sleep without you. You invaded my every thought. I dreamed of you doing things to me all the time, whether I was stuck in rush-hour traffic or walking down the aisle in the grocery store. The mere thought of you made my juices flow. I was determined to make the night special, something neither one of us would ever forget.

It was a Friday evening about 6 P.M. when you left your office, tired but elated that the workweek was over. We didn't have any plans and hadn't spoken, even by telephone, for the past few days, which is why the note in the white envelope with lace trim on your windshield took you by total surprise.

As you lifted the note from under the wiper, you could smell the scent of my perfume, all too familiar to you now, breeze past your nose in the brisk October wind. It was a cold evening, but I had plans to warm you up.

You opened the note and read it:

Hey Baby,
   I know we didn't have plans for tonight, but I have a surprise for you. You have to come to me in order to find out what it is. A friend of mine asked me to house-sit her new home while she is out of town getting her furniture. It is kind of way out, so I drew you a map on the back of this note.
   If you want to experience a night of lovemaking that will stimulate all of your senses and allow me to pamper your entire body as well as your mind, CUM TO ME! Don't bring anything but your sexy ass. Hurry up baby because I need you.

<SMOOCHES>
Zane

You smile as you see the imprint of my lips, in red lipstick, at the very bottom of the note. You can feel your dick getting hard in your pants as you lick your lips and drive off to begin our adventure together.
   The house was indeed hard to find but you accomplished the deed and pulled up in the secluded driveway about an hour later. It was a nice little cottage way out in the country, surrounded by trees. As you got out of the car, you couldn't help but notice how quiet it was. You thought you heard an

owl way off in a distant tree as you approached the front
door.

When you got to the door, there was a piece of paper
attached to it saying:

Roses are red
Violets are blue
Tonight's the night
For me and you

Come in my love
And you will find
In front of you
A glass of wine

You turned the doorknob and opened the door and entered
into my idea of romance. The entire house appeared empty, for
there was no furniture as far as you could see. Every room was
lit up by flickering pillar candles, all vanilla scented, in various
sizes and shapes. In the living room, you could see the fire I had
built for us. A single glass of white zinfandel was sitting on the
hearth. As you picked it up and began to sip on it, you noticed
a white silk scarf and another note lying beside it. You read it:

Quench your thirst
With this glass of wine
Relax a bit
And unwind

Then cover your eyes
Give in to me
I will cum for you
And help you to see

A faint laugh escapes your lips as you finish up your glass of wine. Then you cover your eyes with the silk scarf without hesitation, wondering what I have in store for you next.

As soon as you complete your task, you hear the sounds of Kenny G coming from upstairs. Because of the music, you don't hear my light footsteps descending the stairs and walking up behind you. Once I am very close, you can smell my sweet perfume. You begin to say hello to me, but I reach around in front of you and cover your lips with one of my fingers and say, "Shhhhhh!"

I felt we had talked enough, and I wanted the night to be all about the other senses. I had always wanted to get to know you three ways. I knew you mentally, and now, I wanted to get to know you physically and orally.

I put my hand up to your chest and could feel your heartbeat. I took your right hand and placed it over my heart, and you noticed that my chest was bare. I was already completely nude. For a brief moment, we admired the life emitting from both of us as two heartbeats became one.

I took you by the hand and led you up the stairs to the bathroom where a candlelit bubble bath was waiting. As I began to undress you, you could smell the essence of the rose petals scattered over the top of the bathwater. I undressed you very slowly, admiring every inch of you as it was revealed.

Once you were undressed, I bit my bottom lip with excitement as I took in the splendor of your dick with my eyes. I helped you up the two steps that led to the huge whirlpool garden tub and guided you in. I sat down in front of you with my legs over your thighs and began to bathe you with a soft bath sponge. I began with the top of your head, then moved on to your chest, your back, your shoulders, your arms, your dick, your thighs, and your knees. Finally, I bathed your feet.

One at a time, I took your toes into my mouth and suckled on them, enjoying the reaction on your face and the low moans coming from your sexy lips as the water vibrating out of the whirlpool jets tingled our skin.

When I was done, I stood you up, helped you out of the tub, and began to dry you off with a soft cotton bath towel. I quickly discarded that option and decided to lick you dry instead. Systematically, I licked the remaining water off every inch of you. I remember thinking that I had never in life tasted something so delicious.

I traced a trail with my tongue around each one of your nipples and down the middle of your chest to your belly button. I got down on my knees and licked each one of your thighs and knees and then turned you around so I could lick the back of your thighs and knees. I took the thickness of my tongue and lapped up all the droplets on the cheeks of your ass, licked the entire crease, and then stuck my tongue deep inside your asshole. I could feel you shiver as I turned you around again and took your balls gently into my mouth, suckling the water droplets off of them as well.

What I really craved to lick all over was your beautiful dick, and I did just that. With you still blindfolded by the silk scarf, I devoured every inch of you while you stood there and dick-fed me for the first time. As you ran your fingers through my damp hair that smelled of the strawberry shampoo I used that morning, I took my time enjoying my candy treat. I arched my neck back so that I could take you all in for what seemed like endless moments. When I sensed you were about to explode, I reached up and removed the blindfold from your eyes, and you saw me for the first time that day and the first time ever in the nude.

As your eyes adjusted to the light, you saw me sitting there on my knees with my cherry-colored lips surrounding your dick, my nipples harder than diamonds, and water trickling down my bare back onto my succulent ass. There among the candlelight, with Kenny G still emitting through the master bedroom door into the bathroom, you looked down and removed the hair from in front of my eyes just in time to look deep into them as you came into my mouth for the very first time.

We both lost control as your warm, sweet nectar trickled down my throat and lined my insides with your essence. After I had partaken of every drop, I stood up and whispered in your ear that it wasn't over yet, and the only response you could muster was "Dayummmmm!"

I took you by the hand and led you into the bedroom, where you spotted the single piece of furniture in the whole house, a king-size sleigh bed covered with black satin sheets. Candles also lighted the bedroom, and the single white rose I had gotten for you was lying on a pillow in the center of the bed. I laid you down upon the satin sheets. As lightning began to invade the room from over the horizon, tracing both our bodies with its presence, I took the single rose, began at the top of your head, and moved it all the way down the center of your body. I paused it for a moment at the tip of your nose so that you could admire the essence of it. You laughed a little as the rose petals tickled your skin.

I reached over to the side of the bed onto the floor and returned with a bottle of scented body oil and two more silk scarves. I tied your hands to the headboard and proceeded to give you a full body massage, working my small delicate hands over your smooth skin. I massaged you from head to toe, making sure that you were totally relaxed. Then I reached over and got the bottle of honey I had waiting beside the bed and squeezed a few drops over both of my breasts. I fed them to you, one at a time, as you laid there with your head on the pillow.

After breast-feeding you for a few moments, I took the honey and squeezed some all over my vagina and ass. Then, I climbed on top of your face in the sixty-nine position and felt you begin to suck on my clit with a desire no other man had ever shown. I poured some honey on your dick and began to lick it all off, making long, circular strokes around the shaft with the tip of my tongue. We sucked on each other for a long time, and the CD player kicked over to the next one in sequence, Maxwell's *Urban Hang Suite,* as we both had orgasm on top of orgasm.

We devoured each other until we were both completely exhausted, our mouths were sore, my pussy was swollen, and your dick had the kind of tender soreness that comes about when too many orgasms are reached at one time. We both fell asleep just like we were positioned, with my pussy on your face and the head of your dick in my mouth, your hands still tied to the bed.

The music eventually faded out sometime during the night, and all the candles burned completely down, leaving only the lightning flashes and the distant claps of thunder to invade our private paradise.

In the morning, you awoke to find your hands untied and me standing there with a silver tray, holding the breakfast I had prepared to serve in bed. We fed each other the chocolate-covered strawberries, grapes, and freshly baked blueberry muffins with our fingers.

There, in the first sunlight of the day, you and I made love for the very first time, and I finally got my wish. I felt you inside of me. Now, years later, with our fifth wedding anniversary approaching, we both smile at each other with the secret only the two of us know every time we visit my friend in the country, the godmother of our firstborn son. Whenever life seems to pale in comparison, we remember the night I first seduced you and welcome the challenge of making our next night of passion top every one before it. Guess what, baby? You never, ever disappoint me.

Nervous

For as long as I could remember, I had always been nervous. Nervous about school. Nervous about friends. Nervous about relationships with men. Even nervous about talking to my own mother. I don't know whether it was something deep-rooted inside of me from an early childhood experience or whether it was something that was just meant to be.

I lived in my own little world by the time I was twenty-two years old. I was fresh out of college and working as a project coordinator for a nonprofit organization in Philadelphia. I selected that job because I wouldn't have to deal with too many people on a daily basis. I only had face-to-face dealings with a few of the people from the office, mostly women, and I was very thankful for that. My daily routine consisted of going to work, stopping off at a carryout on the way home to pick up dinner, and then retiring to my cozy but cramped one-bedroom apartment for the rest of the night, only to repeat the same exact steps the next day. When it came to dealing with a man on an intellectual level, any man, my palms would get sweaty, and my knees would tremble a little. I am not sure how noticeable it was to anybody but me. However, it was definitely a regular occurrence.

I had managed to make it all the way through my high school and college years without a single boyfriend. But I was not a virgin by far. The weekends were HER time. They were the times that SHE came out into the light. SHE was my wild side, the one who craved to be fucked. The one who wanted to fuck just about any man because SHE felt that, simply put, a man was a man and a dick was a dick. The one that felt conversation was never needed, nor were games, because SHE knew within five minutes after SHE laid eyes on a man whether SHE wanted to fuck him or not.

SHE first appeared back in my freshman year of college. At that time, I would spend lonely nights in my dorm room masturbating myself to sleep by playing with my nipples and rubbing a sheet or towel in between my legs. I imagined having wild, passionate sex with men that had no faces until I climaxed and the sheet or towel was soaking wet with my nectar.

I have always been a pretty girl, above average even, I would say. It was never a question of whether I thought I looked good enough to get a man. I was just too nervous to talk to the men who pursued me. They came in all shapes and sizes and from all walks of life. Most were extremely nice and attractive. I wanted to wait and give my virginity to the man I would ultimately marry, but SHE could not wait.

One cold winter night of my freshman year, I was studying in the university library when SHE saw him. He was average height, about five-nine, and not what one would call *foine* yet attractive. It was his eyes that made him desirable. His eyes seemed to have a passion burning inside of them. SHE sat there, at a table across the room from where he was standing at a bookcase flipping through some pages, and SHE could feel her panties becoming damp from the growing desire to feel him inside her. SHE crossed her legs and moved them back and forth, creating a light friction against her vagina and making her desire even more intense. SHE didn't realize that SHE was sucking on the eraser of her pencil and staring at him until SHE felt him staring back. SHE moved her eyes up from where they had locked on the bulge of his pants to his face, and for what seemed like an endless moment, their eyes met. He broke the stare and smiled at her. It was then that SHE noticed he had the softest-looking lips. SHE yearned to draw the bottom one into her mouth and suck on it.

SHE looked back down at the economics books SHE was studying for a brief moment, contemplating her next move. When SHE looked up, he was gone. SHE panicked, scanning the library quickly, until SHE noticed him getting in the elevator. He looked at her and smiled as the doors were closing. Something within her exploded, and SHE knew what had to be done. SHE jumped up from the table, leaving her books, coat, and purse and ran out the exit door, going down the steps two at a time, hoping to catch up to him before the elevator reached the ground floor.

When SHE reached ground level, it was too late. The elevator was empty, and he was gone. SHE went out the front door of the library into the cold, brisk winter air, hoping to catch a glimpse of his red ski jacket, but saw nothing. As SHE turned around to go back into the library and retrieve her things, with disappointment in her heart, SHE looked up and he was standing there. In fact, SHE bumped right into his chest and could feel her heart pounding in her own as he looked deep into her eyes, up close and personal for the first time.

He opened his mouth to say something, probably to ask her name, but SHE put her finger over his lips. For what reason SHE was unsure, but SHE knew that talking would only ruin it. Maybe SHE feared that I would rejoin the situation, bringing all my shattered nerves with me at the thought of a mere conversation with a man. Who knows?

SHE smiled at him, took him by the hand, and pulled him back inside the library with her. SHE pushed the button for the elevator. When they got on, instead of pushing the button for the floor where her belongings were, SHE pressed the button for the basement, where all the stacks were located. SHE knew it would be basically deserted and dark down there. It was the perfect place for what SHE had in mind.

When the elevator began to descend, SHE took his hand and placed it between her legs. SHE had on a black skirt with a white bodysuit underneath and silk panties. SHE could feel his fingers push the crotch of her bodysuit and panties aside and explore her wetness. He brought his face closer to hers and was about to explore her mouth with his tongue when they reached the basement level and the doors came open.

Just as SHE imagined, the stacks were deserted. He left his backpack right beside the then closed elevator, picked her up with her legs straddled around his back, and carried her to the rear of the stacks, where a few scattered desks were located. He sat her down on top of one of them.

Their clothes came off quickly, both of them ripping at the other's until they were completely naked in the dimly lit room. SHE took one of her fingers and rubbed it against her clit, taking it and putting it into his mouth, letting him savor her juice off of it. SHE rubbed the finger against her clit again, this time sucking her own juice off her finger. Then they began to kiss, both savoring her sweetness at the same time.

He pushed her back on the desk so that her head was hanging halfway over the rear and her nipples were protruding upward into the air. He suckled on them one at a time, not only taking her dark pearls into his mouth but licking the entire breast, starting at the base of each one with the tip of his tongue and making light, circular strokes until he reached the hardened prize. SHE was in ecstasy. So many nights had been spent alone rubbing her nipples between her fingers, and now a man was devouring them just like SHE had yearned for all that time. He took them both up, one in each hand, pushing them together and then sweeping both nipples into his mouth at the same time. Her moans became louder.

Still palming her breasts, he made a trail with his tongue down to her belly button, pausing just long enough to take a quick dip into it before moving down to explore between her thighs. Before SHE could even prepare herself for what was about to come, he took her hardened clit into his mouth and began to let it vibrate on the tip of his tongue. SHE came for the first time in a matter of seconds; the intensity of having his mouth touch her there was too much to handle.

He continued eating her pussy for the next fifteen minutes or so, and SHE came at least five or six more times before he had sated his hunger. Then he walked around to the other side of the desk, where her head was still hanging over the side, and SHE came face to face with his delicious-looking dick. SHE hesitated not for a second and took the head of it into her mouth with a heightened desire to know what he tasted like.

And there, with her head upside down, SHE sucked a dick for the very first time. SHE held the base of it while he dick-fed her, pushing his manhood in and out of her mouth with increasing speed. SHE relaxed her throat so that he could eventually get it all in. SHE loved every minute of it. As his body began to tremble and his knees began to buckle, SHE was given the added treat of tasting semen and was immediately hooked for life on the scrumptious flavor. SHE lay there, savoring every single drop, and secretly hoping there would be more to come. Never had SHE tasted anything so yummy.

82   Zane

He removed his dick from her throat, now a little sore and tender but never the worse for wear. After going back to the other side of the table, he pushed his dick deep inside her awaiting pussy. SHE could feel her hymen break and realized that virginity was now a thing of her past. He fucked her hard. Considering the way SHE had picked him up and led the way to the basement, he had no idea that this was her first time. He just thought SHE had a tight-ass pussy, and he was taken aback at how snugly it fit around his throbbing dick.

He fucked her without mercy because he knew that SHE wanted it that way. SHE was paralyzed at first when he stuck it in, but gradually SHE grew in tune with his rhythm and began to grind her hips, fucking him back. SHE could feel his balls slamming up against her ass and was mesmerized by the sound of his dick invading her pussy, for it was a sound SHE had never heard before. SHE loved it.

After a few more minutes, SHE felt him explode again, this time inside her pussy walls, his sweat trickling off his forehead onto her breasts. Her stomach muscles contracted as he removed his well-satisfied dick from her sweet pussy. He began to say something. SHE intervened, saying, "No, please don't!"

SHE got up from the desk, dressing quickly and looking at his dick with veins bulging from all directions. SHE knew that SHE had to get the hell out of there quickly, for SHE was halfway ashamed of what SHE had done. SHE was even more ashamed at how much SHE enjoyed it.

SHE left him there, in the basement of the library, nude and wondering why the hell SHE demanded anonymity and silence, hoping that one day he would see her again. And one day he did, in the student union. SHE walked right past him and pretended SHE didn't recognize him. He turned to go after her and beg her to at least tell him her name. With the same haste SHE had entered his life, SHE exited it. He looked for her, and SHE was gone.

Gone like SHE was when all the other men looked for her. SHE always fucked them quickly, in silence, and then left them in awe. There was the man SHE saw in the grocery store line, waiting for him patiently in the parking lot and then fucking him right there in the backseat of his car. There was the gas station attendant SHE took into one of the garage bays and fucked while SHE was waiting for another guy outside to change her tire. There were the two guys SHE saw playing basketball one day at the local park that SHE tantalized into the woods and there, on a secluded picnic table, fucked them both. And, of course, there were all the men SHE had picked up at hotel bars, nightclubs, and virtually every place else over the past five years. A total number of which SHE has lost count of long ago.

Her appetite is insatiable and undeniable. SHE can never get enough when SHE appears. As for me, I am still nervous, but hopefully one of these days, SHE and I will become one and settle down with one man who can satisfy both our needs. Until then, SHE will just continue to have her fun, ruling the weekends, and I will continue my boring-ass weekdays. One thing is for sure, though. When I masturbate now, I have multiple orgasms and enjoy my body in ways I never imagined before. Maybe SHE and I have already become one. Or have we?

Side Note: The female character from this story is the main character from a novel I have in progress entitled *Nervous*. *Nervous* will be the second in a series of novels featuring a prominent African-American psychiatrist named Dr. Marcella Spencer. Dr. Spencer deals with an array of clients suffering from different forms of sexual problems. The first in the series is my novel *Addicted*, available from Pocket Books.

Wrong Number

"I'm sorry, you have the wrong number!" It started with a wrong number and ended with the fuck of a lifetime. It was about seven o'clock on a Wednesday night, hump day, and I was worn the hell out after a hard day at the office. My live-in boyfriend, Tony, wasn't home yet. It was his night to play basketball with the boys at the gym. I was sitting there on the couch with my legs up, sipping on a glass of red wine and watching *Judge Judy* while I was waiting for my chicken breasts and baked potatoes to finish baking.

At the time, Tony and I had been living together for a little over a year, and it was all good. Things were going well between us. The lovemaking was very satisfying. I don't know why I did what I did, and I'm not trying to make excuses for it. All I can say is, I had fallen into kind of a rut. Let's face it, shit happens!

When the phone rang, I figured it must have been my mother or one of my girlfriends but had no idea, since the caller ID was in the bedroom. I picked it up and said, "Hello." The man on the other end of the line said, "Hello, may I please speak to Stacey?" I told him, "I'm sorry, you have the wrong number!"

He then asked, "Is this 555-2269?" and I said, "No, this is 555-2268." So he said, "Sorry, my mistake. Have a good evening!" and I replied, "You too. Peace!"

Now, you would have thought that would be the end of it, but naw. About a half hour later, *Judge Judy* had gone off, and *Real Life Stories of the Highway Patrol* was on, where they show people getting their asses arrested and shit in real life. They have cameras all up in their faces. It's mad funny to me for a person to not only get caught in the act, but cold busted on TV in front of millions of people as well. Anyway, I had just taken the chicken out of the oven and thrown a pouch of boil-in-the-bag rice into a pot on the stove when the phone rang.

I assumed the same thing I did the first time, must be my mother or one of the girls. Wrong again, because he called my ass back. I don't know what the fuck happened, but I ended up flirting with him on the phone for over an hour. He had a deep, mesmerizing, sexy-ass voice, and frankly, the shit turned me on.

Why I told him my name was Amber, I have no idea. Probably because it was the logical response to him telling me his name was Rob. He just made me feel so comfortable and at ease. There I was, kicking it with some stranger on the phone about everything from the latest Puff Daddy and the Family CD to our respective careers to my hair appointment the next day. He and I talked about the fact that there are so few black barbershops and hair salons in our predominately white New England town. I happened to mention that I used a stylist named LaLa at this salon called She Thang over on Twelfth Street.

Even though the conversation was stimulating, I finally told him I had to go because it was getting late. He asked me could he call again sometime, and I said, "Absolutely hell fucking no! My boyfriend would kill me if nuccas started calling the house for me while he's home!" He said he completely understood and that it was nice meeting me, even if it was only over the phone, and insisted on asking one question before we hung up. I asked what the question was, and he asked me to describe what I looked like.

I told him that I was five-nine, 145 pounds, and light-skinned, with shoulder-length medium brown hair, and half Native American. He told me, "You sound delicious!" He volunteered his information before I could even ask and told me that he was six-one, 190 pounds, and dark-skinned with hazel eyes. I told him what was on my mind and replied, "You sound delicious too!" That was it except for the formal good-byes.

I made love to Tony that night and fell asleep in his arms fantasizing about a nucca named Rob who I knew by voice and description alone. I was so aroused that I couldn't sleep. I woke Tony up in the middle of the night by sucking on his dick, and it was all good.

The next day at work was a typical Thursday. I'm a human resource manager for a construction company. I left about an hour early, after changing into some casual clothes, so I could get to my 5 P.M. hair appointment on time. I beat the work traffic and got there ten minutes early. Of course, when I got there, LaLa had one client in her chair, one under the hot-ass hair dryer waiting for all that dayum gel to dry up in her finger waves, and another one sitting in the lounge area with a magazine, waiting to get shampooed. I was not fucking surprised, since hair stylists always overbook and shit to ensure they keep clocking dollars whether everyone shows up or not.

I finally got my touch-up in about an hour later. I was sitting in the chair at LaLa's station, waiting for her to blow-dry me when the phone rang at the salon. One of the other stylists, this big-ass girl named Shakia, told me that the phone was for me. I was dumbfounded, wondering who in the hell would be calling me at the hairdresser.

I went to the telephone, and it was Rob. I was fucking shocked. He told me that since I said he could never call me at home again because of Tony, he knew calling me at the salon was the only chance he would ever have to speak with me again. He said that he was only about twenty minutes from there, and he couldn't resist knowing I was going to be coming out looking good with my hair just done and wanted to drive over and meet me.

I was so scared, thinking to myself, Is this man crazy? I was hoping his ass wasn't crazy, but figured what the hell. I might as well take the chance, since I was in public. If I didn't feel right, I would just leave his ass there.

About thirty minutes later, LaLa was done with my hair, and he had not shown up, so I was contemplating leaving. I was sitting there flipping through some magazines when he came bouncing in the door, plopped down right beside me, and smiled this big ole grin. I couldn't help but do the same, because the man was too dayum fine.

I was a nervous wreck because everyone was looking. I walked outside quickly, and we stood in front of the salon talking for a few. He asked me if I would like to go to a restaurant down the street called the Cuckoo's Nest and I accepted. I was tripping hard because this was totally out of character for me. My ass walked down there with him anyway.

We were seated at a table in the corner. I asked him to excuse me while I went to the ladies' lounge to freshen up, but that was not the real reason I needed to leave the table for a few moments. I had to call Tony and make up an excuse for being out so late. I called him from the pay phone in the hall-way leading to the rest rooms and explained how I had run into a girlfriend at the hair salon, decided to go out for a couple of drinks, and would be home about midnight.

I came back to the table and became lost in Rob's voice, eyes, and the whole package. Time seemed to fly by. It was 10 P.M. by the time we finished our meal and went through two bottles of nice Chablis. We left the restaurant and walked back to the pay parking lot where both our vehicles were located. I started up my Honda Accord and decided to sit in Rob's Grand Cherokee while I was waiting for it to warm up. I assumed the night was ending there. I had to work in the morning and knew I was already in trouble, but somehow talking turned into kissing. We sat and kissed and hugged and kissed and talked and hugged some more.

I told him I really had to get going. He leaned over for a final kiss and then whispered in my ear, "I don't want you to leave tonight!" He laid this kiss on me that made me melt, so I turned off my car, got back in the truck, and asked, "Okay, so now what?"

The parking lot attendant had been watching us from his booth a short distance away the whole time. The kissing and hugging went on for a good hour, and I couldn't take it anymore. I told him I knew about this really secluded lake about five minutes away. Off we went with a quickness.

After we got there, he started kissing me again and feeling all over my breasts. That drives me wild because my nipples are the most sensitive part of my body. I was so wet, I could feel the juices squishing between my legs. I had on this thin jogging suit, which wasn't helping matters any.

I figured we weren't going all the way. I'd just give him some hellified head, and that would be that. I unzipped his pants and put my lips to work. He leaned back in his seat and moaned and begged me not to stop. He was getting ready to cum when he said, "Hold up!" Then, all of a sudden, he put his hand down my pants from the backside and pushed his fingers in me, and that was it. I was done! He had me from that point on, and the shit felt *soooooo* good.

Rob said, "I can't let you do me and not return the favor!" He got out of the truck, came around to my side, opened my door, and swung my legs around. He pushed my shirt up and pulled my sneakers and pants off and threw them on the floor of the truck. He spread my legs open and started eating my pussy like a man on death row devouring his last meal.

I kept saying, "Ohhhh, Rob!" I was at a loss for any other words. It was dead quiet out that night. There were no cars. Just the sounds of nature and me and him moaning and ooooing and ahhhing. Then he went into a bag he had in the back of his truck, pulled out a condom, and put it on. He reclined my seat and starting fucking me like there was no tomorrow. I came SOOOOOO HARD! I wanted to scream, but I was still holding back because I really didn't know this man from Adam.

He stopped before he came, had me get out the truck, and bent me over. I was leaned over on the seat with my feet on the ground when he did it to me from behind. I loved that shit. My ass must have been shining in the moonlight, but I didn't even care at that point. He came, and I came again, and needless to say, my new hairdo was sweated the hell out.

We put our clothes back on. I was feeling like a whore, since I had never done anything like that before. He drove me back to my car, kissed me good night, gave me his number, and that was it. Even though the events of the evening were totally uncharacteristic of me, I look back on it now with no regrets because everyone needs to release their wild side every now and then. Men do it all the time, you know what I mean?

Tony and I are still together. I called Rob once, a few days after we fucked in the moonlight by the lake, and asked him did he think I was a slut. He said, "No! In fact, it just makes me want to see more of you!"

Sitting here now, recalling all of this and becoming horny as hell for him all over again, only one thought comes to mind. Dayum, maybe I need to call him tonight and see what he's doing!

A Flash Fantasy

When I arrived at the building in the warehouse district, I was a bit apprehensive. Not because of the neighborhood. It had character—the kind of character it takes generations to acquire.

I was on pins and needles because I hate to have my picture taken. I've been that way ever since childhood. When I was seven, I was a flower girl in my cousin's wedding. I refused to take pictures with the rest of the wedding party. She had to chase me around the churchyard in her bridal gown for ten minutes before she persuaded me to cooperate.

I scanned the nameplates beside the column of doorbells until I spotted the one with "Curtis Givens—Photographer" engraved on it. I hesitated before pushing the little black button. I had to go through with it. It wasn't like I had a choice. My boss demanded I get a professional picture taken for the new corporate brochure he was having printed up for all of our clients.

When the intercom squeaked, it startled me. "Who is it?" a deep, baritone voice inquired.

"Evoni Price from the Grayson Corporation," I replied hesitantly.

The only response was the loud buzzer, letting me know I was free to enter the building.

I took the freight elevator up to the third floor. Before I could lift the gate, a strong muscular hand did the honors. I glanced up into the sexiest damn, brownest damn, most enticing damn eyes I had ever seen.

"Welcome to Givens Photography Studio," he said, grinning at me and revealing a cinematic smile. "Come on in and make yourself at home."

I followed him into his domain. I purposely trailed a few steps behind so I could get an eagle's-eye glimpse of his perfectly formed behind.

He directed me to a black leather love seat. "Please, have a seat, Miss Price. Or is it Mrs.?"

"No, it's definitely Miss," I replied, not sure why I was stressing the point. Maybe it had something to do with the fine specimen of a man standing before me.

He was just the right height, the color of bubbling brown sugar, and he looked twice as sweet. I had the sudden urge to lick him like a lollipop to see if it gave me a sugar rush.

"Would you like a mug of coffee before we get started with the shoot?"

"No, thanks!" Lawd knows, I was nervous enough without caffeine intervening. I was about to get my picture taken, I hadn't been laid since I was promoted to the Vice President of Promotions, and a sexy-ass man was within striking distance to me.

"Maybe some water or a soft drink?"

"No thanks, I'm fine. Really!"

"Indeed, you are!" Our eyes met again. My knee took on a

life of its own. It started rocking back and forth, causing a friction on my clit. "If I had known such an attractive sista would be showing up on my doorstep this morning, I would've dressed for the occasion."

"You look just fine." Hell, he looked better than fine. He looked like a glass of ice cold water in the middle of the desert; mouthwatering. He was wearing a pair of drawstring navy cotton pants and a white body-hugging T-shirt that revealed every ripple and muscle of his toned physique.

"Well, I'm going to grab some coffee if you don't mind. I'm still feeling a little sheepish this morning. I tend to be a night owl."

"Nothing wrong with that," I commented. "I work very long hours myself."

"I hope you're not all work and no play. A young, vivacious sista like yourself needs to paint the town every now and then."

"I wish. The only painting I get to do is touching up my nails."

We shared a laugh, and he headed off to the kitchen. I couldn't help but notice the size of his feet. Umph, umph, umph! Let's just say my peter heater went up about fifty degrees.

While he was gone, I took a quick survey of his place. It was a huge apartment with a loft. I immediately wondered what type of bed he had stowed away. He looked like a waterbed man to me. I was willing to bet he could make a lot of waves.

There were photographs hanging all over the walls of beautiful African-Americans: men, women, and children. I was thoroughly impressed. The walls were an eggshell hue, and they worked wonderfully in contrast to the colorful pictures. The flooring was wooden parquet, and he had expensive throw rugs scattered here and there.

His voice in my ear startled me because I didn't hear him come back in the room, rather less walk up so close to me that

I could feel his breath on the nape of my neck. "Shall we get started?"

"Fine by me," I mumbled, not looking forward to posing for a camera. "Where would you like me to sit?"

He surveyed the room while he sipped on his java and then pointed to one of the windows with his free hand. "I think over by that window would be great. The sunlight hitting up against your beautiful skin would be perfect."

I tried to control the blush, but it simply wasn't happening. I looked into his mesmerizing eyes. "You really think I have beautiful skin?"

He quickly responded. "I think you have beautiful everything!"

We stared at each other, and I suddenly had the urge to jump his bones. He finally broke the trance and cleared his throat before taking another swig out of his mug. He put the coffee down on an end table and then moved a crate over by the window. I watched him intensely while he covered it with a black velvet blanket. Then he held out his hand for me.

I walked over to him. The moment I took his hand, a surge of electricity shot through my entire body. I wondered if he felt it too.

"Why don't you have a seat right here?"

"Thanks!"

He positioned my shoulders and held my chin up until he was satisfied with the pose. "Hold it right there. Don't move."

He quickly retrieved a camera with a long lens and squatted down a few feet in front of me. "Smile for me, beautiful."

I couldn't do it. I couldn't smile. I was suddenly encased by fear. I started gnawing on my bottom lip and my hands began trembling uncontrollably.

"What's wrong, Evoni?"

I looked into Curtis's eyes, but no answer would come to my lips. Instead, tears came to my eyes.

"I'm so ashamed!" I jumped up from the crate, wiping my eyes with the sleeve of my suit. "Look, this just isn't a good day for me. Is it alright if I schedule another appointment? Maybe for next week sometime?"

I was headed to the door, after retrieving my purse and keys off his sofa, when he grabbed me by the hand and swung me around. "What's wrong with you, Evoni?" he reiterated. "Have I done something to upset you?"

"No, it's not you!" I exclaimed. The last thing I wanted him to think was that he had offended me. "I know that this is silly, but—"

"But what?"

He looked so sincere, so comforting, so sexy. "I hate having my picture taken."

He started laughing something terrible. "Is that all?" I lowered my eyes to the floor. "A lot of people get nervous about having their picture taken. Just relax."

He let go of my hand and started caressing my shoulders. It felt so damn good. I still wasn't relaxed enough to pose for a picture, though. I had no idea what I was going to tell my boss. I would just have to make up something. The brochure would have to go out to our clients minus my picture.

I pulled away from his embrace. "I'm sorry. I just can't do this. You've been so kind to me. I'll definitely recommend you to all of my friends. Do you have some extra business cards I can hand out?"

There was an uncomfortable silence for a few minutes. I could sense his eyes all over me, exploring my face, my body. Then it came out of nowhere. *The kiss.*

He took my face in his hands and lifted it until I was lost in his eyes again. He started with my forehead. Short, sweet, tender kisses. His lips moved down to the ridge of my nose and glided down slowly and methodically until they found mine. My mouth gratefully and hungrily accepted his tongue without hesitation. Before I knew it, I was totally engrossed in his arms and he in mine.

Our kisses became deeper. The next thing I knew he had me up against the wall with my legs straddled around his waist, and my blazer was toppling to the floor. Then the kisses stopped as suddenly as they began.

He put me back down on the floor gently and took my hand. "Follow me."

I whispered, "I would follow you anywhere."

He led me into the bathroom and then shut the door. I assumed he wanted to take a shower or bath together. Much to my surprise, he twirled me around until we were both facing a full-length mirror on the back of the door.

"Why don't you like to take pictures, Evoni?" He reached around me and started unbuttoning my blouse. "You're so incredibly beautiful."

I stood there, frozen, and glared in the mirror while he seductively removed all of my clothing, nibbling on my neck and shoulder blades while he went about his task. Once I was entirely nude, he took my pert breasts into his palms and rubbed my hard nipples between his thumbs and forefingers.

One of his hands dropped down and found the cherry between my thighs. I was in a trance, somewhere between reality and heaven's gate. His fingers worked magic on my clit and explored my pussy lips with a tenderness I had never felt.

Then he blurted it out. "Let me take your picture. Let me take a picture of the *real* you."

I was still nervous, but by that point, I was so much into

him that even taking a picture was acceptable. Posing in the nude was something I never imagined doing. Hell, I never even wanted to pose with clothes on, but for this man who went by the name of Curtis, I was not only willing but eager to please him.

"Okay," I replied, taking a hold of the hand between my legs and guiding his fingers deeper into me. I stared at him in the mirror. "Take my picture."

We left the bathroom, and he laid me down on his waterbed. It was covered with red satin sheets. He removed the pins from my hair, letting my hair flow down around my shoulders. He bent over and kissed me. "Wait right here, baby."

He left to get his camera, and while he was gone, I played with my nipples. I had never masturbated in front of a man before, but I didn't stop when he reentered the room. In fact, I put on a show for him.

I masturbated while he took pictures of me. I can't believe I can actually just come out and say it like that, but that's exactly what I did and I have no regrets. I didn't look at the camera, though. I shut my eyes and pretended it was his hands on my breasts and fingering my pussy. I imagined him taking me right there on his bed, grabbing my full hips and pulling them deeper onto his dick, partaking of me from the front and then from the back. I imagined him suckling on my nipples and nibbling on my ass cheeks. I imagined him sliding his dick in and out of my mouth, and his cum trickling out of the sides and down my chin, splattering on my breasts. Then, when I had imagined it all, I came all over his red satin sheets. I came in front of the camera. I came like I never had.

He snapped one last picture, and then I heard the humming while the camera automatically rewound the film. It was that moment I opened my eyes. I was shocked to see that he was naked. To this day, I still don't know when he took off his clothes. All I know is that he looked good. Damn good.

I sat up on the bed and reached out my arms for him. He put the camera down on the foot of the bed and joined me. Then I jumped his bones for real. We did all the things I had imagined when I was masturbating.

Curtis and I have been living together for more than a year now. Our wedding is next month. I just can't wait to see how the wedding pictures turn out.

A Time for Change

Drake and I had been married for less than two years when I was ready to pack my things up and leave his ass for good. Don't get me wrong! He wasn't physically or emotionally abusive or anything of that nature. It wasn't from lack of attention or quality time together either. I was on the verge of deserting him and heading home to Momma for one reason and one reason only. He didn't fuck me right.

I know what you're thinking. Why didn't I know he couldn't fuck before the marriage? I agree it is a logical question. I only wish I had a logical answer. Drake was very romantic during our dating relationship and extremely sincere. I guess I let those qualities overshadow his lack of sexual skills. I didn't feel putting sex in front of other priorities was the *mature* thing to do.

On my wedding night, I realized my horrid mistake. Throughout the engagement, Drake and I always talked about how we were going to save some things for the honeymoon, such as performing oral sex on one another, and that was cool with me. I wanted something special to look forward to just like him.

We had a beautiful wedding ceremony in my mother's back-
yard in Cleveland. By that time, we were already settled down
in a cozy little apartment together in Akron but still abstained
from oral sex until the wedding. It was on my wedding night
that Drake made it apparent he only planned to go downtown to
window-shop and never intended to actually purchase anything.

The sex on our honeymoon was swift and effortless, boring
even. I should've gotten an annulment, but I truly love Drake.
For almost two years, I suffered through lying in the dark in the
missionary position, exactly two times a week, while he had his
way with me. I never had orgasms because he was done before
I could ever become aroused enough to come. Half of the time
I was so turned off, he fucked me dry, and it became painful.

I tried everything I could possibly think of, including romantic, seductive evenings, wearing sexy lingerie, etc. He was
totally unreceptive to all these things. He would just fuck me
quick and then go to sleep, assuming the satisfaction was mutual.

I tried reading erotic material aloud to him in bed, buying
him skin mags, and even renting pornos. He would listen to
the erotica, although it obviously made him uncomfortable,
but flat-out refused to look at the mags or porno movies.

Despite constant temptation from men at the office and
the gym where I work out, I couldn't bring myself to cheat on
Drake, so I did the next best thing. Men made love to me the
way I wanted them to in my mind. I became a mental
nymphomaniac, thinking about sex every second of every day,
no matter where I was or what I was doing. It satisfied my sexual urges for a little while, but not for long.

Then I asked a female friend of mine, who always seemed
so sexually in tune with herself, to tell me how to masturbate,
and she gave me blow-by-blow instructions. I would sneak and
do it whenever I could, while Drake was working late at the

office or gone out to the store. I tried to make every private moment an erotic one. Once, I even masturbated in the bathtub while he was right in the other room.

I was going nuts! The daydreams and masturbation were cool, but I needed Drake to make love to me in all the ways I desired. He just wasn't responding though.

Desperate times call for desperate measures. So one night, over a dinner of fried chicken, mashed potatoes, and peas, I told Drake when my vacation from work came up in a couple weeks, I was going home to visit my mother. Then I added, "I may not be coming back!"

They were the most difficult words I had ever spoken, but they had to come out. He asked me, "Why? What do you mean? Are you saying you want a divorce?"

I got up from the kitchen table, walked over, and leaned on the counter. "Drake, I love you more than anything in this world, but there are some issues we need to work out."

"Then we'll work them out, if you just tell me what they are. But you're not leaving me, Bridget!" I could see the anger and hurt all over his face. It was killing me inside.

"I've tried to talk to you about them. Given you every hint in the book, and you never give me a positive response!" We were both raising our voices. It wasn't a pleasant encounter because we had never argued in our marriage, partly because I was so submissive to him and accepted everything without question.

I'm so glad I confronted him, because he came over to the counter and held me, telling me how much he loved me and was willing to do anything to make it work.

We retired to the bedroom and lay there in each other's arms. I told him everything about my daydreams, the masturbation, the things I desired. He admitted he had a problem opening up sexually, saying it would make him feel like he was disrespecting me to do certain things.

I reminded him of how we had agreed to save oral sex until the honeymoon, but to that day, it had never once happened. I also told him I wanted us to experiment with different positions and toys. The toy statement threw his ass for a loop. I suggested we just go to sleep because it was getting late and we both had to work in the A.M. Since the next day was Friday, I suggested we go shopping after work together.

After Drake got off from work, he swung by the apartment and picked me up. I had already looked up the address of the store I was looking for in the yellow pages and called to inquire about their business hours. My girlfriend, the same one who taught me how to masturbate, mentioned the place to me, saying it was where she purchased all her sexual playthings.

We found the store, called the Pleasure Palace, in a secluded alley downtown. It was off the hook! Drake was ready to turn around and leave the moment we walked in the door. I was expecting a few interesting items but nothing close to what they actually had. They had some shit I had never imagined.

They had the normal stuff like vibrators, dildos, adult videos and magazines, vulgar-printed tees, sexy lingerie, etc. They also sold adult board games, oils that get hot when you blow on them, novelty items such as penis ballpoint pens, male and female strip pens where the people lose their clothes when you turn them upside down. All sorts of wild stuff. They even had penis and asshole pen holders and a monkey-jerking-off key chain. They had turbo-powered vibrators, vibrators in neon colors, and even vibrators with tongue and anal sleeves. They had anal beads, Ben Wa balls, butt plugs, the whole nine yards.

They sold neon condoms, vibrator cleaner and lube combos, hand-job lubrication lotions, nipple drops in different flavors such as guava/pineapple, orange/mango, and strawberry/kiwi, edible climax gel, anal eze gel, and cherry-flavored stay-hard creme. They had leather whips and chains, masks, three-snap leather cock rings that came with or without spikes, studded cock-and-ball harnesses, three-piece leather cock-and-ball dividers, handcuffs. My personal favorite was the gates of hell, a cock-ring set of three or five held together by a leather strap that a man wears on the shaft of his dick while he fucks you.

After much convincing, I talked Drake into staying, reminding him of our conversation the night before. He agreed, but said he did have his limits. I reassured him I would never ask him to do anything that made him feel humiliated or uneasy. From that point on, it was cool. We shopped together, going up and down each aisle, as if we were at the local supermarket.

We left the Pleasure Palace about an hour later with a shopping bag full of goodies, got into Drake's car, and headed home. I could tell Drake was very tense in the car and reached over, caressing his leg. He was as stiff as a board. I knew that if I could just get him to relax and let his inner sexual desires escape from the stronghold his mind had constructed around them, our sex life would be extremely gratifying.

I reached into the shopping bag and pulled out one of the items I had selected: a big black, ribbed dildo. Drake's eyes lit up when I put one of my feet up on the dashboard, lifted my skirt, pushed my panties to the side, and slowly inserted the tip of it into my pussy walls.

He almost lost control of the car, but I continued pushing more and more of it in until only the bottom of it was sticking out and started fucking myself with it. I used my other hand to caress my nipples through my cotton blouse and really started getting into it, licking my lips and moaning from the intense pleasure derived from the hard, thick dildo.

Drake managed to say, "Bridget, how come you never told me you were like this?"

I looked him right in the eyes and replied, "Because you never asked, baby!"

I let go of my breasts and started caressing his dick through his pants instead. I could tell Drake was turned on by it. What man seeing his woman masturbate in front of him wouldn't get turned on? Even though I had never used a dildo before, I had developed quite an expertise in the masturbation arena, so it was easy for me to cum all over the leather seat of his car. He was done in when he saw it because, as I mentioned before, I never came when he and I had sex.

We were driving past a city park, and I told him to pull over in a parking space. At this point, he became the submissive one in the marriage. I loved it then and love it now. Drake loves it too.

I got out the car and walked over to a park bench by the large water fountain in the center of the park. It was dark and deserted as Drake followed me over to the bench. I lifted up my skirt, bent over the backside of the bench, and told him to rip my panties off. He walked up behind me but didn't rip them off, so I said it louder, "RIP MY PANTIES OFF!" He not only tore them off but also tore them bad boys to shreds.

Then my husband, the one who would never turn the lights on, would never have oral sex, would never try anything new, fucked the hell out of me from behind, and I was thrilled beyond compare. The only noises were the trickling of the water cascading from the fountain, filled at the bottom with pennies tossed in by people who made wishes, and our heavy breathing.

Drake pulled my hair back and started fucking me real hard. He asked, "Am I hurting you?"

I told him, "No, fuck me harder!" He did just that until we came in unison.

Afterward, I sat there in his lap on the bench, and we laughed and giggled like we never had before. We went home, and Drake did everything I asked him to. He fucked me with the dildo, played a sexual board game with me, stuck anal beads in my ass while I was riding his dick and pulled them out as I was cumming. He even handcuffed me to our bed, blindfolded on my stomach, and fucked me from behind again. Then we took a long, hot shower together and performed oral sex on each other for the very first time.

I had waited so long for the moment, and it was more than worth it. We have oral sex just about every day now, not to mention all the other things we do to each other. The Pleasure Palace has become our favorite store in Akron, and we are two of their biggest customers. We can't get enough of trying out new things, and our marriage is fantastic.

Recently, one of my friends from high school surprised me with a call. My mother gave her my new number, and we played catch up over the phone. She started telling me how her married life was depressing her. Ironically, when I asked her why, she had the same problem I had in the beginning—an unreceptive husband. I recalled the phrase "Each One, Teach One" and thought about how a friend had helped me out in my time of need. I started telling her the basic techniques of masturbation, all about sex toys and things she could do to spice up her sex life. She was concerned her husband wouldn't do any of it. I told her she had to put her foot down like I did and tell him, "It's time for a change!"

Get Well Soon

I never saw the car coming until it knocked me ten feet up in the air. As soon as I hit the asphalt, I knew my leg was broken. I heard the crunch. The pain was unreal and worse than anything I could have ever imagined.

The driver, some teenager who looked like she should be at home playing with dolls instead of driving a car, and her two friends jumped out and crowded around me along with other people who brought their cars to a complete halt. One of the pedestrians was a med student. He told everyone not to move me until the ambulance arrived. He talked to me and asked me where it hurt, what my name was, and all the usual questions.

I could hear the sirens approaching as I watched the driver fall into one of her friends' arms and start to wail. I got the distinct feeling she was more concerned about whether or not she would lose her driver's license than my welfare.

Two days later, there I was, laid up in the hospital with my left leg elevated in a cast and suffering from a severe case of depression. You had been to see me on a daily basis, but when the nurse told us visiting hours were over, I was devastated.

You were the only thing that brightened up my day, and they made you leave.

After you left, I found some late-night talk shows on the tube and nibbled off the fried chicken dinner I asked you to sneak in for me so I wouldn't have to eat the nasty-looking meat loaf and processed mashed potatoes they served me for dinner.

I was in a private room with no one to talk to, so once midnight rolled around, I decided I might as well give it up and hit the sack. The night nurse, whose attitude left a lot to be desired, had already come in and taken my temperature and blood pressure, given me some painkiller, and checked the dressing on my leg, so she was off my back, at least for a little while.

I had just dozed off into a light sleep, with the television still on, since I can't sleep without noise, when I heard the door to my hospital room creak open. Much to my surprise, I opened my eyes to find you standing over my bed with a bottle of champagne, two flutes, a picnic basket, and a dozen roses. You are always such the romantic, but you had outdone yourself this time.

I asked you what the hell you were doing there, and you told me about the covert operation that you undertook to sneak in the hospital and into my room. That is when I noticed you had on surgery scrubs and a stethoscope. You looked dayum sexy in the dim light coming from the bathroom and television screen.

You told me how you snuck in through the delivery entrance, found the laundry room and put on the clothes, and found the stethoscope at one of the nurses' stations on your way up. I asked you what the hell you would have done if someone asked you what the roses and picnic basket were for. You said you would have just told them you have one hell of a bedside manner.

As it turned out, you did have one hell of a bedside manner. For a little while, you made me forget I was laid up in a hospital bed with a broken leg. You took me to another world.

First, you fed me some chocolate-covered strawberries and champagne and recited poems to me. You had written them because you missed me at home so much, even though it had only been a couple days.

Then, you fed me wheat crackers along with some Brie cheese and finished it all off with my favorite cheesecake from the deli across the street from our house. You always tease me about being such a cheese fanatic, saying I should have been born a mouse. For a second, we heard someone walking down the hallway and figured we were busted, but whomever it was walked on by.

After you sated my palette, you decided to sate yours. You unfastened the top of my hospital gown and let it droop down over my shoulders. When you broke out the bottle of honey, I knew I was in for a special treat, and indeed I was. You squeezed some over my breasts and licked it slowly off my hard nipples. Normally, I would have wrapped my legs around your waist and gyrated my pussy on your dick, but I couldn't. One of them was a foot above the bed and in shambles. I had to just lie back and enjoy the ecstasy your tongue was bringing me. My pussy was thumping like a rabbit's foot and pussy juice was leaking through my panties.

That is, until you removed them and stuck your beautiful, bald head between my thighs and found the cherry you were looking for. You sucked on each one of my pussy lips individually and then made your way to my clit like a gerbil running through a maze. Instead of a gerbil, your tongue was doing the running. You ate me with such intensity, determined to ensure I would cum at least three times. I came four.

You raised the back of my hospital bed with the automatic

button on the side and then managed to position yourself in front of me so I could get to my *real* dessert, your dick. I helped you undo the drawstring on the surgical pants and whip it out. You glided it in and out of my mouth for me so I wouldn't have to do a lot of work. You knew I was drugged up on painkillers, so you did it slowly. I savored every bit of it. I lifted it up, flicking my tongue over the corona on the bottom, which made you shiver and grab hold of the safety rails.

My desire for you grew until I took your whole dick in my mouth, grabbed a hold of your ass cheeks, and made you pump your dick into my throat faster and faster. My saliva trickled out the corners of my mouth as your dick took up all the room, forcing it out. I sucked and sucked until you exploded in my mouth. We both moaned and shivered because you got to cum and I got to taste you.

We heard a gurney being pushed down the hall and some voices, but once again, we were safe. We figured it was someone being admitted to the hospital late at night, being pushed to his or her assigned room. I suggested you leave before someone walked in on us. You weren't even having it. You said you weren't leaving until you made sure I was completely satisfied.

It took a whole lot of maneuvering but somehow you managed to get your dick in me, even with the elevated leg. You reached over on the nightstand for the stethoscope you had swiped from the nurses' station and put the plugs to your ears. You put the cold part against my chest and listened to my heart pulsating in my chest as you fucked the hell out of me. It made you go crazy. I was wondering why it got such a reaction out of you until you put the plugs on my ears and let me listen to your heart. It was breathtaking; feeling your dick pumping in and out of me and listening to blood pump through your heart at the same time. I had the biggest orgasm ever. In fact, we were both shocked when cum squirted out of me like it does from your dick. Once you saw that, it was all over. You came big-time and laid there in my arms with your chest on top of mine. Both our hearts were jumping out of our chests.

You still didn't leave, saying you had one more thing to accomplish. You pulled out a jar of fudge sauce from the picnic basket you had warmed in the microwave before you left home. Miraculously, it was still warm. You poured some of the sauce on my elevated foot and then licked it all off, sucking each one of my toes at a time. You know how much I love to have my toes sucked. It is the closest a woman can ever come to knowing what it feels like to a man when he has his dick sucked.

You took it to the other foot, pouring sauce on my toes, and then began sucking them one at a time, swirling your tongue around them while they were in your mouth. I came again.

Finally, you decided you better make a dash for the border. It was nearing 3 A.M., and we both knew the nurse would be coming to take my temperature and give me some more painkiller. You gave me the book of African-American poetry you bought for me, kissed me good night, and then snuck out. I laid there reveling in the passion you had shown me, fantasizing about you until I fell asleep.

Dinner at Eight

"Honey, I was in such a rush to get ready for tonight, I completely forgot to put on my panties!" I grinned at you, whispering those words in your ear as the valet pulled off with our car.

We had just arrived at your company Christmas party, being held at a luxury hotel downtown. Your company, one of the biggest brokerage firms on the East Coast, rented out the revolving restaurant on the top level.

We entered the lobby of the hotel, and the bellman suggested we take the glass elevator up instead of the regular elevators in the center of the building. It was a beautiful, clear December evening, and the view of the city was magnificent as the elevator ascended to the restaurant on the fortieth floor. There were two other couples on the elevator with us on their way to the party. We spoke to them, and one of the men was from your department. The two of you discussed a client on the way up.

I was standing behind you, and none of the others could see my hands. I lifted up the back of your dinner jacket and started feeling up your ass. You jumped a little at first, startled that I would even do something like that. I'm usually very conservative in public, but I had been horny all day and couldn't resist you, Christmas party or no Christmas party.

By the time you arrived home, time was of the essence since the sit-down dinner was scheduled for eight. We had to rush out the house. My plans for a quickie were ruined. I was still horny and knew I would be until you broke me off a little sumptin' sumptin'.

When we got upstairs to the rooftop restaurant, the maître d' informed us we would be seated at the table with the head of the company and his wife. You turned to me and looked at me with your sexy-ass eyes. "Boo, you better behave."

I rolled my eyes and straightened your tie for you, moving close enough up on you so I could brush my pussy up against your dick. "Okay, boo, if you insist!"

I gave you a devilish grin and then we followed the maître d' to the table. You put your hand on the small of my back as we were walking, and it gave me goosebumps. After all this time, even your touches arouse me.

All the others were already seated at the table when we arrived. We did the usual greetings. Your boss's wife complimented me on my black evening gown. I returned the favor. We ordered a round of drinks to sip from while the dinner was being prepared.

I ordered a piña colada, and you ordered a vodka and orange juice. When the drinks arrived, I took the cherry out of mine, popped it in my mouth, and did that thing with it that drives you wild. I tied the cherry string into a bow with my long tongue and then sat it down in front of you. You were in the middle of a conversation with your boss, but almost lost it when you saw the cherry string. I could tell it made you horny, thinking about how I use my tongue so methodically on your dick.

The dinner salads and rolls were served while the boring chitchat continued. I asked you to pass me the butter, and when you did, I caressed your fingertips, engaging you in a stare. Saying I would behave and actually doing it are two totally different things—especially when I'm as horny as I was that night.

By the time our dinner finally arrived at the table, my pussy was so moist that I feared it might cause a noticeable stain on my dress. I excused myself, saying I was going to the ladies' room to freshen up. I got in the ladies' lounge and wiped some of the wetness off with a damp paper towel, followed by a dry one.

I returned to the table, took my hand, and pulled your face close to me so I could give you a peck on the lips. I purposely ran my index finger up under your nose so you could get a whiff of my pussy. You shook your head a little, then leaned over to whisper in my ear. "You're so bad, boo. Quit!"

I just looked at you, giggled, and started eating my food. The chicken breast was really dry, but I lied and said it was "succulent, juicy, and delicious." Only you and I knew I was really referring to your dick. Those are the words I always use to describe it.

I kept running my fingers up and down your thigh during dinner and slipped a shoe off so I could rub my toes up your pants leg. You have a foot fetish and love sucking on my toes. I know the idea was running through your mind like wildfire. No one noticed anything because the white linen tablecloth was hiding our discreet activities.

Once the sherbet arrived for dessert, I did some wicked things with my tongue as I licked it off of the long-handled spoon. I stuck my spoon up under the table and inserted the head of it in my pussy very quickly. Then, I scooped up a spoonful of my lime sherbet and told you to taste how delicious the lime was, since you had requested raspberry. The expression on your face gave away the fact you knew the sherbet was well-seasoned.

The pussy sherbet was the straw that broke the camel's back. We opted to skip the after-dinner dance. You made up some cock-and-bull story about our baby-sitter having to leave early so we could haul ass out of there like two bats out of hell.

No sooner had the doors on the glass elevator closed when we were all over each other. You repeated your earlier statement. "You're so bad!"

"Yes, I'm bad. That's why you married me, right?" I grabbed your dick as the elevator began its descent to the lobby. "I just usually save my bad side for home, that's all. But you're looking so sexy and debonair tonight, I couldn't resist you."

I started working at your pants, trying to get *my dick* out, when you inquired, "What the hell are you doing, boo?"

"I want to suck you dry right here in the elevator." I got *my dick* out. "Ummm, you look so scrumptious, boo. Can I have a lick?" I pulled the bottom of my dress up so I could get down on my knees without ripping the material.

You told me to hold up a minute because the elevator was already halfway to the lobby. You pressed the emergency stop button. I started deep-throating your dick, just the way you like it done, while you looked out of the elevator at all the city lights and cars going by on the street. They all looked like colored ants from where we were.

The red phone in the elevator started to ring. No way in hell we were answering it. I kept sucking away, caught a rhythm, and started contracting my cheek muscles on *my dick*. You pulled out of my mouth before I could make you cum and told me to stand up right quick.

You threw me up against the glass, facing the outside and pushed my hands up against the cool surface. You used your foot to spread my legs and then put your dick in my pussy, which was soaked again with my juices. Sucking dick always gets my pussy juices flowing. It's my favorite.

The red phone continued ringing, and you grew concerned. "Maybe we should stop before we cause a panic."

"Hell, no, fuck them! Better yet, fuck me!" You fucked me, too—fast and hard, until we both came about ten minutes later. It was a wild experience, gazing at the stars while you knocked the bottom out of my pussy. I knew from that moment on, having sex in unusual places was a definite must.

We restarted the elevator and straightened our clothes out while it completed its journey to the ground floor. When we got out, the night manager and some maintenance men started to ask us a bunch of questions. We avoided them all, saying they were lucky we didn't sue the pants off their asses.

As we waited for the valet to retrieve our car, we laughed and joked about how much fun it was to fuck in the elevator. In fact we both thought it was so good, when we got back to our apartment building and got on the elevator in the parking garage, we decided to do the shit all over again. Now, I see elevators in a whole new light.

Animal Farm

Making love in unusual places has always turned me on. I've always been creative when it comes to making love to you. One evening, I decided to surprise you by planning something particularly special. I wanted to do something outrageous.

You grew up on a farm and often talked about how much you missed the days of your youth. You always compared the city, where we now live, to country life. I decided to take you back there—if only for one night.

It took quite a bit of doing and a hell of a lot of negotiating to find someone who was willing to let me use their facilities. I finally found an older couple, who were still romantic at heart and gracious enough to let me carry out my plans on their property.

I took the day off of work and drove out to the country to make all of the preparations. You had absolutely no clue I was not in my office that day. I put on a business suit that morning, left the house, and pretended like it was just another day in the grind.

By the time you got off work, I was all sexy for you in a white, skintight dress with a split going all the way up the side. After waiting for you to come out your office building, I told you I had a surprise for you, that I decided to pick you up instead of letting you ride the subway home as usual. I handed you a garment bag and told you to go change into the clothes inside it.

I waited out in the car while you went to change into a black suit, white shirt, and silk tie. When you got in the car, you asked where we were headed. I told you it was a surprise; you would just have to wait and see. The drive was a good ninety miles, and just as I suspected, it was almost nightfall when we arrived at the farm. As I drove up the driveway past the main house, you asked me whose place it was, and I replied, "Just a couple of good friends. You'll meet them later!"

I parked the car directly in front of the barn, letting the high beams highlight the barn doors so we could see how to enter more easily. I told you to get out of the car, and you complied. I asked you to close your eyes, took you by the hand, and led you inside the barn.

Once inside, I told you to open up your eyes. You were shocked to see a king-size bed adorned with huge, fluffy pillows and wildflowers wrapped up in ivy flowing around the bedposts. There was also a small bouquet of wildflowers sprawled across the bed for you.

There was a round table with a white linen tablecloth about ten feet from the bed. The table had white taper candles burning on it and was set with fine china. A bottle of wine was chilling in a silver cooler, and I had a vase of wildflowers placed in the center of the table.

The barn had four horses in two stalls on one side and six

cows in stalls on the other side. They were all pretty calm at the moment, doing what animals do, like eating hay or grass—whatever.

I told you to have a seat at the table, left for a moment to kill the headlights on the car, and got ready to spring my other surprises on you. They were all waiting on the other side of the barn.

I came back in and found you looking all around in dismay from your seat at the table. You laughed at me and said, "You're so crazy, girl! That's why I love you!"

I replied, "I love you too, baby!"

Just then, the doors to the barn opened up, and the violinist entered, wearing a black tuxedo. He started playing for us, and it only made you laugh harder.

You were really shocked when the waiter entered next, also wearing a black tuxedo, pushing a rolling cart covered with a white tablecloth, the kind they use for room service in upper-crust hotels. The catered dinner I ordered earlier that day was on it.

The waiter poured the wine and then proceeded to serve us the lobster in butter sauce, wild rice, steamed vegetables, and buttered rolls while the violinist played soft music throughout the entire meal. It was an extremely romantic evening, just like I had hoped. The animals were still chilling out in their stalls the entire time.

After dinner, I had the waiter and violinist clear out so we could be alone together in the barn. I stood up, took your hand, and led you to the bed. I started kissing you as I pushed you back on the bed and climbed on top of you.

I began to tell you all the things I love about you. I told you how much I love your humor, your compassion, your honesty, your sense of adventure, your romantic nature, the way you make love to me, the way you look, the way you walk, the way you kiss, the way you taste.

Then I handed you the bouquet of wildflowers that were held together by my final surprise. I blurted out the question really fast before I lost my nerve. "Will you marry me?"

I don't know what stunned you more, the question or the gold man's engagement ring on the stems of the flowers. You made me the happiest woman in the world by saying, "Yes!" It was the most beautiful word in the English language at that very moment.

I took the ring off the flowers and placed it on your ring finger. Then I asked you to make love to me with the passion and fire that you always do. We began kissing again. I was still on top of you, but we were sitting up, with my legs hooked around your back.

I undid your tie and practically tore it off because I couldn't wait another minute. We both began ripping at each other's clothes until we were completely nude. You stuck your dick inside me with such ease and grace, I never even saw it coming.

Then you stood up and carried me, dick still inside, over to one of the horse stalls and started fucking me up against it. The sound of my ass banging up against the wooden gate to the stall startled the horse inside, and it started bucking its head and making noises. Before we knew it, the other horses started making noises too, and so did the cows.

Suddenly, I felt the horse rub his head up against the nape of my neck, and I couldn't help but laugh. It tickled and took me by surprise. I reached over my head and started petting the horse, in an effort to make it calm down before it decided to kick its way right out the stall.

You had a better idea, though. You opened the stall and carried me inside. You took your dick out and let me down on the ground just long enough for you to climb on the horse bare-back. Then you took both my hands and lifted me up on the horse, facing me away from you toward the horse's head.

After you lifted me up on your thighs, I reached down and placed your dick back in my pussy and started riding it. The horse really went wild then. Who knows, maybe it was horny. It started pacing around the stall, slowly at first. When we both started moaning and fucking harder, the horse seemed to completely lose it. He took off out of the stall into the main part of the barn.

All we could do is laugh and try to hang on for dear life. I grabbed a hold of the horse's mane and started trying to tell it to chill, having absolutely no clue what to say to a horse, since I had never been on one in my entire life.

I tried to get off, but you grabbed me around the waist and told me not to. I was scared it was going to throw us, and we would both be in traction by the morning. Your crazy ass kicked your heels into the sides of the horse and made it go faster. Before I knew it, we were outside the barn, butt-naked, fucking on a horse in the moonlight. The shit was mad funny.

The horse ended up in the middle of the field of wildflowers, the same field I picked flowers from earlier that day. You made another gesture, making the horse come to a stop, and then we both got down on the ground.

We started going for it then, right in the middle of the field, paying no attention to the insects all over the place. We got in the sixty-nine position and started partaking of each other for dessert. Both of us were cumming all over the place within a few minutes. It was great.

You made love to me in the field with a greater passion than ever before. Then we went back to the barn on the horse's back and finally made good use of the bed. We made love all night long until the rooster woke up half the country-side the next morning.

We got dressed and got back in the car. I drove up to the main house so you could meet our benefactors. Ma and Pa, as I call them, were happy to hear that my proposal went over well and had a huge breakfast waiting for us. Of course, we were both itching like all hell because of the mosquito bites we got out in the field of flowers. They had really torn our asses up. Ma gave us some ointment and sent us on our way.

We've been married for two years now and drive up to see Ma and Pa regularly. Of course, they were seated on the first pew at the wedding. Every now and then, we even make love in their barn, reliving the night two hearts decided to become one.

Harlem Blues

The club was standing room only that night, and the smoke was thick as I took the stage. Singing the blues classics, by sisters like Ms. Holliday, came extremely easy to me. I had been severely depressed since I walked in on Kendall getting a blow job from the slut who lived across the hall from us. Imagine walking into my own fucking place of residence and seeing the bitch with my man's cum all over her mouth and his dick swinging like a willow tree in front of her face.

I got medieval on both their asses, packed all the shit I could possibly carry, and caught a cab to my sister's place near 135th and Fifth Avenue in Harlem. As I began to sing "Good Morning Heartache," I thought about how drastically my life had changed over the last month. How I had given myself completely to a man who treated my love like a disease instead of a blessed gift. How he turned out to have so little respect for me that he would let a woman suck his dick in the place we had decorated and made a home out of together. How he could do his dirt with a woman I saw on a regular basis, that I borrowed flour and sugar from on occasion, that I trusted.

How the one I gave my heart to could hurt me so bad. How I had been such a fucking fool.

Then something strange happened while the people in the audience were applauding and whistling at our first set. Glancing over at you sitting on the piano bench and watching all the passion from your soul escape through your fingertips, I began to fantasize about how it would be if we made love, what your passionate fingers would feel like all over my body. Would you play my body with the same intensity as you played the piano, would you make me forget all the shit Kendall had done, would you show me what making *real* love was all about?

When we finished our final set a little after two, you approached me with the intention of simply shooting the breeze, but I was so horny for you, I couldn't take it and dashed outside to catch a cab without even taking the time out to change my clothes. I know you were wondering what made me leave in such a rush. I had never fantasized about a man the way I did about you onstage that night. I wanted to rub my fingers over my nipples and finger myself, but sure as hell couldn't in front of a crowd of people.

However, doing it in the cab was a totally different matter. The driver, a foreigner who could barely understand my destination when I told him, almost wrecked the car when he realized I was masturbating in the backseat. I know it seems raunchy, but I *had* to do it. I *had* to cum right then and there, so I made it happen.

I lowered one of the straps on my sequined evening gown, licked one of my fingers, and then rubbed it over my hardened nipple. I took my breast in my hand, pushed it up as much as I could, and flickered my tongue over the nipple. I could see the cabdriver looking through his rearview mirror at my little show. Eventually, when we were at a stoplight, he even adjusted it so he could get a better view. We never said another word to each other, not even when we arrived at my sister's place. I tried to pay him the amount shown on the meter, but he smiled at me and gave me a hand motion, letting me know he didn't want me to pay. Of course, this was after I had fingered myself in front of him and cum all over the backseat of his cab, moaning and flinging my head all over the place because the orgasm was so profound. I guess he figured he should probably be the one paying me.

I slept like a baby that night. All of my dreams were filled with you. It was so wild because we had been friends for so long, working closely together and all of that. I had never thought of you in a sexual way until that night. In my mind, I wanted to be with you, but I feared losing your friendship by coming on to you.

The next afternoon, when I arrived at the club for rehearsal, we were all alone. You informed me that the club's owner, Ralph, had gone across town to pick up some liquor for the club. I started feenin for your ass right off the bat. You had on one of those tight-ass body shirts that revealed all of your muscles and some jeans that showed off that well-defined ass of yours. I was so fucking nervous. Apparently it showed, because you asked me what was wrong.

I had danced around what happened between me and Kendall when I told all of you I had moved in with my sister, but I sat there and spilled the whole story to you that afternoon. You listened intently and looked me in my eyes while I talked. Your dark eyes hypnotized me. The whole time I was talking about Kendall, I really wanted it to be about the two of us.

We decided we better get some rehearsing done. I leaned over the edge of the black grand piano and began singing as you played. The rehearsal went great, and we were about to end it when you told me to come there. I was shook and not sure what you meant. You took me by the hand and pulled me closer to you so that I was standing in between your legs, facing you, while you sat on the piano bench. My round, succulent ass was resting on about a dozen of the eighty-eight keys as you took your hands and traced the outline of my chest with them.

I had on a black, loose-fitting above-the-knee skirt and a white crop top that left my pierced belly button exposed. You palmed my breasts in your hands and took the round earring onto the tip of your tongue and licked my belly button gently. My pussy was instantly wet. All I could do was caress the back of your head. I couldn't believe you wanted it too. Just the night before, I figured you would tell me to get lost if I came on to you. Yet there we were, the situation totally reversed, with you coming on to me.

You lifted my shirt up over my breasts, reached behind my back, unfastened my bra, and devoured my breasts, giving them both an equal tongue bath. We both moaned softly. I was wiggling my ass on the piano keys 'cause my pussy was yearning for your touch. You must have read my mind because you stood up and tongue-kissed me while you lifted me up on top of the grand piano. My feet were on the piano keys, playing an unrecognizable tune. I spread my legs to meet your hardened dick grinding in between them.

You laid me back on the piano, lifted my skirt, and ripped my panties off, not wanting to go through the effort of pulling them down and off. You caressed my nipples, one in each hand, as you began to suck on my anxiously awaiting pussy. I arched my back so that only my ass and head were actually resting on the piano top as you partook of the life source of my pussy. No man had ever eaten me out like that before. I realized that you were answering all the questions I was wondering about the night before onstage.

As I came in your mouth, I could hear your pants unzipping. I could barely wait to get some of your dick. My wait was short. You stood up on the piano stool and entered my pussy as it rested on the edge of the piano top. I pictured what it would be like if the cramped yet cozy club was standing room only at that moment, with people nursing their drinks, smoking cigars and cigarettes, making the room cloudy as they watched you grind your dick into me. You fucked me so hard, the rest of the day I had trouble walking straight, but it was well worth it.

That night, during our live show, I was not too much for singing the blues. I was ready to skat my ass off and dance the jig, jumping for joy because I was so hooked on you. I still am hooked. In fact, we are hooked on each other. The past five years as your wife have been the best years of my life. We still perform together four nights a week at the club and raise our baby girl, Harlem, together during the day. From now until the end of time, I know the only blues in my life will be onstage. You have turned my real world into heaven on earth, and I love you, boo!

Lust in a Bus Depot

"Simone? Is that you?"

I turned around to see who was calling out my name. "Wendell? Wow! Long time, no see!"

It had indeed been a long time since Wendell and I had laid eyes on each other—at least four or five years. We walked up to each other and engaged in a long, comforting embrace.

"Damn, Simone, you look fantastic! How long has it been?" His smile was still the same. So beautiful, I wanted to jump his bones.

"Hmmm, it has been quite some time. Funny how time flies." I was in shock, but tried not to show it. Ever since my freshman year in high school, I had wanted Wendell. I was always too shy to tell him, though. I spent hours upon hours daydreaming about him in class, but he never knew it. He was so busy dating all the cheerleaders and school queens, I'm not sure he even cared.

In high school, I was dumpy and far from a sex goddess. My mother used to imply that I purposely made myself look unattractive so boys wouldn't pay me any mind. Looking back on it, I realize she may have not only hit the nail on the head but all the way through the fucking headboard.

I got lost in thought, daydreaming again, when the woman over the loudspeaker started blaring out the bus arrival and departure schedule again. Her voice was nothing short of obnoxious and knocked me out of my trance. Wendell wasn't saying anything either. He was too busy checking my new and improved ass out.

The Simone from high school and the Simone standing before him in the bus depot were from two different planets. I was shy all the way through high school, but everything changed when I got to college. Two people are responsible for the dramatic changes in me that came about freshman year: my roommate and my man.

Melinda was my roommate freshman year and was a real wild chile. She insisted I shed the dumpy look and threw hoochie clothes on me instead, did my hair and makeup, and even showed me how to seduce a man. At first, I thought she was plum foolish, but after being bored to death too many weekends in a row while she was out on dates, I decided to give it a shot.

It didn't take long for the Melinda Mind-Bender Plan, as she called it, to work. I met Duncan at the very first club we hit on my virgin voyage into the nightlife. The areas Melinda couldn't help me in, Duncan damn sure did. He taught me how to free myself from the imprisonment I created in my mind growing up. He taught me how to experiment with my feelings and emotions, wants and desires. In other words, he taught me how to fuck.

Duncan used to get this pussy anywhere and everywhere and at anytime. I never complained. I was glad I had waited for the right lover to come along because he broke my ass in right. I never loved him, though; never that. It was almost like fucking a play brother or something. I cared for him, but not in a relationship kind of way.

Eventually my feelings, or lack thereof, caused our demise. That was perfectly cool with me. It's not like I was sweating it or anything. I left the relationship with more than I entered it with, and that's all that matters.

Wendell, on the other hand, is a different matter altogether. I always wanted the real deal with him. Now that fate had intervened, I wasn't about to let the opportunity slip by to get with him. "So, Wendell, what are you doing in a bus depot in Charlotte in the middle of the night?"

He laughed. "I might ask you the same thing. I'm on my way from NYC to Atlanta, and you?"

"Oh, you still live in the Apple, huh? I live in D.C. now. I'm on my way to meet my parents in Florida for a few days. Gonna do the mouse-ears thing." We both giggled like a couple of kindergarten students.

"How long before your bus leaves?"

"Hmm, about an hour or so, but you know how it is with buses. An hour could mean three."

People were walking past and bumping into us, since we were in the direct path of the main pedestrian traffic inside the terminal. Wendell suggested we find a couple of seats and helped me with my duffel bag. The bag was extremely heavy, and it was a relief not to have to drag it for a moment. As usual, I had packed everything but the kitchen sink and would end up not wearing even half of the clothes in it.

Wendell and I sat there, reminiscing about the good old days for about half an hour. Underneath my calm and cool exterior, I was working myself up into a frenzy. My eyes kept wandering to the gigantic clock on the depot wall, and I was dreading the moment when we would have to split up again.

What if I didn't see him for another four or five years? Ten years? Ever again? The mental anguish was too much to bear. Even though there had been drastic changes in my personality since high school, in an instant, I reverted back to those days and was shy all over again.

The time Wendell and I had together was seeping away like sand in an hourglass. I couldn't imagine not knowing how good the sex between he and me really would be. So I went for it! Wendell was talking about the weather when I blurted it out. "Wendell, how about a quickie?"

"Wha, wha, what you mean?" He started stuttering.

"How about you and I going somewhere right quick and fucking the shit out each other?" I looked him dead in the eyes so he would realize I wasn't kidding.

"Let me get this straight, Simone!" He started blushing. "You want to fuck me? Right here? Right now?"

"Word!" I put my hand on his knee and started caressing his thigh. "So where do you suggest? We don't have that much time."

"Ummm, let's see!" Wendell starting looking around the depot for a suitable spot, as did I.

As an afterthought, I asked him, "Do you have a condom?"

He looked at me with that damn-I-can't-get-none look on his face and replied, "Naw, boo, you?"

"Nope! Where there's a will, there's a way, though." I jumped to my feet and told him, "You look for a spot, and I'll be right back!"

The little convenience store inside the depot had closed at midnight, so I was shit out of luck on that end. I was about to go tell Wendell maybe we could hook up some other time when I spotted what I was looking for. Standing over in a corner were three guys in army uniforms. I knew one of them, if not all of them, was packing a condom, so I simply went over, tapped one of them on the shoulder, pulled him aside, and asked, "Got a condom?" He was a bit surprised, since he probably was expecting me to ask the time or to bum a cigarette and wanted to know if he was going to get the privilege of using it on me. I told him, "No, not tonight." He and I both laughed while he gave me one from his wallet.

I went back to look for Wendell. Our bags were there, but he was nowhere in sight. I heard someone whistle and turned around. I spotted him by the ladies' bathroom area and rushed over to him. We only had about twenty minutes left before my bus was due in. That was the one and only time I was hoping to have a transportation delay.

Once I entered the enclave, I noticed there were two separate ladies' bathrooms, each with its own door. The only other things in the enclave were a row of three pay telephones and a cleaning cart containing a mop, broom, cleaning supplies, rolls of toilet tissue, and packages of paper towels.

Wendell asked me to go into the one on the right and see if it was empty. I went in and checked to see if all the stalls were vacant. One wasn't, but I heard the toilet flush. I went back out and told Wendell it should be empty in a moment, and it was. An elderly woman, who appeared very down on her luck, exited the bathroom and walked away.

Wendell grabbed the Closed for Cleaning sign off the side of the cleaning cart, which I didn't even notice at first, and put it on the door. We rushed inside, and I sat on the countertop area, where there were about five or six sinks lined up along a huge mirror.

"Are you sure you want to do this, Simone?" I was hoping his ass wasn't having second thoughts, worried about being faithful to some lover he had waiting for him back in NYC.

"I've never been more sure about anything in my entire life!" I motioned for him to come over to me, opened my arms, and said, "Come here, baby!"

If he did have any reservations, they didn't show any longer, because he hurried over. I wrapped my arms around his neck and my legs behind his back. We started kissing and taking off each other's clothes.

We didn't take off everything. There wasn't enough time. He pushed my coat off my shoulders, and it landed sprawled out on the countertop. I lifted my shirt and bra so he could get to my nipples. He pushed my panties to the side.

While I was lying back, with the rear of my head pressed against the glass of the mirror and Wendell sucking on my nipples, I ripped open the condom packet with my teeth and pulled it out, tossing the wrapper into one of the sinks.

I undid the zipper on his jeans and whipped his dick out. I was overanxious, we both were, but I was determined to get some of his dick before I got on any damn bus. I told him to let up off my tits for a minute so I could slap the condom on. I had a little trouble getting it on 'cause his dick was so thick. We really needed one of those extra-large condoms, but beggars can't be choosers.

After managing to get the condom halfway up the shaft of his juicy dick, I made a special request. "Now, boo, fuck me like this is the last pussy you'll ever get!"

Wendell must have taken the shit to heart because he rammed his dick up in me and tore my little pussy up. I pressed his head between my breasts and worked my pussy all over his dick.

I heard a little girl outside the rest room door and told Wendell to stop for a second. He raised his head up, stopped pumping his dick into me, and we both listened intently. The only sounds were water dripping from a couple of the faucets and our heavy panting.

"Mommy, over here!" The door to the bathroom started opening, and I was thinking, "Oh, shit, no! Don't let that little girl come in here!"

As if someone was answering my prayers, I heard her mother say, "No, Lisa, that one's closed. We have to go in the other one."

We were both relieved and went back to fucking. Wendell started fucking me so hard, my head was banging against the mirror. I was getting one hell of a headache, so he told me to get up and bend over the counter. No sooner had I assumed the position before he was at it again. As usual, being fucked doggy-style made me cum something fierce.

Just then, the obnoxious sounding woman on the loud-speaker announced my bus was now boarding. All I could say was, "Shit, not now!"

Wendell was about to take his dick out, but I told him not to. "No, boo, I want you to cum too. Just fuck me faster until you do!"

That's when I had to control myself from having spasms and shit. Never had I been fucked so royally. For it to finally happen in the bathroom of a bus depot was a trip. He fucked the hell out of me, and I know I came at least three more times in the few minutes that followed. Wendell finally came and pulled it out real quick when they announced the final call for my bus.

I pulled my shirt and bra down and flung my coat over my arm while Wendell got himself together real quick, ripping the condom off and making a nothing-but-net shot into the trash receptacle.

We rushed out the bathroom, and I noticed there was now a little crowd of people outside the enclave area. I really didn't give a fuck though, because I got mine. Wendell grabbed my duffel bag from the seating area and hurried behind me outside to the bus loading area. I located the bus that had a sign for Orlando, handed the driver my ticket while Wendell flung my bag underneath the bus in the luggage area, and then got on.

I didn't have a pen on me anywhere and asked the driver for one so I could scribble my number on the envelope my ticket had been in. I wrote it down, handed it to Wendell, gave him a long wet kiss, and told him I would be home on Monday.

As the bus was pulling away, I waved at Wendell and drew a heart with my finger in the dew that had gathered on the cold window. I fell asleep before the bus made it thrity miles from the depot. I dreamt about him and woke up with his scent all over me. I could still feel his saliva on my lips and breasts.

I got home the following Monday afternoon, and Wendell called me that evening while I was doing the dinner dishes. I was thrilled, because I wasn't sure he would call. We talked for hours on end, and he told me how he wanted to get with me all through high school as well, but didn't know how to approach me.

Wendell and I spend at least one weekend together a month now, sometimes more. He and I catch the bus back and forth from D.C. to NYC to see each other. Every time we pass a bathroom in the bus depot of either station, we remember the time we did the wild thing in Charlotte. I told Wendell one day I want us to take a long cross-country train trip and get a private compartment so we can fuck in about ten states all in one shot. His reply was, "Hell, boo, why not?"

The Bachelorette Party

       I knew my gurls were gonna throw me a party the night before I jumped the broom, but dayum. They went all out for my bachelorette party. After the rehearsal dinner, I figured they were going to take me to one of my bridesmaids' houses and have a stripper or something. I couldn't have been farther off base if I tried.

       Instead of taking me to a house, we drove about an hour out of town to what appeared to be an abandoned warehouse. However, there were tons of cars outside and people walking in and out the front doors, mostly women.

       When we went inside, it was the wildest shit I had ever seen. Dick for days! Days, I tell you! I had been to my share of strip shows in my day, but I had never been to one where all the men were dancing butt-naked. There was no sign on the door, but once inside, there were neon signs everywhere with the club's name, the Black Screw, on them.

       The gurls and I, about ten of us altogether, found a couple of tables in the rear, since all the tables up front had long been taken. A waiter came to take our drink orders, and the man was fine as all hell. I wanted to lick a piña colada off his ass, but I refrained from my nasty thoughts. After all, I was marrying the love of my life the next day, and faithfulness was a must. It was hard to keep the faith with the waiter's big, juicy dick dangling in my face, though.

A few minutes later he returned with our first round of drinks while this other fine-ass guy with about a ten-inch dick was sitting in my maid of honor's lap, blowing in her ear. I was totally shook and couldn't believe I never knew the place existed. It had to be some undercover club because mad laws must have been thrown out the fucking window in order to have all that dick floating around the room.

The Black Screw was huge, too. Imagine a warehouse turned into a big-ass fuck palace, and then you are halfway there. "Doin' It Again" by LL Cool J kicked in, and this fine-ass guy (hell, they were all fine) took center stage and began to do some of the most amazing acrobatic fuck moves I had ever witnessed. The way he was pretending to grind his dick in some nana made me wanna scream, Have mercy! He continued with the grind moves until the song ended, but when "Big Daddy" by Heavy D came on next, he got buck-wild and buck-naked. Dayum shame all those big dicks were in the house.

The gurls and I got tore up by the third round of drinks, and by the fifth round, we were all horny. I was sitting there wishing I could get my hands on my fiancé's ass right then and there, because I would have fucked him like I hated him. I'm not quite sure who was wilder, the male dancers or the women patrons. There was some truly freaky shit going on up in that place.

Men had women bent over tables, grinding their dicks up against their asses, they were palming tits, sucking toes, fingering pussy even. As for the women, aw shit, they were even worse. The women were pulling their shit off too, jacking dicks, riding dicks with their clothes on, everything except actual fucking, but don't take my word on that. I didn't exactly do a panty check or anything of that nature.

One man after another took the stage and did his thing. I must say there is no way any woman who even remotely loves herself some dick wouldn't be drowning in her own pussy juice up in the Black Screw. There was a stage right smack in the middle of the club, like a boxing ring in the middle of an arena, with tables surrounding all four sides of it so all the women could get a little look-see. In addition, there were circular risers in the four corners of the club with male dancers, who had already performed and taken it all off, on them getting mad freaky. I'm telling you, the shit was all that! They were so naked the only place they could put the dollars women tipped them was in their boots. I noticed they were all wearing some sort of boots, mostly cowboy ones. Cash-and-carry, I suppose.

As much as I loved it, it was getting pretty late. Two A.M. was rolling around, and the wedding was at noon sharp. I told the gurls we should bounce and thanks for taking me there. My maid of honor, Shari, told me the party wasn't over and then called the fine waiter over and whispered something in his ear. I sat there nervous as all hell because I figured they were planning on having some guy come over to the table and freak me or something. I had managed to keep my hands to myself all night, even though the temptation was killing me.

About five minutes later, the waiter returned with three other waiters and a cake. While our waiter set the cake—which, by the way, was chocolate and shaped like a huge dick—on the table, the other three clapped and recited some rehearsed congrats-on-your-wedding verse. I was relieved that the cake was the surprise and loosened up a bit.

My relief turned to panic when the finest guy in the place

walked up to me. If Mother Nature made anything better, she kept him for her dayum self, because the man was hitting. He was about six-foot-four tall, 210 or 215 pounds, dark-skinned, with jet-black curly hair and deep brown eyes. He stood out in the club because he was clothed with stonewashed wide-legged jeans, a suede vest, and of course, cowboy boots.

He leaned over the table, reached for my hand, and I was likely to faint. Shari told me, "You better get your ass up!" I asked her, "What the fuck is going on?" She replied, "Just a little something extra I have planned for you! This is your last night of freedom. Now, GET THE FUCK UP!"

You could tell from the expression on her face that she could barely prevent herself from breaking out into a full grin. I was drunk, and his hand was still reaching out for me. I threw caution to the wind and took it.

A couple of minutes later, he and I walked through a set of double doors into the rear of the Black Screw. He had yet to say a word to me. I figured Shari had paid him to give me a private dance, sort of like a male lap dance. To be honest, I was still nervous as shit, though. If he had been just average, cute, or even remotely fine, I would have had no problem whatsoever. The problem was, he was past all those, and I was tore up. My pussy was throbbing and shit for him just by the hand-holding alone. I was getting the distinct feeling my ass might get in some serious trouble once he did his little show. I should have stopped it right then. I should have told him I felt uncomfortable and was about to rejoin my friends so we could leave. But I didn't, and before I knew it, we reached our final destination.

There was a long hallway in the back of the club with several rooms. All the rooms had neon signs over the doorways. He led me to one called "The Red Light District" and held the door open for me to go in.

The room was dimly lit with red lightbulbs, and there was a slow jam playing. Much to my surprise, there were four couches in the room, one on each wall, and two of them were occupied. I tried to pull my hand loose after I saw what was going on in the room, but he held onto it tightly and spoke to me for the first time: "Don't run away, baby. At least let me do my dance for you. Don't worry about them!"

He had the deepest, sexiest voice, and when he looked at me with them there eyes, I was at his beck and call. So, I didn't worry about *them* and went and sat on the couch farthest from the door while he walked over to the compact shelf stereo system and changed the CD. *Them* referred to the two other female customers in the room with male dancers. There was absolutely no dancing going on, and when my private dancer was putting on his performance music, I could hear *them* moaning and shit. Not to mention the fucking and sucking noises.

You see, one sister was over on the couch by the door, and her ankles were pressed up over her shoulders while a big, mandingo-looking brother was fucking the shit out of her. The other was not quite as bad. However, she was sitting on the couch on the left wall sucking another brother's dick like a Hoover vacuum cleaner. Apparently, the lap dances they received were slamming, because they were all about knocking boots.

All sort of shit started going through my mind faster than the speed of light. I know I should have been thinking about my baby, my boo, my husband-to-be, but he never crossed my mind. In fact, looking back on it now, I don't feel guilty because I know about all the shit that goes on at bachelor parties. His ass probably fucked some hoochie that night too.

He put on his music, "My Body" by LSG, and began his dance. He told me, "My name's Warren, by the way. What's yours?" I told him, "My name's Mira," as he began to do his thing, grinding all in my face while I sat there on the couch with a serious case of locked knees.

Warren slowly removed his vest, and like I had suspected, he was perfect. I tried to keep my eyes fixed on him, but it was hard with all the other shit going on. The other two couples had done some shifting, and the one who had been sucking dick was now bent over getting fucked doggy-style. The other one, who previously was shaped like a pretzel, was now in the sixty-nine position getting her freak on.

I began to feel light-headed as Warren started to break out of his jeans. I recuperated fast when I saw his dick protruding out his black thong bikini. Just like I like them: big, long, thick, and chocolate. That was the very moment I knew I was gonna fuck him if he was down. Judging by the way he was looking at me, I suspected he was.

Warren confirmed my suspicions when, once naked, he knelt down and pried my knees open with his strong hands, exposing the black lace panties I was wearing underneath my black knee-length skirt. I wore no stockings with my heels because it was midsummer and extremely hot out, so it was easy for Warren to run his fingers all over my smooth, creamy thighs. He began to kiss my kneecaps. All I could do was look, being I was overcome by a desire I had never known, a desire to make love to a complete stranger. A desire, it appeared, I was destined to fulfill the night before I married the man of my dreams.

That is exactly what I did. I fulfilled the desire to make love to a stranger, and I have not regretted it a moment since. In fact, I think the night with Warren has significantly helped my married life. I know that sounds sick, but I was able to open up more sexually with him than I could previously do with my boo. Because of the events of that one night, I have become a much better lover for my man.

Warren started running his tongue up and down the inside of my thighs, spreading my legs wider with his hands. My pussy was soaked by that time. He pushed me back on the couch, so I was lying down, pulled my panties off, and then lifted one of my legs up so it was resting on the headrest of the couch.

He wasted no time getting his eat on with my pussy as the main course. I thought I had died and gone to heaven because I came like crazy. The wild part is that I didn't even give a fuck what the other people in the room were doing. That's totally uncharacteristic of me, because I tend to be very inhibited. At least, I was before that night.

His warm, thick tongue played magnificent tricks within my pussy walls, and I got lost in the music and the red lights while he did the thing he does so well. He reached up, with his head still buried between my thighs, and caressed my tender breasts through the white poplin-sleeve blouse I was wearing with the black skirt. I took the initiative, unbuttoned it for him, and unfastened the clasp in the front of my bra, letting my hard nipples escape their prison.

Warren moved his tongue from my pussy, over the material of my skirt, which was up around my waist at the time, and started sucking on my nipples. I went fucking berserk. I'm not sure whether it was the liquor or the fine-ass nucca licking me all over, but I just kept cumming and cumming.

I'm not sure when the other couples got up and left the room. I didn't see them because I was too busy sucking Warren's dick, which was, by the way, extremely pleasing to my taste buds. I sucked him so good he exploded in my mouth twice before we moved on to the main event—the main event being knocking boots.

The man fucked me every which way but upside down. If

time had permitted, we probably would have gotten to that position eventually. I needed about three days to fuck him the right way. Instead, I only had about three hours. We made good use of them, though, and he tore my coochie-coo up. He gave a whole new meaning to the phrase "dick-whipped."

Never before, or since, have I ever begged a man to stop fucking me because it was too much for me, but I begged his ass to stop grinding his dick into me in such a fashion. Warren didn't let up, though, and ended up giving me the fuck of a lifetime.

When I rejoined my friends, after quite some time, they were about the only ones left in the entire club. Some of the gurls had left already. The only ones remaining were the ones I was riding with, including Shari, my maid of honor. They were all laughing and grinning at me. I didn't even attempt to fake the funk because there was no way they would have believed I had been back there talking for the past three hours plus.

I did the next best thing and told them all about it on the way home in the car, blow by mother-fucking blow, and they were all ears, probably envisioning every second of it the way I related the story to them.

By the time we got back to my hotel suite, the sun was coming up over the horizon. I only had an hour to get to my hair appointment, so I showered and dressed and headed for the land of hot-ass hair dryers and curling irons. At noon on the dot, I walked down the aisle of the church I had attended since I was baptized in it and married my boo.

I exchanged vows with him and meant every word of them. I love him dearly and would never forsake him for another man again. Like I said earlier, though, I think the night with Warren improved my bedroom skills, and therefore has helped keep my marriage together. My boo thought he was marrying his shy, conservative baby, but on our wedding night, he found out he married a sexual diva.

I can't say for sure what men do at bachelor parties, but I can say this. Any woman who has her bachelorette party at the Black Screw is in for one hell of a great time!

Sweet Revenge

He was sitting all alone by the fireplace in the great room when I arrived. It was a cold, windy night. I used the key she keeps under the welcome mat by the garage door to let myself in. I knew he would be alone. She called me at my office earlier in the day and told me she was leaving town on a business trip that afternoon.

I knew it was then or never before I lost the nerve to do it altogether. I decided to go through with the plans I had constructed over and over again in my mind. I wasn't sure whether or not he would go for it. There had been signals here and there—glances, smiles, body language—but I still wasn't sure. If he wasn't a willing subject, my plan could never work. I crossed my fingers and went for it anyway.

There he was sitting by the fireplace, sipping on some expensive cognac and listening to classical music, his favorite. He didn't even hear me come in. Once I saw him, I started to hurry back out the same way I came, but it was then or never. So I spoke. He was startled to turn around and see me standing there. I told him I used the key to let myself in and I hoped he didn't mind. He told me she was out of town. I made him aware I knew that already. That I was there to see him, not her.

He asked me was something wrong, and I replied, "Not at all!" Then a dead silence fell over the room as one CD track ended and another began. I looked at him, he looked at me, and I think he got the point right away. If he didn't get it then, I'm sure he got it once I removed my trench coat, letting it fall to the floor, revealing my nude body clad only in high heels.

There was a brief moment when I thought he was going to curse at me, tell me to get the hell out of his home, call her at whatever hotel she was staying, and tell her the whole sordid story, making sure her love for me would turn to hatred in a heartbeat.

However, none of it happened that way. Instead, he got up from the fireplace hearth and walked over to me. The look of astonishment on his face turned to lust as he made the first move, saving me the trouble. He kissed me very lovingly, like an old lover who had just returned home from overseas. He and I had known each other for years, but it was time to take it to another level.

I pulled the cable-knit sweater he was wearing up over his head, removing it and letting my hands gain the freedom to explore his massive chest. I sucked his bottom lip into my mouth and dug my fingers into his breasts. Our kisses gained momentum as he picked me up, carried me up the stairwell to the master bedroom, their bedroom. Once inside, he laid me on their bed, and I watched as he removed his jeans and silk boxers.

There were no words, and that was just as well, because I had no clue what to say at such a moment. My reasons for coming there had been clear-cut, but once he laid his hands on me, other reasons for doing it came into play, such as passion, yearning, and lust.

He lay on top of me, pressed my arms up over my head, and began to drown me with his sweet tongue. When he moved down to my neck and then my breasts, I held onto the headboard of their iron canopy bed with both hands. That made my hard nipples even more prominent and manageable to suck.

He licked all around my breasts, starting from the bottom and going all the way to the top like he was licking an ice cream cone. His tongue was nothing short of magical as he used the tip of his tongue to trace a line down the center of my stomach to my belly button.

I pulled his head back up to mine, after letting go of the headboard, because I yearned for more of his passionate kisses. I caressed his dick, feeling it grow to massive proportions as he and I both moaned with delight. I grabbed his ass cheeks, one in each hand, and helped guide his dick inside my hot, awaiting pussy. It welcomed him with much enthusiasm.

I held onto an ass cheek with one hand and retook hold of the iron headboard with the other while he fucked me harder and harder. All we could do was look each other in the eyes, visually confirming that the lovemaking was what we both wanted.

I never expected it to be like that. I thought he and I would have a rough little quickie, and then I would leave and go about my business after about fifteen minutes or so. At that point, it became clear we were going to go at it all night long. He came inside me, and the flow of hot cum shooting up my pussy caused a chain reaction. I came a few seconds later.

He rested on top of me for a moment, both of us breathing heavy and savoring the fruit of our labors, before he lay on his back beside me. Their bedroom ceiling is covered with mirrors, so we could look at each other without actually facing one another. I didn't know whether the look on his face was one of guilt, confusion, or happiness.

A few moments later, after moving down some on the bed, I leaned over him and began suckling on his dick. The added seasoning of my pussy on his dick was thrilling to my senses, and I couldn't get enough of it. It was like having the best of both worlds, the pussy I was eating being my own. He put his hands behind his head and reveled in the penis massage I was performing with my warm mouth. I wouldn't stop until he came in my mouth. The reward was well worth the effort.

Afterward, he told me to turn over on my stomach. He left the bed for a few seconds to retrieve a bottle of lubricant from the master bathroom. Upon his return, he took his fingers and rubbed it all up and down my ass and his dick. He finger-fucked my ass for a few moments, probably to judge my reaction and figure out whether anal sex was my sort of thing or not. I moaned with delight, so he knew the deal.

As I laid there on my stomach, with his dick grinding in and out my ass, screaming and holding onto the headboard for dear life, I wondered what she would say at that very moment if she walked in. Half of me wished she would return from her trip early and catch us in the act. However, that was not part of the plan.

He exploded in my ass. It was a wonderful feeling. We fell asleep just like that, with his dick in my ass, and we slept for a few hours. He woke me up by ass-fucking me again, since his dick had hardened once more while he was sleeping.

We took a long, hot bath together. I rode his dick till we both came as the bubbles tingled against our skin. A few words began to exchange between us, but not many. We both knew it was wrong to be together in such a way. Neither one of us was about to put a stop to it, though.

Unfortunately, it had to end. She may have been out of town, but my husband wasn't, so I had to leave him there, naked, dazed, and confused. I needed to rush home and make up a lie about my whereabouts. That's exactly what I did. If by some chance my husband chose not to believe me, it wouldn't have come as a big surprise. Most cheaters think their spouses are cheating too.

You see, there was more than just my whereabouts that particular evening my husband was unaware of. He was unaware I had walked into his office two weeks earlier while he was fucking my best friend on his desk. He was unaware that I paid both their asses back in spades by letting myself into her house and fucking her husband.

It is true what they say. What goes around really does come around. In my case, the revenge was oh so sweet, and so was the dick.

Blind Date

The whole idea was strange right from the onset, but I told myself that once I hit thirty, I was going to take that sexual-prime theory to heart and let go of all my inhibitions. So when my friend Tamlyn told me about this guy she knew who was into all kinds of kinky eroticism, I asked her to hook me up, and she did.

His name was Xander, and he called me the same night Tamlyn gave him my digits. He was all about the nana and couldn't wait to fuck me, sight unseen. I asked him did he get freaky with strangers often. His only reply was asking when his tongue could touch mine. Tamlyn told me he was fine and all. She even described him to me, and he sounded delicious, so when he related the fantasy over the phone he wanted me to help him out with, I told him I was down. Besides, his voice alone had my pussy feenin.

The sexual-prime theory must be true, because the day after I turned thirty, my pussy gained a mind of its own. I was daydreaming about dick all the time, masturbating every dayum day, and began asking myself one question: If I can't wake up to a bagel with cream cheese and a stiff dick, why wake up at all?

I arranged to meet Xander at a hotel of his choice the very next day during my lunch hour, and it was to be a quickie. Since I was still a bit hesitant, I figured meeting him on my lunch hour was the safest bet. I could always use the excuse of having to get back to work as an easy out.

When I arrived at the cozy downtown hotel a few blocks from my office, I saw no one that fit his description in sight. A male desk clerk asked was my name Jocelyn. I told him it was. He gave me a room key, informing me that my husband asked that I meet him in the room upstairs.

Once I reached the room, he wasn't there. I began to get a slight sense of fear in my heart. There were a bottle of chilled champagne and some flute glasses on the table with a dozen roses. There was also a blindfold on the table and a note. The note read: "Welcome! Drink some champagne and then blind-fold yourself within the next five minutes so I can come in. No cheating!"

I wasn't surprised to see the blindfold; Xander and I had discussed it on the phone. However, I thought he planned to blindfold me after we met, not before. He really wanted to take the blind date idea to an extreme.

I drank some champagne. It was nice and cold. Afterward, I sat on the edge of the bed and put on the blindfold tightly. I couldn't see a thing. My knees were trembling. I had never come close to doing anything of that nature before. I figured, if nothing else, I would gain an interesting memory to hang onto in my old age when my fucking years were far behind me.

No sooner had I sat down on the bed than I heard footsteps approaching the room in the hallway. I could hear him whistling as he unlocked the door with the card key. When he entered the room, so did the sensuous aroma of his cologne. Then, I heard the familiar voice from the phone say, "Hello Jocelyn. What's up?"

I gave the typical reply of the '90s: "Just chillin'."

Xander said, "Cool," and I could feel the bed sink down some beside me as he sat down. He was so close to me, I could feel his breath on my cheek when he said, "Tamlyn was right. You're an extremely beautiful woman, Jocelyn."

I replied by saying, "Thanks, but you have me at a disadvantage. Other than the description she gave me, I have no idea what you really look like. Can I take off the blindfold for a second?"

He came back quickly with a resounding "NO!" Then he lowered his voice again and said, "This is all part of my fantasy. Having a woman make love to me who has never seen me before. Once we are done, I will make sure you see me. I promise! Is that cool?"

I started to take the blindfold off and tell him I was leaving, but a part of me was enjoying the whole mystery man scenario. I told him it was cool, and he asked me to lie back on the bed with my head on a pillow. I complied and heard him get up and start walking around.

The hotel was pretty quiet. It was early afternoon, and most people hadn't even checked in for the night. I could hear the faint noise of horns blowing on the busy city street five floors below. Xander came back to the bed and turned on the small alarm clock radio on the nightstand beside the bed. I could hear him turning the tuning dial until he came upon a station playing soft music.

I decided I should make him aware of my time constriction once more. "Don't forget I have to be back at work by one, so please tell me when it is getting close."

Xander said, "Don't worry! This won't take long!"

I wondered when he was going to get started doing whatever he was going to do, and then I started wondering if he was a lousy fuck or something—a two-minute brother. He didn't seem worried about the time at all. While I was lying there, letting all those thoughts flash through my mind, suddenly I smelled the essence of a rose.

He put the rose up to my nose and used it to trace a path down to my chin, then my neck, and around my nipples. He told me to hold the rose and placed it in my left hand. I could feel him straddle me and begin to unbutton my blouse. He pulled my breasts out of the cups of my bra and started rubbing my nipples around between his thumbs and forefingers.

Xander told me he wanted to see me naked and helped me get completely undressed. I was beginning to feel more comfortable. There was something about him that seemed all too familiar to me. A feeling that maybe I had known him in another life. It was very strange.

Once I was nude, I realized that at least half my lunch hour must have expired by that time. I contemplated the fact that, if he didn't hurry up, there would be no fucking at all. Once again, I told him we needed to hurry up. He told me to relax again and not to worry. Then he asked me to turn over on my stomach.

He straddled himself over the back of my thighs, and I could sense him reaching for something off the nightstand. A few seconds later, I felt something cold trickling down my back and recognized the sensation right away. It was some sort of lotion. Xander began to rub the lotion into my skin with the expertise of a masseuse. He started by digging his fingers gently into the small of my back, moving outward to the sides of my stomach and all the way up until he reached my shoulders. He gave me a wonderful shoulder massage, then proceeded to pour some more lotion, but this time onto my ass cheeks. He massaged my ass for me and moved down to my thighs. It felt so relaxing that I almost fell asleep.

I could feel him get off me and sit down at the foot of the bed. He poured some more lotion, massaged my calves, and then gave me a foot massage that made me want to say, "I love you!"

Xander told me to turn over, and I quickly complied, figuring it was time to get busy. Instead, he massaged the whole front of my body. He started from my feet and worked his way upward to my hips and to my stomach. When he poured lotion in my belly button, it made me flinch and bite my bottom lip, since I am ticklish. He massaged both my arms and then, once again, caressed my breasts with the added sensation of lotion the second time around.

He asked me, "Are you enjoying yourself?" All I could manage to do was nod yes. I thought he would somehow disappear if I responded, and the dream would end. He told me to spread my legs, and I did.

With the most gentle hands I had ever felt, he reached inside my vagina with a single finger, pulled it back toward the lips of my pussy like a person motioning for someone to come there, and located the spongy area beneath my pelvic bone that most men live their entire lives and never find. He caressed my G spot with such tenderness, I not only came but also *literally* squirted out of my pussy like a man.

Never before had that ever happened to me. I had heard of women squirting when they cum, but I never, in a million years, imagined it would happen to me. I moaned so loud and my body trembled so much, I thought I might have a seizure. I was still recovering from what had just happened when Xander gave me one single kiss on my lips and said, "Don't move! I will be right back!"

I assumed he was going to the bathroom to get me a towel until I heard the door to the hotel room open and shut quickly. At that moment, I was utterly confused. I didn't know whether to take the blindfold off and leave or wait for him to come back. I couldn't imagine a man arranging a midday meeting with a stranger in a hotel room just to give her a full-body massage and see her cum. I figured he was coming back, and I didn't give a shit about the time anymore. I would call the office and take the rest of the day off if need be. I wanted to fuck the man so bad, more than I had ever wanted to be with a man before in my life.

My desires were shattered when the telephone in the room rang with a loud blare, startling me. I reached around for it on the nightstand, but couldn't find it. I ripped the blindfold off by the third ring and picked it up. It was the desk clerk, informing me that my "husband" had to leave and had left a written message for me at the front desk.

I looked at the clock radio and saw it was ten minutes to one. I hurriedly got dressed and caught the elevator down to the lobby. The clerk handed me the note, probably noticing that my clothes were not as neatly put on as they were when he handed me the room key less than an hour earlier.

The note read, "Jocelyn, thank you for the lovely afternoon. I hope you enjoyed yourself, because I sure did. A woman like you deserves to be treated like a queen every day of your life, and like I said, I promise you will see me. I just didn't tell you when it will happen, but it will be sooner than you think."

The rest of the day at work, I was no good. I kept trying to reach Tamlyn at her office, but her secretary kept saying she was in a meeting. I got the distinct feeling she was avoiding me. There was something strange about the whole thing. Why would a man do such a thing? Then again, why would I meet a stranger in a hotel room to fuck him?

I went out to happy hour with some friends from work that evening. Once I left the bar, I decided to swing by Tamlyn's house and see if she was home. When I got there, I saw her car, but there was also another car in her driveway. I hesitated about going to the door. I thought she might be getting her freak on with a new man but decided, since she had been a friend since first grade, she would just have to forgive my ass if that was the case. I had to know what the hell was going on, and I had to know how to get in touch with Xander. I had fallen hopelessly in love with a mystery man.

I knocked on her front door and heard a bunch of rambling around inside, and voices talking low. I was beginning to turn around and leave. I figured I was right about her getting freaky and didn't want to disturb them. Suddenly, the door flung open. Tamlyn said, "Hey, Sis!"

I told her I really needed to talk, and she told me to come in. When I entered her living room, there was indeed a man there, but it was her baby brother, Phillip. I had not seen him in about seven years since he joined the military. The last time I saw him he was eighteen, tall, lanky, and looked like a nerd. The man standing before me in Tamlyn's living room was tall, dark, handsome, built like an Adonis, and far from the nerd of the past.

Even though he had changed drastically, I immediately recognized him and rushed to give him a hug before he could say a word. He didn't need to say a word. I knew the moment I hugged him. The scent of his cologne was a dead giveaway. His breath on my cheek was all too familiar. When he finally did speak, it was not in the wimpy voice of baby brother Phillip but the sexy, deep voice of Xander. All he said at first was, "I never told you my middle name, did I?"

By the time I turned around to confront Tamlyn, she was headed out the front door. When her car started up and pulled out the driveway a few seconds later, I was still standing there gawking at him. I was in a state of shock. No wonder he felt so familiar. No wonder I felt comfortable around him. He was the baby brother of my best friend in life, and he had turned my ass out in the span of a lunch hour.

I sat down on the couch. More like fainted. He sat beside me and took my hand. "Look, Jocelyn, whatever you do, don't blame Tamlyn. This is all my doing! I asked her to set me up with you because I have always been in love with you. Ever since I was about ten years old and first started thinking about girls in that way. You were older, though, and wouldn't have shit to do with me. The whole time I was away, no matter who I was with, all I could ever think about was you. Now that I am back in town to stay, I wanted the opportunity to show you I am a man now. I thought the hotel thing was the only way."

I just looked at him in disbelief and couldn't utter a word. He continued, "If I had come to you and asked you out, you would have refused, if for no other reason than who I am. It wouldn't have mattered if you were attracted to me now or that I have changed a lot. You still would have seen me as Little Phillip. I wanted you to know how much I feel for you, how much I desire you, how much I want to make you mine."

I can't possibly explain what happened at that moment. The tears just started flowing. They were tears of joy, and that night, Phillip and I made love for the first time. It was the single most meaningful experience of my life, and every day since then, Phillip has treated me like a queen.

Tamlyn and I are closer than ever. In fact, she will be the maid of honor in my wedding to Phillip next month. What started out as a quest to let go of my sexual inhibitions and test the sexual-prime theory turned into the adventure of a life-time. Instead of making a memory I can think about when I become an old lady whose fucking years are way behind her, Phillip and I have one hell of a story to tell our grandchildren on the porch one day. There is a hell of a lot to be said for blind dates.

Vacation of a Lifetime

       I arrived in the Bahamas at approximately 11 A.M. having taken the six-hour cruise from Fort Lauderdale upon the *Sea Escape*. The cruise had been very relaxing—good food, great entertainment, and a nice casino—yet depressing all the same. I was so fucking upset at Kevin for canceling out on me at the last minute because of some dayum business conference in Chicago. I told him to fuck off and decided to take the vacation all by myself. I thought it would be cool, vacationing all alone, until I got aboard the ship and saw all the people paired off or traveling with little kids. There were a few groups of females traveling together, but none of them seemed friendly enough to approach, so I stayed to myself. They sat me at a table with this elderly white couple at the first breakfast sitting in the dining hall, and after that, I just put my sarong and halter top on and laid out on the admiral deck on a lounger until the ship was about to dock.

       I had to wait about an hour to retrieve my luggage because they were so slow unloading the large racks from the ship. Customs was pretty quick, but I had to wait quite some time for a cab because everyone had to catch them to their respective hotels. I finally arrived at the Bahamas Princess Country Club around 1 P.M. I was exhausted by the time I checked in and got to my room. It had been a long day. The shuttle left the hotel at 4 A.M. for the dock, and I had only checked into the hotel in Fort Lauderdale about 1 A.M. Needless to say, I was worn the hell out.

The one thing that did cheer me up was how nice the hotel was—beautiful rooms, nice restaurants, and a bad-ass pool with a cascading waterfall. I took a long bath in some aromatherapy bath beads. My mom had given them to me for my birthday six months before, but I had never used them. Afterward, I flipped through *Essence* magazine when I was done soaking and then decided to draw the curtains and take a quick nap. I always need noise to sleep, so I turned on the television. Lo and behold, Oprah was on.

I tried to fall asleep, but couldn't because I was horny as all hell, so I did what comes naturally. I masturbated my ass off, came a few good times, and then fell off to sleep.

Boy, was I tired! I slept until almost 7 P.M. and felt vigorously refreshed when I woke up. I decided it was time for me to dump the fucked-up attitude, stop worrying about Kevin's skank ass, and have a great time—even if it killed me. I put on this banging two-piece black outfit with a tight crop top and a long slim skirt with a slit going up the back along with some black three-inch heel slides and decided to go check out the scenery.

They were having an all-you-can-eat barbecue by the pool. I decided to jump on it and was glad I did. The ribs and corn on the cob were slamming. I washed it all down with a Bahama Mama and was feeling a little buzz when this fine-ass Bahamian approached me and asked could he take my picture. I had been scoping his ass out all night while he worked his way through the crowd, taking photos and clocking dollars. I told him to go for it, and he snapped a quick shot of me holding the remains of my drink. While the picture was developing, I asked him how much the photo cost and was reaching for my purse, but he said that mine was on the house. He told me that he should pay me to take my picture because I was so beautiful. I began to blush. I was flattered—not to mention that his accent was turning me on.

I began to take a real good look at him. His fine face was obvious, but it was time to check out the rest. All I could think to myself was, *dayum, dayum, dayum.* The man had a body that looked like it was chiseled out of stone, deep chocolate skin, and beautiful everything else. Simply put, the man was all that, a bag of chips, a Popeye's three-piece, and a pack of Bubblicious. I knew right then that I had to have him. He could definitely get it.

What else is a girl to do but flirt her ass off? For the next two hours, he forgot all about taking pictures, and I forgot where the hell I even was as we sat poolside and became better acquainted. His name was Joseph. That tripped me out. I was expecting some exotic-sounding name from an island man, but it was Joseph just the same.

I made a couple of dick-size glances throughout the evening. I came to the conclusion that the brother was hung like a fucking horse. I could tell even with his pants on, and I could hardly wait to ride that sucker until the saddle broke. The reggae band was playing this bumping-ass song. He asked me to dance, so we hit the floor. I decided it was the time to make a move. While we danced with our bodies grinding up against each other, I just happened to mention in passing that I was uncomfortable because my black thong bikinis were riding up my ass. He said, "So take them off." I asked him, "Right here?" and he said, "Sure, why not?" I was still a bit tipsy, so I thought to myself, "Fuck it!" I lifted up my skirt right there on the dance floor, until it was right above my thighs, and then pulled my thongs off. Everyone was looking, but I didn't give a shit. He took them out of my hand, sniffed them, closed his eyes as he savored the sweet aroma, and then put them in the pocket of the white pants he was wearing with an island-print shirt.

Finally, after much chitchat about the differences between American and Bahamian culture and some provocative-ass dancing, I suggested that we cut the bullshit and retire to my hotel room for the rest of the evening. I didn't have to say it twice. He reached for my hand, asked my room number, and off we went.

To make a long story short, the lights came on and the clothes began to come off. I wanted to see every precious inch of him, and a magnificent sight he was. I pushed him up against the closed door, and our kiss began. His tongue was long and thick, just the way I like them. My pussy was so dayum wet by that point, I was convinced I would cum a couple of times from kissing alone. And guess what? I did!

I tore his shirt open, and the buttons hit the carpeted floor. I traced a trail with the tip of my tongue down his chin, down his neck, and all the way down the center of his chest. When I got to his pants, I quickly took his dick in my mouth through his pants for a brief second and then moved my way back up to his nipples, suckling on each one of them in turn. We began to tongue-kiss again as I unbuckled his belt and unzipped his pants, reaching in to fondle his juicy-ass dick.

He turned me around so my back was up against the door instead of his and pushed both my hands above my head. Holding them in place with his own hands, he bit lightly on my still-clothed nipples and with one hand pulled my shirt up with a yank, exposing my breasts and hardened nipples. He began to devour my nipples, one at time, while I still stood there with my arms pinned above my head. I could feel my pussy juices trickling down the inside of my thighs.

He let my arms go and got down on his knees, simultaneously pulling my skirt up around my hips. He took my leg and positioned it so that it was resting on his shoulder and went to town on my pussy with his mouth. My mind wandered for a second. I thought about Kevin, but then I said, "Fuck it!" The shit was on now.

Joseph picked me up in the air, his head still buried between my legs, carried me to the table over by the window, and laid me on it, still eating my pussy. The curtains were open, and I could look up at the stars in the beautiful clear night as I caressed the back of his head. He ate my pussy for what seemed like an eternity. I savored every moment of it, losing count of how many orgasms erupted from me.

He told me that he was going to spell the alphabet out on my pussy lips with his tongue, and he did just that. He started with the A and moved his tongue up one pussy lip and down the other and then made a horizontal line going across. Then on to the B, and all the way down the line to Z.

His long, thick tongue brought me so much pleasure. He pushed my legs up over his shoulders farther so that my ass was raised off the table and began to eat my ass out too. The shit was the bomb.

Then he told me to get off the table, turn around, and bend over it. I gratefully complied. He spread my ass cheeks, holding them open with his strong hands, and ate it out some more, sticking his tongue completely in my asshole. I had never had a man take total control of me that way. I became totally submissive to him.

Joseph stood up, and I could hear him lowering his pants to his ankles. I could feel that huge dick of his caressing up against my ass, but he didn't stick it in right away. He just rubbed the head of it up and down the center of my ass cheeks, making my desire for him to enter me grow.

He took me by surprise and yanked me around, picking me up again and sticking his luscious tongue down my throat, now covered with my sweet nectar. He carried me over to the bed and sat me down. He stood before me so that his dick was right in my face. All night I had thought of nothing else but tasting him, so I gladly undertook the task.

He was huge. I knew there was no way I would ever be able to take the whole thing down my throat, but I was willing to give it the old college try. I looked up into his eyes as I licked my lips and then moistened the head of his dick with my tongue. I was in heaven.

I decided to tackle the balls first. I lifted his dick up with one hand and caressed his balls with the fingertips of the other. I took his ball sack into my mouth and sucked on it gently. He began to tremble, and I knew at that very moment that I was truly going to enjoy watching him give in to me.

I found the corona of his dick on the underside of it and flickered my tongue all around it. He was shook. Precum started to trickle out the head of his dick, and like a bullfrog catches a fly with his tongue, I caught every drop of that shit. I took the head of his dick in my mouth and contracted my cheek muscles on it, squeezing all the precum I could find out of that bad boy. It was dayum delicious.

I got a good grip on the base of his dick, applying a little pressure to it, and put my lips to that shit, taking as much of the thick shaft into my mouth as I could possibly fathom. I placed my other hand on his thigh for leverage and sucked harder, moving my head back and forth on his magnificent dick. Kevin had a good dick too, but dayum, it was not nearly as big as this one, and not as juicy either.

My own saliva, mixed with his precum, began to trickle out the sides of my mouth, and I had to prevent myself from gagging on it. I let my throat muscles vibrate on the head of his dick like I was gargling. That drove him wild. I could feel his hot cum shoot down my throat, which sated my anxiously awaiting taste buds. He tasted like candy to me. Ummm, I just love the taste of a man's cum.

Joseph stood there for a moment, knees trembling, recovering from what had just happened. We stared at each other as I sat there with the head of his dick dangling from my mouth, cum trickling down my chin onto my breasts.

We both had too much to drink that night, so we ended up falling asleep with one of my nipples in his mouth. The oral sex alone had worn us both out.

When the sun came up the next morning, so did Joseph's dick. We fucked all day long. He called in sick to work, and I forgot all about catching the shuttle bus from the hotel to the beach like I had planned.

We fucked on the bed with him on top, me on top and, of course, doggy-style. We fucked in the shower and ate each other's asses out while we were at it. I had never eaten a man's ass before, but I must say that it was quite a delightful experience watching his reaction. Kevin is a very lucky man now, 'cause he gets that extra treat, thanks to a man named Joseph who lives across the ocean, who he will never meet.

Joseph fucked me up against the wall from behind. He fucked me on the balcony, on the dresser, on the bathroom floor. I never knew a man's dick could stay that hard. My vacation that started out fucked up because Kevin had to go to a conference turned out to be the mother-fucking bomb.

I will never forget Joseph because he helped me discover things about myself sexually that I had never known. I will not forget him because he had the biggest dick I have ever had the pleasure of having inside of me. I will never forget him because he ate my pussy with a hunger so intense that it was overwhelming. But most of all, I will never forget Joseph because of the pictures I keep locked away in my top left desk drawer under a bunch of folders, paper clips, and rubber bands.

The pictures we took of each other with the camera provided by the hotel in the Bahamas to sucker some extra cash out of tourists. The pictures he took of me sucking his dick, of him fucking my pussy till it was sore, of his dick up in my asshole, of him cumming all over my face. The pictures I took of him sucking my toes, of his head buried between my thighs, of my nipples in his mouth. Whenever I am feeling down and having problems with Kevin, whom I am now married to and have a precious little baby girl with, I can always sit down, relax, sneak into my study, pull out the pictures, and savor the memories of my vacation of a lifetime.

Mailman

   While I have always had a predilection for men in uniform, I had never acted on the urge before. I mean, after all, the clothing doesn't make the man. What's inside the man does. Then again, if a man in uniform looks like my mailman, the theory goes straight out the freakin' window.

   I remember the first day I laid eyes on him. Richard and I had just moved in together after deciding one rent was better than two. We had been practically shacking up for more than six months anyway. We just decided to make it official. Besides, I needed more space than my one-bedroom in Adams Morgan. I had joined the masses of computer junkies, quit my job at a graphic design firm in Georgetown, and decided to start my own Web publishing firm. So after a romantic dinner of seafood linguine and Moët down by the waterfront, Richard and I decided to rent this sprawling four-bedroom house in Northwest. It is an old house and needs a lot of renovations, but I love being creative. Interior decorating is just another expressive outlet to entertain me.

   Working from home definitely has its benefits. First off, if I want to, I don't even have to get dressed all day. I can sit in front of my computer in my nightie and grab a quick shower half an hour before Richard comes in from a long day at his accounting firm. Sometimes I sit in my desk chair (yes, it is an ergonomic one) butt-naked. I love the way the Italian leather feels against my smooth skin. At times I feel myself drifting off into another place and time, daydreaming of places I have never seen, fantasizing about men I have never met.

That's what I was doing that day. The day I first saw him. I was sitting there in front of the bay window at my computer, spanking butt-naked and daydreaming about making love to a mandingo somewhere along the Ivory Coast. Much to my surprise, I glanced up, and there was a mandingo coming up my very own front steps.

He was tall, very tall. He had to be at least six and a half feet. Luscious full lips, creamy dark skin, sparkling dark bedroom eyes, and curly jet-black hair. He had a perfect smile, too. I noticed his teeth the moment his mouth fell open after spotting me in the window.

Now normally, I would have been totally embarrassed, but I just sat there and gazed at him. We gazed at each other for a good two or three minutes. I think he was trying to decide whether or not he should bring the package he was grasping up to my door. I made up his mind for him. I stood up so he could get a better look at my birthday suit and marched straight over to the door.

I swung the door open and startled him. He probably assumed I had gone to put on some clothes, but not in this case. I wanted him to see me in all of my naked glory. You see, Richard hadn't exactly been handling business lately. In fact, his sex hadn't been hitting on anything at all since we moved in. It was like he did all of the groundwork to get me to commit and then figured his work was done. *Nada!*

"Can I help you?" I asked abruptly, like it was just a normal day-to-day thing for me to be an exhibitionist.

He started stuttering. "Uh-uh-uh, I have a package for you."

"I can see that," I said sarcastically. "It's pretty large. Could you bring it in and put it on the couch?"

"Ma'am, I'm not supposed to enter a residence. It's against postal regulations." Once I saw him up close, I realized he was just a manchild. He couldn't have been a day over twenty. No wonder he was nervous. Men closer to my age, thirty and up, would have been in the house with a quickness.

I decided I liked playing whatever game it was we were playing. I took a quick survey of the street, and there wasn't a soul in sight. Another perk for working at home. All of the neighbors were gone during the day, and I could have peace and quiet. Once I made sure the coast was clear, I set about torturing the young buck.

I reached my right hand down between my legs and starting fingering my pussy. I took my moistened finger and held it up to his lips, rubbing my juices all over the bottom one. "Couldn't you please make an exception in my case? Pretty please, with pussy on top."

He took a step backward, letting my hand fall from his mouth, before replying, "I dunno about this. I could really get into a heap of trouble. I still have a lot of mail to deliver."

"This will only take a second." I moved aside and held the door open, leaving him no choice but to either bring it in or be rude by refusing me. I knew which one he would do even before he did. He came in the door reluctantly. I quickly closed and locked the door behind us and then went into the living room. I pointed at the couch. "Could you place it right over there?"

He set the large package down, and I noticed it was from my sister in California. I assumed it was the housewarming present she'd been promising me over the phone for weeks. I was curious to know what it was, but I was more intrigued by something else at that very moment.

"There you go, ma'am." He had one of those country-bumpkin voices. He couldn't have possibly have been from the D.C. area.

"Where are you from?" I asked seductively, letting my eyes drift down to the increasing bulge in his slate blue uniform pants.

"Alabama."

Ummmmm, Alabama black snake! "I've never seen you around here before. Are you new?"

He chuckled slightly, loosening up a bit. "This is my first week on the job."

"I see. I figured as much, because I'm sure I would have noticed you before. This is my first time getting a package since I moved in here, though. I've never paid attention to whoever puts the mail in the box, but I know I wouldn't have missed your fine ass. I couldn't have."

He started blushing something terrible. "Thanks, ma'am," he replied, letting his eyes drift all over my nude body before narrowing in on my hard nipples.

"First of all, please don't call me ma'am. My name is Rayn."

"Rain? Like the rain that falls?"

"Not exactly. It's spelled R-A-Y-N."

Beads of sweat started forming on his forehead. I could tell he was eager to get his freak on, but he had no clue how to get started. He opted to try the coward's way out. "Listen ma'am, I me-me-mean Rayn, I really should be going."

He turned and headed toward the door, but I grabbed him by the elbow. I walked up to him from behind and slid my arms around his well-toned waist. "Before you do, care for a little afternoon sex?"

I could hear his breathing become shallow, but he didn't respond. I dropped my left hand below the belt and let my right one move upward until I was caressing his dick and one of his nipples at the same time. He was ready for me alright. Damn, was he ready!

"What's your name?" I inquired.

"Everyone calls me P.J.," he managed to utter as I made my way around to the front of him.

He started trembling when I went down on my knees, unbuckling his belt on my way down. "Well, P.J.," I said while I worked on getting his dick out of his pants, "I'm starving. I haven't had a thing to eat all day. Mind if I have a little snack?"

Again, no answer. Then again, I wasn't really waiting on one.

I hungrily took in the head of his penis, letting my tongue slide in and out of the slit. Some of his juices immediately started to escape. "Oh, damn," he whispered. "Oh, shit," I whispered back. Then I went for the gold. For the next thirty minutes, I sucked on him like he was royalty. He came the first time in less than five minutes, but I wouldn't let it go at that. I intended to teach his young ass how to last more than one time. That I did.

I could tell he had never been sucked off like that before. To be honest, I'm not sure I've ever given head so well before. Not to Richard. Not to anybody. That mere fact only served to motivate me.

After I deep-throated that bad boy until he came in my mouth three times, I glanced at the grandfather clock in the entry hall when the chimes announced it was three o'clock. Two more hours before Richard left his office. Damn, the possibilities!

We didn't exchange many words. Who needed them? I led

P.J. into the kitchen, climbed up on the table, and spread my legs. Eating pussy was something he obviously didn't need to be schooled on. He ate me out big-time. My clit was swollen by the time he got through with me, but it was the good kind of soreness. The kind that lets a sistah know she's been done right.

Richard's imminent arrival was barreling in on us, and I should have probably ended the escapade right then and there. I had yet to actually get fucked, though. I told P.J. to follow me up the stairs. He was at my service and would have done any and every thing I wanted.

We bypassed the master bedroom I shared with Richard and went into the guest bedroom. It was still in heavy stages of renovation. However, I chose that room for a particular reason, and I spotted it the second we entered. There was a huge antique mirror with an authentic bronze frame propped up over by the window. I purchased it at a flea market for a steal from an old woman who didn't realize what a treasure it was. I instructed P.J. to carefully lay it down in the middle of the floor on top of the tarp that was sprawled about because of the painting in progress. Richard planned to add another coat the following weekend.

P.J. still had on his uniform, even though his pants were halfway down. I wanted to see his ass naked. I demanded, "Take off all of your clothes."

He complied in silence while I took my place on top of the mirror, getting down on my hands and knees. I wanted to do the doggy stroke. It's always been my favorite position. After he was naked, he joined me on the mirror. He was too fucking fine.

"Take this pussy, baby!" Once again, he complied, entering my pussy gently from behind. He began to stroke me slowly but I wanted him to fuck the living daylights out of me. I moved my hips back and forth on his dick to encourage him to intensify his efforts.

The real turn-on was watching it all take place on the mirror. I had been taken from the rear dozens of times without having the benefit of watching my lover. That day I could see it all. We both could. I love the way his fingers squeezed my nipples. The way his balls slammed up against the back of my thighs while his dick caught a rhythm. The way he gritted his teeth when I tightened my pussy around his shaft. That damn Thighmaster tightens up more than just thigh muscles.

I could tell he was seconds away from cumming when his eyes started rolling around in his head. I knew he came when his semen trickled down onto the mirror along with my own juices. After we were done, we laid there on the mirror with his head on my chest, trying to get our breathing under control. I heard the grandfather clock strike five. Richard would be on the way to his car in the underground garage. I had less than fifteen freakin' minutes to cover my tracks.

I got P.J. out of the crib with a quickness, promising him we would do it again sometime. He left out with a gigantic smile on his face. I don't know if he got in trouble because he delivered his mail late, but I'm sure he felt it was worth it. I wiped off the mirror with glass cleaner, propped it back up against the wall, broke out the air freshener, and sprayed the entire house. I turned on my potpourri Crockpot on the kitchen counter and threw a turkey breast in the oven. Then I jumped in the shower just long enough to wash the vital parts with a loofah sponge and my herbal body wash. I brushed and gargled before slipping into a pair of sweats and one of Richard's T-shirts just in the nick of time. He walked through the door ten seconds after I got to the bottom of the stairs.

"Did you have a productive day, sweetheart?" he asked me.

"Absolutely!" I chuckled. "Very productive!"

Several months have passed since I first met P.J. The house

is all fixed up now, and Richard is acting more romantic. Even so, about once a month I stand up in front of the bay window in my birthday suit when I see P.J. approaching the mailbox out front. It is our version of the bat signal. I call it the fuck signal. Those days are always interesting. As for that antique mirror in the guest bedroom—it gets put to a hell of a lot of use.

Body Chemistry 101

His name was Professor Vaughn Mason. To me, he was simply heaven on earth. I was lucky enough to be in his organic chemistry class my freshman year at State. I started lusting after him the first day of class. One glance into his captivating bedroom eyes, one flash of his charismatic smile, and I was hooked.

I used to daydream during his class lectures, undress him with my eyeballs, and wonder if he was a tender or rough lover. During one of our lab periods, I almost spilled a beaker of hydrochloric acid on my thigh. I'd lost my concentration, fantasizing about milking his dick with my mouth.

After freshman year, I didn't get to see Vaughn that often. A wave here, a smile there, an occasional greeting when we passed each other on the steps or in the halls of the Natural Sciences building. It was depressing.

Senior year rolled around, and purely by the luck of the draw, I ended up snagging his student assistant position. It was like winning the lottery. I would get to spend time with him, talk to him privately, and maybe even brush up against him on the sly every now and then.

So there I was, his assistant, and excited as I could possibly be about it. Vaughn, who I never addressed by his first name to his face, was so dayum fione. He was about five-eleven, 180 pounds, deep chocolate with dark bedroom eyes, and had a sexy-ass bald head. His body, dayum, what I say except the man was cut and looked like his muscles were chiseled out of stone. If ever there was a man who could make a woman's pussy get wet by looks alone, he was the one.

I had just celebrated my twenty-first birthday during the summer. He was much older than I was, about forty, but I never asked. When a nucca is that fine, who gives a dayum about a number? He had never married, but he was shacking up with some nurse from the university hospital. Did I care? Hell, naw!

You can never control the way you feel. Which is why what happened just two weeks into the fall semester was beyond my control. Whenever I reflect on that day, I realize it was the single most erotic experience of my entire life—one that I wouldn't trade for anything in this world.

I remember it so vividly, like it was yesterday. Vaughn had a faculty meeting that morning. I stayed behind in the chemistry lab to grade some exams for him. I was sitting at his desk, grading papers, and my mind began to wander as usual. I imagined him and me alone in the lab as we often were, but instead of just going about the course of a normal day, he had me bent over his desk and was fucking me doggy-style from behind. The thought of it made my pussy so wet.

Even though it was mid-September, it was terribly hot that day. The form-fitting white button-down oxford shirt I had on with a navy above-the-knee skirt, white slouch socks, and a pair of Nikes was clinging to my breasts. I had the windows ajar in the lab. The Natural Sciences building was one of the oldest on campus and without central air. The only real breeze in the room was coming from the box fan I had strategically placed on the top of one of the long laboratory tables.

The mere thought of his hands on me was driving me berserk. I masturbated in my dorm room all the time thinking about him, but on that particular day, I needed some fast relief and couldn't stand the thought of having to wait until I went home. I analyzed the whole situation like a silent movie in my mind. The faculty meetings would usually last at least two hours, and I didn't have a dayum thing to satisfy myself with. Unfortunately, I didn't tote my vibrator around in my book bag. I would have done anything to have it at that moment.

I locked the door to the lab and went to sit back down at the desk. I leaned back in the comfortable leather desk chair with the reclining back and swivel base. I closed my eyes and fantasized about him kissing me on my lips, and my hands suddenly became his hands. I caressed my nipples through the cotton of my shirt. They were ripe and hardened. I unbuttoned the top three buttons and pulled both of my nipples out so that they were protruding from my bra.

I licked my lips, fantasizing about Vaughn sucking on them one at a time. I threw one of my legs up on top of the desk and, pushing my underwear aside, began to finger my pussy. It was so hot and moist, longing to feel his tongue. I stuck one finger in at a time until I was working three of them inside. I still had my eyes closed. In my mind, Vaughn was feasting off my sweet, tender pussy.

Finger-fucking myself was pleasing, but it wasn't enough. I wanted to feel something deep inside my pussy walls. I took my fingers out and licked my pussy juice off them, savoring my own flava. I opened my eyes and took a quick survey of the lab looking for something, *anything,* to use to fuck myself with.

Most of the items, like the microscopes and Bunsen burners, were out of the fucking question, but suddenly I spotted something that would do the trick. As I got up from the desk, I peeped the wall clock and realized that Vaughn hadn't even been gone a good hour. I assumed there was enough time to finish myself off. I walked over to the closest lab table to the front and retrieved a large test tube, one that held 500 ml, and went back to the desk, positioning my leg back on the desk.

I moved my panties out of the way again and gently inserted the test tube into my pussy. I had it inverted so that the bottom, round part was the entry point of the tube. It was made out of unbreakable Pyrex, so I wasn't afraid it would break and cut me if I got too carried away. To be honest, though, even if the glass had been breakable, I was so horny that it wouldn't have mattered much.

The cool glass felt great as I slid it in and out my pussy. It even tickled a little. After I got a good rhythm going, I closed my eyes and began to fantasize about Vaughn again, imagining him sliding his hardened dick in and out my sugar walls. I began to moan as I caressed my nipples with my other hand, lifting one of my breasts as high as I could and flickering the tip of my tongue over the nipple. I moved the test tube in and out faster and faster and the pleasure was so intense that—

I never heard his key in the lock or the door open, but I heard it close. I opened my eyes, and he was standing there, with a look of shock on his face and his mouth hanging wide open. I was so embarrassed to be caught like that, with my leg on his desk, breasts hanging out everywhere, test tube in my pussy with juices all over it. I should have taken it out, gotten up, and fixed my clothes but something happened.

The look on his face was not one of disgust but one of desire. I don't know how I could tell for sure, but I could. I was about to remove the tube when he said, "No, don't stop!" Vaughn locked the door, came over, and knelt between my legs. We looked at each other with desire, even though we both knew we had no business being together like that.

He said, "Let me help you!" I could manage nothing but "Okay!" He put his left hand on the inner thigh of my right leg, the one that was raised on the desk, and with his other hand, he took control of the test tube. He fucked me with it, and the experience was so intense. I pinched my nipples and, with both hands available at that time, I pushed my breasts together and pushed then up toward my mouth, licking on my own nipples.

I was about to explode, and apparently he could tell that I was about to cum, because he took the test tube out of me and said, "No, I don't want you to cum yet!" He put the test tube up to my mouth and said, "Lick it! Taste yourself for me!" As he held it in place, I placed my hand over his and began to lick my pussy juice off the test tube while we gazed in each other's eyes. I licked it clean, and he gave me a kiss on my lips and sucked on my bottom lip, withdrawing a quick sample of my nectar from it.

He slowly put the test tube back into my pussy and began to fuck me with it again, but this time, he sucked on my breasts for me. I cupped my left one in my hand and fed it to him. He was grateful to have it. After a few moments, I fed him the other one too. He pulled my hips down a little farther on the seat and reclined it so that my ass was exposed just enough for him to finger it.

I couldn't hold back any more. I came harder than I had ever cum before. I can't be sure, but judging from his reaction, I think he came also, even though his dick never left his pants. He pulled the cum-drenched tube from my pussy and devoured every last drop of it.

For at least ten minutes after that, we were speechless. I sat there recovering from what had just taken place. He stared at me while he ran his fingers through the baby-fine pussy hair on my swollen vagina. I cannot explain how it feels to make love to a person and never have actual intercourse. It was so sexy.

We were still sitting there, basking in the afterglow, the only sounds in the room being the rotating blades of the box fan and voices of coeds walking across campus far below the ajar windows, when a knock came at the door. We both snapped out of our trance instantly and I struggled to get dressed while Vaughn told the dean of the Chemistry Department that he would be right there. It turns out Vaughn had left the meeting to come retrieve some notes for a proposal he was supposed to give to the rest of the professors in the department and was due to go straight back. I guess the sight of a woman fucking herself with a test tube could throw most any man off track.

He left the room grinning from ear to ear, and I went back to grading papers with a smile on my face as well. I couldn't believe what had happened, but I have never regretted it to this very day. Vaughn and I never mentioned it for the rest of my time at State. I remained his assistant and continued to call him Professor Mason.

I am now a chemist for a pharmaceutical company in Texas. Recently, I was going through some old boxes from college, and guess what I found? A 500 ml test tube made out of Pyrex. I wonder where that came from!

Alpha Phi Fuckem

We are a sorority. You won't find us on any college campus, though. Nor will you see us participating in step shows or collecting canned goods for the needy or having parties at a sorority house. We walk alone. We are as close as any sisterhood can get, and we would lay down our lives for each other. We are professional, well-educated women from all walks of life: bankers, lawyers, accountants, doctors, teachers. We are the proud sorors of Alpha Phi Fuckem Sorority, and we are here to stay.

We were founded over twenty years ago in a penthouse overlooking the Potomac River in Georgetown, an upper-class area of Washington, D.C. Most of the founding members have moved on, but they're always around to guide us if ever we need their wisdom. A classmate at law school inducted me into the sorority eight years ago. Her name's Patricia, and she's my mentor, having been in the sorority a good two years before myself.

Currently, there are twenty-four active members of the Washington, D.C., chapter. Yes, there are other chapters. There are seven chapters altogether, with sistahs in about three or four other cities trying to form groups now. We have the D.C. chapter and others in New York City, Chicago, Los Angeles, Detroit, Atlanta, and Miami. We even have an annual convention under the ruse of an African-American female business organization. At least, that's what we tell the hotels where we stay.

It takes a significant amount of time to start a chapter because it takes a certain type of woman to be eligible for membership. What are the requirements? First of all, you have to be able to pass an initiation. Every aspect of your life is scrutinized and gone over with a fine-toothed comb. We have to all feel comfortable around you and feel you have that edge about you that sets you apart from other women. We have to feel you are deserving enough to participate in our erotic adventures.

Secondly, you must be trustworthy, secretive, and willing to take all the freaky shit we do to your grave. No one outside the sorority can ever know the things we do. You must be willing to lie to your husband or boyfriend or, in some cases, your girlfriend about where you're going and what you're doing. We all lie, but the sexual gratification we get as our reward is well worth it. We give a whole new outlook to the word *creeping*. The men we engage in our little escapades are not in the position to tell on us, mostly because they have no idea who the hell we are. We're just faces and bodies, tits and ass, to them. However, the members of the sorority all know who the others are, and therefore, it's important that the trust is there. We could all lose our reputations, possibly even our careers, if the existence of Alpha Phi Fuckem ever came to light.

Thirdly, and this is by far the most important qualification, you have to straight up love fucking. There is just no getting around that, but it goes beyond the normal spectrum of society's definition of fucking. You have to be down for whatever, whenever, and with whomever. No limitations, no inhibitions, and no mental hang-ups are allowed. You must be a woman looking to take sexuality to another level.

Let me give you a quick overview of our mission. We have two "gatherings" a month. The first one is indeed a business meeting. Like I said, we're all professional women. We have an investment club where we pool our resources and invest in certain stocks and bonds. It's each member's responsibility to bring detailed information to the meeting pertaining to at least one corporation and/or product. After all of the options have been discussed, we decide as a group what new investments we will undertake. We also discuss the profits and losses of the stocks already in our portfolio and decide whether to increase or decrease our shares. We have quite a portfolio established. It is a very lucrative investment for all those involved.

The second "gathering" of the month is what we affection- ately call Freak Night. Each month, two members are selected at random to organize an activity for the month. The activity chosen must be both sexually stimulating and completely off the hook. Allow me to elaborate. For example, two months ago in January, Yolanda and Keisha decided to host a night of checkers. Yes, I said checkers. Checkers with a twist. Our two sorors rented a ski chalet up in the Shenandoah Mountains of Virginia, a couple hours drive from D.C. It was a huge chalet with six bedrooms, huge whirlpools, a great room, and a breathtaking view of the ski slopes.

It was snowing heavily when we arrived at the top of the mountain. We all met up at the chalet. Patricia and I rode up together in her Mercedes ATV. After all the young ladies had arrived, Yolanda and Keisha went over the agenda for the evening before the men showed up. As usual, the men my sistahs selected were right on point. We all have the same general taste in men, and that's a good thing, because there are never any complaints. Where they found them, who knows? They were somebody's sons, somebody's husbands, somebody's lovers, somebody's baby's daddies. Who cares as long as the sex is good!

The men arrived one, two, and three at a time. Some knew each other already, if they were "picked up" together. All of them were taken off guard when they entered the chalet. In every room throughout the house, there were butt-naked women strategically positioned in front of a checkerboard, including myself. They were informed by the two hostesses, both of whom greeted them naked at the door, that they could challenge the lady of their choice to a game. Imagine their shock to arrive at what they were told would be a cocktail party and discover a virtual smorgasbord of pussy instead.

So play checkers we did, after asking all the men to get naked as well. They were all down because they knew something like that would probably never happen to them again. Maybe in a wet dream, but not during waking hours. We played checkers everywhere—at the dining room and kitchen tables, on the coffee table, on the hearth of the fireplace, on all the beds, on huge stuffed floor pillows. Everywhere. We chatted with the men about the typical things people would talk about at a cocktail party and served them drinks when they requested them so they could see our tits and ass as we walked across the room to get their drinks.

Their dicks were all degrees of hard and came in all different lengths and degrees of thickness. I love dick more than I love my next breath, so they were all mighty appealing to me. I played checkers with a guy from Baltimore. He offered his name. I declined to accept it and refused to give mine. Instead of calling each other by our real names when men are present, we call each other by nicknames like Soror Deep Throat, Soror Cum Hard, and Soror Ride Dick. Yeah, it's silly but we're not trying to impress anyone. It's extremely vital that our real identities remain sacred.

We sat there in the snow-covered chalet for most of the evening playing checkers and shooting the breeze. Wet pussies were everywhere because all of us are multiorgasmic. Just looking at all the dick in the house made us horny as hell. Then came the highlight of the evening, and just in the nick of time too. One more game of checkers without getting some dick, and I was going to start fingering myself and eating my own dayum pussy.

Yolanda and Keisha told everyone it was time to get busy and turned some classic fuck songs on the boom box, the kind of songs that immediately bring fucking to the mind and cease any and all other brain activity. You know the kind. At that point, we all went to fucking. We each fucked the gentleman we had played checkers with the first go-round, and then it turned into a straight up fuckfest. Dicks, tits, ass, pussy everywhere.

Soror Deep Throat, an ophthalmologist during the day, sucked off about every man in there. As usual, I thought she was going for the title in the world records book. My sistah loves sucking some dick more than any woman I have ever known. She comes to the gatherings more to suck dick than to fuck. Soror Cum Hard, a professor of paleontology, is the exact opposite. She loves to be eaten, and by as many men as she can muster up the energy to feed in one night.

Soror Ride Dick would be none other than myself, an assistant district attorney. I avidly believe in the more the merrier. I don't know what it is about riding a dick that turns my ass out, but I love it. Maybe it's having all the control and watching men shiver and lose command of the English language when you're an expert on riding a dick like I am. It takes skills to ride a man in such a fashion that he wants to get in the fetal position and cry afterward because it was so dayum good.

It was a great orgy, as they all are. Everyone left completely sated and with smiles on their faces the next morning. Patricia and I discussed the highlights of the night before as we cautiously descended the icy mountain road, passing a family of deer walking in single file, tracking footprints through the snow.

Anyway, that was the gist of our January activity. February was just as intriguing. Sorors Lisa and Melanie undertook the task of planning a very special Valentine's Day dance. They paid the owner of a sleazy strip club an exorbitant amount of money, in cash of course, to rent the entire place for one evening. They filled the small place up with men in suits, and we each took turns taking the stage and stripping our asses off. All of us wore masks—the kind with feathers you find in abundance at the Mardi Gras. We wore all sorts of sexy lingerie, but ended up in the raw by the end of our individual performances.

Once each lady finished her performance, she would get the opportunity to choose which man she wanted to sit with at a table. At that point, she had to continue her exhibition by sitting facing the man, with one leg thrown up on the table. This enabled him to get an eagle's-eye view of her pussy. He watched while she fucked herself with the ten-inch dildo placed on each table by the hostesses, along with anal beads, butt plugs, and Ben Wa balls to use later on in the evening.

After the last performance, Soror Three Input, a network analyst, pulled a man onstage and showed us a captivating rendition of ass-fucking. It's her personal favorite. Once her interpretation of the fine art of anal sex was over, we had a free-for-all. I made the man I was with get down on his knees underneath the table and eat my pussy while I sucked my own pussy juices off the dildo, and we proceeded from there. He was a great lover, and sometimes I hate the fact that we can never see these men again. It's such a waste when they have the bomb-ass dick.

Just two nights ago, Patricia and I hosted the March gathering. We decided to go back in time and get a little psychedelic thing going. We convinced this guy to let us use his photography studio for the evening. It was in a huge loft, so we had plenty of space. We told all the sorors to wear some bell-bottoms, platforms, crocheted tank tops, halters, or whatever, along with Afro wigs, and meet us there. We found some cool-ass men for the night, including the photographer. That was part of the deal for letting us use his place. Once everyone got there, we turned on the black-light bulbs and strobe lights and danced, getting butt-naked as we went along. Once everyone was nude and doing the hustle, the bump, and the dog to old-school jams, we passed out tubes of neon body paint in various colors and had everyone paint each other. We even had small paint rollers so the men could roll paint onto our asses and wherever else.

Patricia and I had completely covered the hard wood floor with white sheets so we didn't leave a mess. The way everyone was naked and glowing in the dark was wild, especially when the fucking began. We had the photographer take several rolls of film. This was definitely one for the scrapbooks. It was safe because it was so dark in the place that only the body paints and outlines of bodies were visible. Seeing the mass orgy of neon bodies rolling around on the floor was nothing short of amazing.

Well, that brings us up to date. Next month, Sorors Diane and Cynthia are in charge. I can hardly wait to see what they have in store. I realize all of this must seem crazy to outsiders, but trust me, it's not as preposterous as it sounds. The sorority of Alpha Phi Fuckem has already survived for twenty years, and we will survive for a hundred more. One of the founding members is now a governor. She was keynote speaker at our last year's national convention. We're not just some group of women who have fly-by-night ideas, do something for a little while, and get tired of it. We're determined to keep this sorority alive. Just as determined as we are with all the other aspects of our lives.

You would never be able to pick us out as we walk down the street, volunteer at community events, bake cookies for the church bake sales, and act as cheerleaders on the sidelines at our kids' Little League games. Most women have an undercover freak in them yearning to get loose. If we can free our bodies, then we can also free our minds. Soror Ride Dick, over and out!

Room 69

I arrived in Charlotte on a Monday night about 9 P.M., rented a car at the airport, and got checked into the hotel by ten. I was exhausted. It was a cold and rainy night in December. I forgot to pack an overcoat or umbrella before I left California, so I was soaked and freezing by the time I got in the room. The room they gave me was cozy and had a nice king-size bed. I laughed when the clerk handed me the room key because it had the number 69 on it. That brought all kinds of interesting thoughts into my head.

I had been to Charlotte before on business trips and always had a boring time in the evenings. I didn't know anyone there outside of business, and so most nights, I would just grab a pizza or sub and eat in the room, do a little work on my IBM Thinkpad, and go to bed.

There had been one exception. About six months before this particular trip, I had ventured out and gone to breakfast with a man I met at a business meeting. We had a nice breakfast, and then he showed me around town in his car, kissed me good-bye on the cheek, and that was it.

After I got back home, we talked on the phone quite often. Both of us joked about how the chemistry was there between us, and yet we were both too nervous to act upon it. I told him if I ever ran up on him again, I would fuck his fine ass on sight. He agreed it was definitely a plan of action because he was feenin for me too.

I was so cold and damp when I got in the room. I decided I would just take a warm shower and call him in the morning to discuss the possibilities. Needless to say, that's exactly what I did. I called him the next morning at work, and he was elated to hear from me. We made plans to meet up at my hotel after I had completed my business meetings. We planned to go out to dinner around six in the evening.

When I got to the hotel, he was parked in front of my room and leaning on his car, awaiting my arrival. I was about ten minutes late. I decided to stop by a drugstore and pick up some condoms. There was no way I was gonna let anything disrupt the plans I had to get busy.

We went into my room and chatted maybe ten minutes, if that, and then it was on. I enjoyed being with him because he was very passionate. He kissed me with conviction, and his tongue made me melt. We laid there in each other arms for a good while, just enjoying exploring each other's mouths.

Then, he got up from the bed and turned off the evening news, saying he didn't want any noise distracting our lovemaking. The room was completely silent except for the faint noise of the heat escaping from the vents, an occasional car door slamming, and the distant clatter of someone getting ice from the machine in the courtyard.

He came back to the bed and pulled my black cable-knit sweater up and over my head, removing it. He kissed me again, this time even more sensually than before. I remember thinking he was the greatest kisser I had ever known. I imagined his tongue tracing patterns on my pussy lips, on my clit, and inside my pussy walls. Having oral sex performed on me is always the highlight of any fuck session for me. I anxiously awaited the point in time when he would quench his thirst with my nectar. I just knew the moment was coming, because that was all he ever talked about during our phone conversations. How much he wanted to taste me. I could tell by the way that he explored my mouth that he would probably be a prime candidate for the Pussy Eaters Hall of Fame.

He lowered my bra straps and sucked on my nipples, getting to know each one of them up close and personal. I pulled his head up so I could kiss him again because it was such a helluva turn-on. I pushed him on his back and straddled myself on top of him, letting my breasts dangle over his mouth. He grabbed both of my breasts, pushed them together a little roughly, and licked all over them at the same time.

I took his tie and shirt off and licked all over his chest, using the tip of my tongue to carve a path from his nipples, down his rippled chest, to his belly button, where I paused to dab my tongue in and out of it. I bit gently on his nipples and rubbed them around between my thumbs and forefingers.

I unfastened his belt buckle and pulled his pants down and off, untying and removing his shoes during the process. I helped him remove his red silk boxers and started sucking on the head of his dick before they even hit the floor. His dick was so good. I enjoyed feasting on it until he climaxed. His hot cum trickled down my throat, lining my stomach with a warm coating.

The moment had finally arrived. I just knew it was my turn to lay back and relax while he got to know me orally. Boy, was I wrong!

He fell asleep, calling the fucking hogs after only a blow

job, and I was pissed. All the anticipation and planning for nothing. I caressed his dick, hoping to arouse him from his slumber, but nothing.

It was only about 7 P.M. at that point. I realized a hard day's work can be draining, but dayum him. He slept until almost eleven, four fucking hours, and when he woke up, I was sitting at the table over by the window going over some figures on my laptop and drinking some wild-cherry-flavored springwater.

I gawked at him with disbelief when he told me to come back and join him in bed. Then I figured, oh well, maybe he was just tired. Now he was gonna do all the shit he claimed he wanted to do to me on the phone. I went back over and lay down on the bed. I had my bra on, having repositioned the straps so my breasts were covered, and my black pants and panties were still on. He hadn't even touched me down there.

Once again, he started in with the kissing, but this time, I wasn't as receptive. The impression was already embedded in my mind that he wasn't even worth my time or effort. He did the nipple thing again, and I was bored.

Finally, he got to the bottom half of my body and started rubbing my vagina through the material of my pants. He pulled them down and off. I was thinking, About dayum time. He was finally gonna get busy and eat my coochie-coo.

Wrong! He started finger-fucking me. I wanted to tell him so badly that finger-fucking went out with bell-bottoms, Afros, and platform shoes, but I tolerated it, hoping it was all a means to an end.

Once again, I was wrong, so I decided to get the whole fucked-up situation over with. I got a condom out the box, slapped that shit on him, and rode him real fast until his ass came. He had the audacity to try to stop me, grabbing my hips and saying, "I don't want to cum yet!" I wanted to say, "Fuck you!" But that would have been dumb, considering I was fucking him—lousy fucking, yet fucking all the same.

I finally got his ass out of there about midnight, after explaining to him why he couldn't spend the night. I had an early meeting in the morning. I was too through and couldn't believe I built his ass up in my mind to be some black Don Juan when he wasn't 'bout shit.

You probably think I just took my ass to sleep depressed or went back to crunching numbers on my computer, huh? *Nope!* My ass was starving, since he and I never made it to dinner, and I hadn't eaten anything except a bagel with cream cheese about 8 A.M.

I took a shower, got dressed, and went to check out this all-night diner. I had noticed it two exits away in the vicinity of the drugstore where I bought the condoms. What a joke! I should have left them bad boys in the store and had a V-8 instead.

The diner was practically deserted when I arrived at a quarter to one. It was a Tuesday, so most people were home snuggled in for a good night's sleep, making love to their mates, or watching late-night repeats of talk shows like *Jenny Jones* and *Jerry Springer*. If it had been a Friday or Saturday night around the same time, I'm sure the place would have been packed with people that developed the munchies after a night at the movies or dancing and drinking at a club.

There were only a few other people scattered around at the tables—some black guy over in the corner suffering from an obvious case of jungle fever, a couple of teenage boys laughing loudly and trying to see which one of them could be more obnoxious than the other, and a black guy in a booth by the window who appealed to me right away.

Why he appealed to me, I'm not sure. He was attractive, but I see attractive men all day, every day. Maybe I was just still feeling horny, sexually repressed even. I still couldn't believe that man talked mad shit about how he was gonna turn my ass out and managed to do nothing but turn my ass off.

The guy in the booth was very nicely built and looked very friendly. I sat there sizing his ass up while I waited for some ditzy waitress named Becky to bring my grilled chicken breast sandwich with fries. He was mocha with dark eyes, a sexy mouth, and juicy-ass lips. I imagined drawing the bottom one into my mouth and sucking on it. Next thing you know, I was wondering whether or not he had a big dick.

I snapped out of it when tactless Becky slammed my plate down hard and asked if I wanted a refill on my iced tea. I was tripping, sitting there fantasizing about freaking some man who had only stopped by a diner to get a bite to eat. He wasn't thinking about my ass. Or was he?

As I was sitting there hitting the hell out of this bottle of slow-ass Hunt's ketchup to no avail, I felt his eyes on me and looked up. Sure enough, he was staring dead at me. He smiled at me, I smiled back, and the wheels started turning in my head. I began to ponder exactly how scandalous it would make me if I picked this guy up and whether it would classify me as a certified hoochie if I did. I let out a sigh of relief when he got up from his table, placed a tip on it, and headed toward the front door.

The ball was no longer in my corner, since he was taking his ass home and going to bed. The night turned out to be full of surprises, because he paused at the door, which his hand was holding halfway open, allowing a cool breeze to come in, and then turned around and headed straight toward my table.

My heart started pounding a mile a minute. The shit was un-fucking-believable. He came up to me and said, "Excuse me. You have a minute?"

I looked up at him and managed to utter one word, "Sure!"

He sat down across from me and just stared me in the eyes, and I was a nervous wreck. He just sat there grinning at me for what seemed like an eternity. In actuality, it couldn't have been more than a couple minutes.

Finally, he asked, "Aren't you gonna eat?" I told him my appetite was gone, and I thought I was hungry when I placed my order, but it was much too late at night for me to actually eat. It was all bullshit, but there was no freaking way I was gonna have him sitting there watching me chew my food.

We started chatting about whatever. I told him about my career and he explained how he was stationed nearby in the military and had just gotten back to the states from a long assignment in Panama.

Then, he just happened to mention the fact he hadn't had any pussy in a good while and wondered if he could have some of mine. I freaked. My first instinct was to cuss his ass out, but I didn't. Instead I asked him what he meant by "have some." He wanted to know what the hell I was talking about. I decided if his ass could be blunt like that, my ass could do the same thing.

So, I laid it out for him and told him how I expected this turn-my-ass-out, toe-curling sexual experience, and what had really happened instead. I told him how much I love my pussy eaten and how I felt like the shit I did a few hours before wasn't even fucking. Then I asked him whether or not he just goes downtown to window-shop or does he actually purchase something.

He started laughing because of the way I phrased it. I asked him, did the laugh mean he wasn't about shit either? He leaned closer to me over the table, took my hand, and adamantly stated that he loved to eat pussy and would love to eat mine. Again, I froze; I couldn't believe the shit was happening. I left California to go on a *business* trip, and all I was worried about was having my coochie eaten.

After a few moments of silence, he inquired whether I was fronting or not. The man was dead serious about going down on me. He told me he would follow me back to my hotel room in his car and lick me clean. I couldn't help but blush. Normally, I would have hauled ass and ran for the hills, but there was something about him. He had such a friendly disposition and seemed like a good old country boy who would eat me like a pot of chitterlings with Tabasco sauce.

I pondered and pondered while he waited and waited for a response, telling me to make sure I was comfortable with it before I made a final decision. Becky kept coming over, asking if we wanted anything else, and we both repeatedly said no. I think she was just being nosy. As empty as the place was, she knew we didn't come in together and figured there was some freaky-deaky shit going on.

Finally, I decided I was a grown woman, and hell yeah, I did want my pussy eaten, was feenin for it even, so I told him to bring it on. He paid my check at the counter, left Becky a tip, and walked me to my car, asking one more time if I was sure. I told him I was very sure.

He followed me back to the room and chuckled when he saw the number on the door. It was three in the morning. Once inside, he told me straight up he wanted to see me naked. I took my clothes off, since there was no point in turning back.

After I was butt-naked, I got up on the bed and embarked upon the wildest oral experience I've ever had. The man was all about the pussy. He was a beast. First, he sniffed all around it like a predator in the woods seeking out some prey. He told me how much he loved my aroma and was glad I was clean. I asked him were there some women who really had bad personal hygiene habits. He replied with a loud "Hell, yeah!" telling me sometimes he could smell a woman's pussy when he walked by her on the street because the odor was so strong and funky. I could do nothing but laugh and tell him I was glad I passed the inspection.

Then came the interesting part. Instead of just spreading my legs open and cleaning my clock, he positioned himself beside me on the bed, lifting my right leg up in the air and putting my thigh up on his back with his head facing toward my left thigh instead of directly at my clit. He lifted my left leg up in the air and pushed it outward so that my legs were spread wide apart and started eating me.

Boy, did he eat! All I can say is the man was starving like Marvin. I lost count of how many times I came. He was not lying—he loved eating some pussy, unlike the sexually disappointing fuck who had been on the very same bed not long before. After a while, my left leg, which was hanging out there in the air, started getting tired. I put it down on the bed. He immediately pushed it back up and told me to hold it there.

I wasn't used to holding my leg up like that. Normally, the man's shoulders would be holding them both up. Instead, his back was holding up my right one, and it was mad comfortable, but my left leg was having problems. He unzipped his jeans and guided my hand to his dick. I started jacking him off, even though that wasn't in the contract. It was cool with me. I was kind of lying there with nothing to do with my hands, so what the hell.

He ate and ate, and I jacked and jacked, and he ate some more until the moment of truth arrived and he detonated. Scared me shitless too. He came so hard and made these sounds like a fucking animal. Never in life have I seen anything like that before or since.

He passed out right there, with his head in between my legs. The right one was still resting comfortably on his back.

The left one was cramped up, but holding its own, since it could finally lie flat on the bed.

The shit was too wild, and I wasn't about to go to sleep, not knowing a dayum thing about the man, so I flipped through cable channels all night with the remote while he drooled on my pussy and enjoyed his slumber.

At 7 A.M., I told him I needed to get ready for a meeting. He woke up, turned over onto his back, and started rubbing all over his own chest and up and down the shaft of his dick. I thought to myself, "Oh, shit! Now his freaky ass is gonna masturbate in front of me!"

He did play with himself until he came. I watched it. It was sort of interesting. Besides, a woman doesn't get to see such a command performance often. Then he got up and asked me did I want his number. I replied with, "Sure, why not?"

He wrote it inside a matchbook cover with the hotel name imprinted on it, and I saw him to the door. I couldn't believe I had done that shit, but bottom line, the first guy wasn't 'bout it 'bout it, I got what I craved in the end, and it was all good.

I took yet another shower, threw on a navy business suit, went to my meetings, grabbed a pizza on my way back to the hotel, ignored the messages the clerk gave me from the lousy-ass fuck who was all talk and no action, and went to bed.

I flew back to California the next day, none the worse for wear, and now I'm sitting here writing my scandalous, yet sexually fulfilling, escapade down in my journal. It may be a long-ass time before I have something this interesting to write in here again. Then again, maybe not! The fact of the matter is, as wild as it was, I truly relished it, so I have learned my lesson. Before that night, I would've told everyone I wouldn't do something freaky like that. The lesson that I've learned is to never say never again.

The Cat Burglar

The first time I ever laid eyes on you was the night Penny and I robbed you blind. She and I had been knocking over places for the past two years. We met when we were both doing a stint in the county jail. She was in for prostitution and I was in for shoplifting a can of soup because I was sick, starving, and cold. What can I say? Life was hard, and I had to make ends meet any way I could. I grew up dirt-poor with a mother who cared more about where her next bottle of booze was coming from than her kids.

Penny and I got to talking about how life was treating us both so shitty and contemplating how we could have the last laugh. They say jail doesn't reform you—it just makes you a better criminal. In both of our cases, that was definitely true. We talked to some experts in the robbery field, since county jail was our little training academy and they instructed us well.

When we got out two days apart, we put all the plans we made in jail into action and started hitting places right and left. The first couple of times I was convinced we were headed to the big house for a long-ass time. When we didn't get caught, I began to relax a little. Robbing people was so much easier than I thought it would be. I didn't feel guilty; I knew they were insured if they had any fucking sense at all.

Basically, Penny and I took turns between doing the actual heist and being the lookout. When we got to your place, we had hit thirty-four homes altogether; everywhere from one-bedroom apartments to mansions. We only took small items from apartments and saved the big stuff like televisions, stereos, and VCRs for houses, where it was much easier to get them out.

I entered your apartment from the balcony door, after using a grappling hook and rope to lower myself from the roof of the building down to the fourth floor. Penny had been very good about constructing your weekly schedule. I knew you were working out at the gym that night. Since she did all the legwork, Penny had seen you several times, but I never had.

That is, until I was going through your dresser drawers, looking for any valuables I could find. There were several photographs attached to your dresser mirror, ones you had slid between the glass and the black lacquer frame. There were seven pictures all together. Three were of a woman that I assumed was your lady, one was of an older woman that I pegged to be your mother, two were of a little boy that I later found out is your son, and the last one was of you.

You were standing on a beach somewhere, in a pair of shorts and a tank top, with your hand up over your forehead as if you were giving a military salute. It was obvious the true purpose was to cut down on the glare from the sun. I had never been a true believer in love at first sight until I saw your picture.

There you were, probably on vacation with the woman from the pictures. She was more than likely the one who took the picture of you. The thing that struck me first about you was your smile. You have this great smile. Then I was mesmerized by your eyes. Most eyes look lifeless in pictures, but yours were so vivid, breathtaking even. A car horn from somewhere down below knocked me out of my daze, and I remembered why I was there in the first place.

I finished looking through your dresser and found quite a load of goodies—some gold jewelry, a couple of watches, and some earrings your lady must have left over there. I was startled when I discovered a diamond engagement ring under a pile of silk boxers in the bottom left drawer. You must have been planning to pop the question soon, and I was halfway disappointed. I took the ring even though, for the very first time ever, I felt kind of bad about stealing.

I didn't even bother going through the rest of your apartment. For some reason, I felt depressed, as if some woman had stole my man from me. Crazy, since we had never met. I was robbing your ass and feenin for you at the same time. I left the same way I had come in and used the rope to scale back up to the roof. I exited the building by taking the elevator back down to the lobby and rushing out like I had a date or appointment. As usual, no one paid much attention to me because people, the male species in particular, never suspect women as burglars. That is part of the beauty of it.

I got into the getaway car where Penny was waiting for me, in the alley around the corner from your building. While we were pulling off, I spotted you jogging down the street on your way home from the gym. Penny pointed you out to me. There was no need, because I knew who you were right away. I also knew I had to have you.

That night in my bed, I tossed and turned, thinking about you. I dreamed of you and me on the beach in the picture, making love in the sand. I dreamed of you smiling at me with your beautiful mouth and looking deep into my soul through your captivating eyes. I began to rub my fingers over my clit with one hand and caress my nipples with the other. I did it until I came all over my bedsheets, sweating from the sex I had undertaken all alone.

A whole month went by. Penny and I had long spent the cash we got for pawning your valuables. I was still dreaming about you, wondering what you were doing at every moment of every day, wondering how often you fulfilled the sexual desires of the woman in the pictures, wondering if you had gotten another ring and proposed to her.

I couldn't take it anymore! I wanted to feel you inside me. I began to think about the best way to go about meeting you and stealing you away from the other woman. She was the other woman, you know? You and I were destined to be together. You belonged to me. She was just borrowing you for a little while.

When you were jogging home from the gym two nights later, you were wearing headphones and never heard or saw me coming until I ran smack into you and fell down on the concrete sidewalk three blocks from your building.

I grabbed my ankle, as if in severe pain. You immediately took the headphones off, knelt down, and asked if I was okay. What can I say? Desperate times call for desperate measures, and robberies are not the only things I know how to plan out.

I pretended my ankle had been sprained in the fall, and you helped me up. I faked a limp and put my arm around your shoulder for leverage. First contact, and it was awesome. You looked ten times finer up close and smelled delicious, even after working out at the gym and running. Something about a sweaty-ass man lights my fire.

I had spent much time getting my running look together. I wanted to look athletic yet sexy at the same time. I had selected some black spandex biker shorts so you could peep my ass, a cutoff T-shirt so my belly button ring was showing, and a lightweight jacket. I left it unzipped so you could get the full view without me being too obvious.

You helped me over to a bus stop bench and sat down with me, apologizing over and over again about the mishap. I told you it was cool and probably my fault anyway. Then we started chatting like old war buddies, and it was fantastic. We exchanged names. You told me your name was Prescott. I told you mine was Netanya.

After we became comfortable with one another, you asked me if I wanted to go back to your place so I could put an ice pack on my ankle. I quickly replied yes, hoping not to seem too eager. I held onto your shoulder as you escorted me back to your apartment. I was hoping like hell that no one would recognize me from the night I robbed you. Luckily, they didn't. The doorman greeted you by your last name, and we went upstairs.

When we got to your floor and got off the elevator, I almost gave myself away by walking toward your apartment before you even told me whether it was to the left or right. I caught my mistake just in time.

After propping my ankle with the imaginary injury up on a pillow, you left me on the couch, went to get a couple of bottles of Snapple fruit juice from the kitchen, and then turned on the television. Chris Tucker was on cable, so we decided to watch, and his ass was hilarious.

I was really watching you and not the tube. You looked so fine, I wanted to drink your bathwater. Now that I was in your place, I had to figure out how to get in your bed. I had to tread cautiously, since I knew you already had a woman, but like I said before, she was just borrowing you from me.

After the comedy hour went off, an R-rated movie came on. When they flashed the warnings across the screen saying it contained nudity and extreme sexual content, I was happy because I was counting on it helping to get you in the mood. I was praying you didn't reach for the remote to change the channel, and you didn't.

My ankle wasn't hurting at all. I was big-time frontin'. The only things aching on me were my breasts and the tender, wet area between my legs. The movie turned out to be a pretty good one—a little bit too good, because you became so enthralled in it that our conversation almost ceased altogether. I just lay there, peeping at you out the corner of my eyes from my position on the couch. You were sitting over on your love seat, all into the flick.

Prescott, I swear, part of me wanted to get up, leave, and let you go on with your life with the *other* woman. After all, I was living a life of crime, destined to end up in the big house or get taken out in a blaze of glory. If nothing else, at least the other woman could have offered you a stable and secure future.

I couldn't do it, though. I couldn't give you up without a fight, so I tried to get you in bed instead. I told you all about my life. Well, some of it. Everything I said was true too. I just happened to leave out the illegal activities. I told you about my abusive childhood, my alcoholic mother, how my first sexual experience had been against my will, how no man had ever truly loved me, how I felt I would never know what it feels like to be cherished and adored.

You forgot all about the skin flick and listened intently. I started crying, and it wasn't fake crying either. I had never come clean with anyone like that before, with the exception of Penny, and it felt good to release all the pain. It was as if I turned the couch in your apartment in to a chaise longue in a therapist's office, because I laid out my heart to you. It wasn't even all about the sex anymore. I began to feel a closeness to you, a sense of warmth overcame me, and it was one of the greatest moments of my life.

You came over to the couch, put your arms around me, and I cried on your shoulder. You held me so tenderly, like a mother holding a newborn on her shoulder in the rocking chair of the hospital nursery. It was then that I knew I had fallen for you bad. My feelings were totally indestructible and irreversible.

To this day, I can't recall everything that happened next. Somehow we ended up lying on your bed together, with my head resting on your chest, and I could hear your heart beating. It was such an intensified moment. Your heartbeat was so profound, it made me feel like I was part of you, inside you like a fetus inside a womb. In a sense, all the love and affection I felt I missed out on from my mother seemed to flow out of you.

You kissed me on my forehead first, then my eyelids, the tip of my nose, and finally my mouth. I partook of your thick, wet tongue gratefully, and we delved into a kiss that knew no boundaries. I relaxed my throat so you could push your tongue even farther into my mouth. You were so passionate, so loving.

You undressed me with gentle, strong hands and made love to me for the rest of the night. In fact, we didn't leave your apartment for three whole days. You called in sick, and I pretended to call in sick when I really called Penny instead. You wouldn't answer the phone at all, letting the voice-mail service answer for you. You wouldn't answer the door, and we barely ate a thing besides each other.

You washed my hair in the shower, gave me candlelight bubble baths and then licked me dry, delighted me with massages, and tempted my taste buds with your delicious body. We made love all over your place, everywhere from the kitchen counter to the balcony, but my favorite was when you banged me slowly up against the wall from behind.

You started off by lifting me up against the wall and sucking on my breasts. You let me down briefly and lifted me up against the wall, upside down this time, and started eating my pussy out. I followed suit and started sucking your dick, even with all the blood rushing to my head. Good thing I'm flexible.

After we did that for a good while, I told you I was feeling light-headed, and you stopped so I could stand upright again. I loved the whole thing and wished I could have held the position longer.

You told me to face the wall and put my hands up. You rubbed the head of your dick up against my ass and then pulled my ass out toward you so it could rub against my clit.

I felt your dick enter me, and I came so hard, the first of many orgasms up against your living room wall. Your dick took on a rhythm of its own as it started going in and out of me, slowly at first, the intensity growing with each stroke. We both came over and over again, and I prayed the episode would never end.

After the three days were up, you knew it was time to go back to work before you lost your job altogether, so I followed suit, lying and saying I had to get back to work too. You never mentioned the other woman. Mysteriously, after my first night there, her pictures disappeared from your dresser mirror. You probably shoved them under some clothes in a drawer when I wasn't in the room.

You went back to work, but we started seeing each other all the time, spending as many nights and weekends together as we could manage. I lied to you and told you I couldn't receive calls at work. I asked you to page me all the time instead.

Eventually, I got sick of all the lies, told Penny my love for you was stronger than my love of money, and quit the business. I found a job as an administrative assistant and worked the old nine-to-five.

Two months later, all of the jewelry stolen from your apartment mysteriously reappeared in a brown envelope delivered by the mailman. It was a miracle, or so you thought. Truth be known, I worked my ass off to get it all back. It wasn't easy either, since the time limit on the pawn ticket had expired. I had to pay extra to get the stuff back. Fortunately, all of the items were still there, except for one—the ring.

One of the guys who worked at the shop owed me bigtime. I called in a favor and got the address of the person who purchased it. I had to cross the blue line of the law one more time and steal it back. I figured it was a better idea than knocking on her door and asking to buy it.

Today, I love you more than ever. You have given me all the things I never thought I would have. You have fulfilled my every desire. One day soon, I hope you'll put a ring on my finger. If not that one, another one. I will gladly say, "I do!"

My Knight in Shining Armor

Journal Entry—June 1990

Dear Diary,

The worst part of growing up is finding out that your knight in shining armor has been eaten by time's dragon. . . .

When I was a little girl, I didn't have the dreams and fantasies that most little girls have. Normal little girls dream of being a beautiful princess trapped in a tower by an evil queen. They dream of a handsome knight on a big white horse rescuing them, taking them to a magnificent castle full of servants, and showering them with diamonds and treasures.

Well, instead of being a beautiful princess, I was an average little darling in my dreams. Instead of being trapped in a tower by an evil queen, I was locked in a closet by my evil stepmother. Instead of my knight riding a big white horse, he straddled atop a big black Harley. Instead of taking me to a castle, he took me to a small log cabin out amid the woods with a fireplace and lots of windows so we could see nature's creatures *and they could see us. And instead of showering me with diamonds and treasures, all I could think about was the way he could make me feel.*

Even though we have yet to make love, my knight in shining armor makes me feel that way. I dream of him all the time. I dream of his lips upon my lips, on my neck, atop my breasts. I dream of his hands touching my face, caressing my behind, between my thighs. Orgasm on top of orgasm.

I dream of him laying me down upon a bed of roses and blowing lightly in my ear. I dream of us sharing every fantasy that each of us holds dear. I dream of making love in a rain shower, on a sailboat, in a clock tower. Orgasm on top of orgasm.

I dream of giving him an oil massage, feeding him chocolate-covered strawberries, licking honey off of his chest. I dream of him entering me from behind and putting my entire body to the test. I dream of candlelight dinners followed by bubble baths. Orgasm on top of orgasm.

One day, my knight will come to me, and when he does, all of my desires shall be fulfilled, all of my dreams shall come true. I know that he is here somewhere, lurking in the shadows of my soul, imagining the pleasures my body shall give to him as well. And when the time comes, he and I shall become as one and our nights will bring us both orgasms on top of orgasms.

Imani

Six years later

Well, just like I always dreamed about as a little girl, I bought my cabin out in the woods. I wasn't rescued by my knight in shining armor, though. Instead, I left home at the age of seventeen, leaving my abusive stepmother alone with my father, which is what she wanted all along.

I got a partial academic scholarship for college and worked

nights as a waitress to make up the difference. It had been a long road, but I had it all—at least, financially and professionally.

After receiving a degree in marketing, I decided to venture out on my own and start an information brokerage firm, marketing information via the Internet. It paid off. I have a nice house in the city, my two dream cars, and the log cabin I always dreamed of.

There was one thing still missing: the man of my dreams. Even though I had all the things most people use to measure success, the most vital part of happiness was still missing from my life. I craved for a man's touch so much. A man who would make all my childhood fantasies come true. A man who would turn my ass out and make me cum at least twenty times in one night.

I would go up to the cabin on weekends to get away from the hustle and bustle of the city, trading all the horns, sirens, and cars backfiring in exchange for the sounds of nature. Small animals scurrying through the bushes, birds singing in the trees, and the leaves rustling in the wind.

The cabin I own is just like the one I imagined in my dreams. It's small and cozy, with huge picturesque windows and a large fireplace. It has a loft bedroom overlooking the living room and kitchen area. There is one huge window that goes from floor to ceiling, so you can see the whole wooded area from either level.

The cabin is secluded, and there are no other homes for miles. My friends always expressed concern about me being up there alone, because if something were to happen, I would be completely defenseless. That is, except for the Glock I kept loaded in the nightstand next to my bed. I love nature, but I am not a fool, so hell, yeah, I was packing.

It was early one Saturday morning when everything in my life changed. I decided to go for an early-morning jog, about 7 A.M.

The cool breeze felt great hitting up against my skin through the thin material of my windsuit. There is a river about a mile from my cabin. I often jogged there and sat by the water and thought about all the trials and tribulations of the hectic week.

On this particular day, I must not have been paying attention to my surroundings, because I tripped over a log within ten yards of the river, twisted my ankle, and it hurt like hell. I was sitting there on my ass in the middle of the woods, holding my ankle and shrieking out in pain, when I heard a noise like some twigs breaking.

I was petrified. My immediate thought was it must have been a bear or a mountain lion or some other type of animal that was gonna eat me alive. My gun was back in the cabin, so basically, I figured I was fucked for sure.

I tried to pull myself up, but the pain was excruciating. I didn't dare yell out for help. I figured that would only allow whatever animal was out there to pinpoint my exact location, as if it hadn't done that already.

I couldn't get up to my feet, so I began to drag myself down toward the river. I had read somewhere, in a mystery novel perhaps, that animals lose the scent of whatever they are tracking in water.

I heard some more twigs breaking and leaves being disturbed, even closer this time, so I broke into an all-out crawl. It was obviously something huge, and it was moving in on me at a fast rate.

Once I reached the embankment of the river, I heard heavy breathing behind me, panting even, and that did it. I didn't dare turn around. I just knew some humongous bear was about to have me for breakfast if I didn't cast myself in the river with a quickness.

I flung myself into the cold water hoping I would still be

able to swim, even with the swollen ankle. Water, especially cold water, tends to dull pain, and I thought it would work to my advantage.

Immediately, I realized it was a big mistake. The current pulled me deeper into the river. I lost my bearings and couldn't even manage to dog-paddle. The water carried me down toward the river floor. All I saw was the sunlight glowing through the water and getting dimmer and dimmer until it disappeared altogether. What a fucking way to die!

All I remember is the pressure of something bearing down on my chest cavity. I could hear myself gurgling as I coughed up the water. The first thing I heard was that same heavy panting. When I managed to open my eyes and adjust to the glaring sunlight, I saw this big-ass nose and long tongue and smelled some foul-ass breath. I was lost like a virgin in a whorehouse. I passed the hell out.

When I awoke, I felt immensely warm; almost feverish. I looked up and saw wooden beams lining a ceiling and flames from a fireplace dancing on them. I was nursing the stomachache of all stomachaches, my ankle was still sore but good enough to walk on, and there was something cold on my head. I reached up to remove it and saw it was a wet rag.

I was nude and covered up with several handmade quilts, which looked generations old, and lying on an old-fashioned iron bed. I saw one of those little washbasins and a pitcher sitting on a wooden table next to the bed.

I looked around, taking in my new surroundings. It was a cabin, but not like mine. There was only one room with a little kitchenette area, a fireplace, a table pushed up against the wall with two chairs, a dresser, a bathroom with a sink and toilet and one of those old-timer silver bathtubs you only see in the movies, and the bed I was lying on. That was it.

Then I saw it over in the corner and began to laugh hysterically. It was a bloodhound, a brown one. I realized it was the beast I had been so terrified of, the one I almost drowned trying to get away from. It looked at me and tilted its head, probably wondering whether I was plum foolish or not.

It became apparent that whoever owned the dog also pulled my stupid ass out the river and saved my life. I had been rescued, but not the kind of rescued I imagined in my childhood fantasies. This person *literally* saved my life. I had been rescued and taken to a log cabin out in the woods. The whole scenario was getting much too amusing, and then it became arousing.

Could it be my knight in shining armor had finally come to me? I thought about how ridiculous it was for me to expect some handsome man to come in there and fuck me for dear life. It was more likely the person who saved me was some sixty-year-old white man with three teeth and a musty odor that came up to the mountains to hunt—maybe even a poacher.

Fear invaded my heart again as it hit me. Maybe I wasn't out of danger yet. What if the person had brought me there to cause me harm, rape me? What if he had only saved me so he could butcher me to death? All the classic horror films—*Friday the Thirteenth, Halloween,* and *Night of the Living Dead*—raced through my mind. I jumped up from the bed, wrapping one of the quilts around me, and started looking for my clothes. I didn't see them anywhere—not that there were many places for me to look.

I pulled out one of the dresser drawers, hoping to find something, anything I could cover up with, just so I wouldn't have to run naked through the woods back to my cabin. Then it hit me that I had no idea where my cabin was. I didn't even know which direction to run in if I did manage to escape. There was nothing in the top dresser drawer, so I pushed it back in. I had trouble pulling out the second drawer. It was crammed with so much clothing that I had to yank on it hard. When I did, something hit the floor on the right side of the dresser.

I looked down and saw a double-barreled shotgun. That did it! It was time to haul ass, clothes or no clothes, swollen ankle or no swollen ankle. The dog was still sitting there in the corner, gazing at me with wonder as I headed toward the door. It didn't have an actual lock on it, just one of those long pieces of wood that slides across into a wooden bracket and holds the door shut. I felt like I was lost in time—the Wild, Wild West and shit.

I managed to get the door open and was ready to make a mad dash for my life, barefoot and naked if the quilt proved to hinder me in any way.

I ran right smack into his chest, and the boomerang effect pushed me back just far enough for me to look up at his face. I exhaled! I had found him, or rather he had found me. After all my dreams, after all these years, there he was in front of me— my knight in shining armor.

Tall, dark, and handsome. He was about six-two, around thirty years old, with a mocha complexion and as muscular as muscular gets. My dream, my fantasy, my knight. I walked backward into the cabin so he could bring in the wood that he had obviously gone to retrieve while I was sleeping. I pictured his muscles and physique as he stood out there chopping wood with an ax and wished I could have witnessed it.

We talked and talked. I told him my name was Imani and explained to him what I was doing up by the river, where my cabin was, what I did for a living, how I thought his dog was a killer bear, and how I ended up at the bottom of the river.

He told me his name was Deon. He was a carpenter in the city who also came out to the woods on the weekends to relax, blend in with nature, and do some occasional hunting. We chatted for hours, and he cooked me dinner out of tin cans. I was in love from the second I saw him.

He had the most beautiful eyes, the most beautiful smile, and the most beautiful skin. Hell, he had the most beautiful *everything,* and he made me feel so comfortable around him. I felt like I had known him all my life.

After dinner, Deon put a quilt on the floor over by the fire and massaged my ankle for me. All I had on was a huge flannel button-down shirt he gave me to put on. My clothes were outside, strewn about on logs so they could dry.

While he was rubbing my ankle, I began to wonder whether my fantasy could truly be completed or I was being delusional. I wanted to know if he could make my ass cum twenty times in one night. Twenty was kind of a high number to shoot for with a fucked-up ankle, but I was willing to give it my best shot.

I didn't know how to broach the subject. Luckily, he did it for me by telling me how sexy I looked standing there in nothing but his quilt when I opened the door and barreled into him. How his heart almost jumped out his chest when I brushed up against it. How beautiful he thought I was when he first dove into the river and pulled me out. How sweet I smelled when he performed CPR on me. How he hadn't been with a woman in over two years, since his wife was killed in an automobile accident two days before her thirtieth birthday. How no other woman had appealed to him since her death until the moment he laid eyes on me. How he wanted to get to know me better, much better, and possibly one day marry me. I was blown away. We had come so far in the span of one afternoon.

I reciprocated by telling him all about my childhood dreams, which had become a repetitive part of my adulthood dreams as well. How I basically remained manless due to the fact that most men immediately turned me off. They weren't romantic enough and simply could not begin to comprehend my physical and mental needs. How I felt a closeness to him already as well, and how I thought he was my *real* knight in shining armor, my destiny.

Then, I told him how much I wanted to make love to him right then and there. How I wanted to finish the feelings, how I wanted to feel him inside me, how I wanted our bodies to fuse together, and how I wanted for us to give each other orgasm on top of orgasm.

Deon took his hand and brushed his thumb gently over my cheekbone and across my lips. He rubbed it over my eyebrows and then from the bridge of my nose back down to my lips. I exhaled again! At that very moment, I became positively aware he was the one.

We were both on our knees, facing each other, when I removed his hand from my lips and pressed my fingertips lightly upon his own. I took his hand, brought it back toward my mouth, and began to suck his fingers one at a time.

We gazed into each other's eyes, the only light in the cabin emerging from the roaring fire. I unbuttoned the flannel shirt I had on and removed it altogether, letting it fall down around my succulent ass.

My hardened nipples looked like black pearls. He took one of my breasts into his hand, pulling it up to meet his descending mouth. He sucked on my breast like it contained his life sustenance. It brought me immense pleasure.

I pushed him backward so that he was lying flat on his back. Then I straddled him and started to remove his clothing with my teeth. I broke off all the buttons on his shirt and made him sit up just long enough for me to get it off. I unbuckled his pants and then unzipped them with my teeth and got them off. I pulled his underwear all the way off with my teeth and on my way back up from his ankles, where they eventually landed, I took his dick in my mouth and tickled my palette with its sweetness.

Sucking dick is the one thing I've always enjoyed, and I sucked Deon's for a very long time, licking all around the shaft of it with my tongue, taking his ball sack in my mouth and suckling on it gently. I love the way a man shudders when I suck on his balls. I enjoyed feasting on his dick, and when he came in my mouth, it was like hitting the lottery to me, because we both came. What a reward!

The fire was still going strong when I sat on his face and let him taste my honeydew. Just like I imagined, he was remarkably talented with his tongue. Nothing is more satisfying than having a man eat your pussy who makes no bones about enjoying it. When a man does it just to please you, it's not as arousing, but when he does it to please you both, it's such a turn-on. I came over and over again, orgasm on top of orgasm.

Once he had been well nourished, I moved down to his dick, letting my pussy juice and cum smear along his chest as I inched my way toward his hips. I felt the head of his dick bouncing up toward my pussy like it knew it was coming and wanted to break out the welcome wagon. I sat all the way down on his dick, pausing for a moment so I could get used to the head of it all the way near my stomach.

Then I rode his dick like a champion, and he brought his hips up to meet my every thrust. His dog had been sitting quietly in the same corner the entire time, but started whimpering when our moans began to grow in volume. The fire was roaring, and I was still a bit feverish, so the sweat of my body covered him as it trickled down my breasts and my spine. We were like two wild animals in heat.

We could hear the animals out in the woods making noises

like they knew we were mating. I took hold of both his hands, and we clasped them together so I could ride him harder. I collapsed on his chest as we both came again, holding his hands back over his head, and started tongue-kissing him for the first time. We had saved the best for last.

The intensity of our kiss was electrifying, mixed with the taste of each other's body juices on our tongues. We bonded in a way we both knew was forever. We made love the rest of the night. Deon carried me to the bed and did it to me in every position we could manage without putting too much pressure on my ankle.

The next morning he filled up the old-fashioned bathtub and put it in the center of the cabin by the fire. He had replenished it with fresh wood. We both sat in the tub, washed each other, and made love—orgasm on top of orgasm.

He drove me back to my cabin, which I almost forgot even existed, in his Jeep. We spent the next two days there, both of us putting our businesses in the big city on hold. We fell in love in such a short span of time and wasted no time with fears and hesitations.

The very next weekend we took the plunge and got married. We had the local justice of the peace marry us in front of a select few of our friends on the riverbank. Deon and I were both barefoot. He looked debonair in black slacks and a white cotton shirt hanging loosely instead of being tucked in. I wore a white cotton dress with a wreath around my head made out of vines and red roses. Even Zeus, who is now my dog too, had a great time.

We had the reception at our larger cabin, the one that used to be just mine. We decided to keep both of them and go back and forth on our weekend excursions. I'm pregnant with our first child, and Deon seems like he has more morning sickness than I do.

Well, my knight in shining armor may not have come to me in the exact way I planned, but it was sure as hell close. This is forever, there is not a doubt in my mind. So you see, fairy tales do come true, and people do live happily ever after. From now until the end of time, Deon and I will bring each other orgasm on top of orgasm.

Valley of the Freaks

Welcome to the Valley! The Valley of the Freaks has been around for about a decade now, and I've been general manager for about three of them. My name is Grace, and I would just love to sit on your face.

The Valley is an underground galleria of interesting business establishments. Sexual hang-ups, moral issues, and other matters of such nature must be left at the gate. The customers here don't need to be judged, ridiculed, or harassed by those who aren't sexually free.

We get all types down here, from wealthy socialites to women who have to put their hair weaves on layaway, famous athletes to drug dealers, bikers and truckers, even priests. No one gives a shit who you are down here. As long as you have the cash, we have the ass.

We have regulars—some are here every dayum day—and then we have tourists and others who just want to take a brief walk on the wild side. We even have a special parking section for trucks, recreational vehicles, and buses. Most people don't believe we even exist until they actually see it for themselves.

It's kind of like the person who's quick to believe there are 500 million stars in the sky, but if you tell the same person that a bench has wet paint on it, they have to touch it to make sure. Very, very strange, but human nature itself is strange.

We have several different establishments in the Valley. It's my personal responsibility to make sure they all run smoothly. We're one of the biggest employers in this city. I have stacks and stacks of applications from people who are just dying to work here. I have plenty of fine mandingos to back my little ass up if there's any trouble. They give a whole new meaning to the word *bouncers,* because I bounce their dicks all the time in my office. Hell, I can't help but be horny around here. Once I explain what goes on down here, you'll most surely see my point.

There's a huge metal gate at the entrance, manned by employees who check your ID to make sure you're legal. If you are, they'll let you in so you can walk down the ramp to the underground area. There's a huge neon sign stretching across the ceiling of the walkway: "Welcome to the Valley of the Freaks." There's also a list of rules posted on the wall informing you what type of behavior will and will not be tolerated as well as a warning that no flash photography is allowed. This is very important, since we have to protect our clients; many are famous entertainers and politicians.

Of course, we have the things you might expect like bars and strip joints but ours are a bit different. Off da hook, you might say. We have one club called Fetishes, where we cater to every fetish from a love of sucking toes to a love of eating ass, from a love of drinking breast milk to a love of swallowing sperm. We have a couple of strippers in there who are pregnant and squirt breast milk on the customers while they are dancing. They'll also squeeze some in a shot glass for $20 a shot. Check this out, though, and I know this will shock you—

men are not the only ones who pay for breast milk shots. On the other hand, women are not the only ones with sperm fetishes, since plenty of men pay to drink sperm. You follow?

Whatever the customers want, they get. We have a little cart that looks sort of like a snow-cone cart with bottles of different flavors on it so the customer can choose whichever one they fancy.

We have another strip club called the Pit where women strip down to nothing and then wrestle each other in a big pit filled with mud. Sometimes there are as many as ten women in the pit at a time. Customers are allowed to take the female mud wrestlers on if they like. The Pit is a favorite of the bikers and truckers. Something about crawling around in a grimy substance with naked women turns them on.

Truckers and bikers also love to prove how strong they are, so we have a nightly contest for them to strut their stuff. We took the regular arm-wrestling competition done at most truck stops and biker bars and put a twist on it. The bravest of the brave face off with each other in a Dick-Tug-O-War. The loser generally walks away with a very tender dick, and the winner gets a coupon for a free blow job.

Then there's Temptation, our biggest strip club and the closest we come to getting normal. There are two separate performance rooms, one where we have female strippers and one where we have male dancers. Most of the housewives and businessmen hang out in Temptation, stuffing dollar bills in the bras, thongs, and bikinis of the dancers. They pay extra to get lap dances. If they really want to come out of pocket, they can get sexed up for real in a back room.

Hmmm, what should I tell you about next? Let's move on to our sex shop, the Diamond in the Ruff, where you can find any kind of sex toy, lotion, lingerie, or S & M gadget made in the hemisphere today. We pride ourselves on having the largest collection available, and we clock a lot of dollars up in there. People get so horny in the Valley, they often stop by the sex shop on their way to the exit to purchase something freaky to use when they get home.

Next, we have our massage parlor and bathhouse, Different Strokes, where people can get regular massages, hand jobs, clit massages, enemas, douches, whatever floats their boat. They can also rent a room with a hot tub and get their freak on with their date or with one of the employees. We have a lot of police officers who love to get their groove on up in there. Don't think it's strange, because the police department makes up at least 10 percent of our overall client base.

We have a porn shop, Indecent Exposure, where we sell every porno movie, magazine and book on the market today. The sign over the counter says, "If You Can't Find It Here, You Can't Find It Anywhere!" We mean that shit *literally,* too. We have it all from books on how to really fuck to pornos featuring farm animals.

We also have booths in Indecent Exposure where you go in, pull the curtain behind you, put a crisp dollar bill in the machine, and get to see a brief trailer of a porno flick before you purchase it.

There are other booths as well where you slide a dead president through a hole in the wall, either a ten, twenty, or fifty, sometimes even a hundred, depending on what you want to see. After you insert the money, the curtain in front of you is raised, and a live naked man or woman appears behind the glass. You can talk to them and tell them what your pleasure is, such as watch them masturbate, watch them fuck themselves with a foreign object, or even have them call another person in the room so you can watch the two of them get it on. Two women, a man and a woman, two men—whatever's clever.

For those who want the ultimate memento to take home with them, we let them make a porn movie of their own, with themselves as the star. We have a costume room, makeup artist, the whole nine yards. This is one of the services normally sexually repressed people soak up like gravy. It is their opportunity to prove to themselves and the rest of the world that they can let go of all inhibitions and get downright nasty. Lots of married women make tapes with other women and give it to their husbands as anniversary gifts and stuff like that. Young studs, from college age to about thirty, love to make movies too. They take them home and pop them in the VCR after the football games on Sunday so their buddies can see what a man's man they are.

We have the Body Bar, where customers are seated at a table and can see the food prepared in front of them. There are a couple of catches, though. All the food served in the Body Bar is room temperature, and instead of being prepared on a grill attached to the table, it's prepared by a chef on a nude body. That's right, chile! Customers select a man or woman, and the person disrobes and lies on the table. At that point, everything from sushi to grilled chicken salad is strategically placed on their body by the chef, and the customers use chopsticks to eat the food off of them.

There's also another restaurant in the Valley, Freedom Café, where customers are required to check all their clothing at the door. It's a plush restaurant, dimly lit with television screens all along the walls and in every booth as well as a gigantic movie screen in the middle of the dining area. All the screens show the same porno movie, whatever the night's selection is, at the same time for the customer's viewing pleasure.

Freedom Café serves everything from hamburgers seasoned with pussy to chef salads tossed with cum dressing. We also have special cakes for those celebrating their birthday with us. The wait staff, also nude, comes to their table to sing "Happy Birthday" to them and present them with a cake. We have cakes shaped like big black dicks and others shaped like black tits. To each his own.

We do have a *normal* dance club, where people just dance and socialize. It's called the Freak Dome and it's mad cool. It has a huge dance floor, and we have nude dancers on pedestals throughout the club. There's only one requirement to be a dancer in the Freak Dome. You must be over three hundred pounds, or you must be a midget.

The disc jockey in the Dome is one of the best on the East Coast. He has his own morning radio show and works the Dome at night. He never complains because he's paid very well and never has to go home alone. Women practically throw pussy at him. Hell, I even threw mine at him a time or two.

Well, that about covers it except for the Go-Between. The Go-Between is a little place we have by the exit for those people not fortunate enough to have a lover with them or waiting for them at home. It's for clients only, and basically what we do is play matchmaker. Customers give the receptionist some quick information, which she types in the computer, telling what they are looking for sexually. She then asks them to have a seat in the waiting room.

After a while, usually within minutes as it nears closing time, a suitable match is located, the two are introduced, and they take it from there. I've had several customers write me thank-you notes and send me wedding invitations after meeting their soul mate in the Go-Between. Often the people who leave together are so incredibly horny that they end up having some hellified sex and fall in lust by the time the sun comes up.

The Valley of the Freaks can't be located in the phone directory or by calling 411. We have no billboard ads on the highway, and we don't pass out flyers. We don't need any of those things, because we stay packed. If you really want to check us out, ask enough people, and you'll be surprised who can give you directions. Your friend, your coworker, your boss, your brother, your sister, your lover. Hell, maybe even your own mother. Bottom line is, seek and you shall find!

Stakeout

His name is Detective Dwayne Stewart, and from the moment we first laid eyes on each other, there was a spontaneous combustion. There was one problem, though. The Police Department has a policy that basically means, when translated, "You can't shit where you eat!"

I'm also a detective in Homicide, Detective Jessica Minor. I had been a homicide detective in the Fifth Precinct for three years when Dwayne transferred to my unit.

For months, it was easy for us to avoid the inevitable because we were always assigned to different cases. We only held brief, nonchalant conversations and smiled at each other across the room during the weekly meetings held by the captain.

One day everything changed and the lust for each other came crashing in like a Mack truck. I owe it all to one felon, a murderer even. His name was Aaron Redmond, and he was a straight-up son of a bitch.

I drew the case of a woman who had been murdered on her way home from a step aerobics class one night. She left the gym and never got home. About a week later, some boys playing hooky from school discovered her remains in a field behind the junior high school.

Everything about the case smelled like Aaron. He had killed before, was convicted, and served only seven years of a twenty-five-year sentence. They should have locked his ass up and thrown away the key, but due to prison overcrowding, they cut his sentence short so they could get rid of him.

Dwayne was the detective who originally busted his ass in the first case, back when he first became a detective in the Third Precinct. When the latest murder occurred, he was highly upset and frustrated. He and I both agreed it was fucked up they even let a person like Aaron out of jail. They should've known he would kill again. Once you're determined to be a fucking loony bird, that never changes.

That's how Dwayne and I ended up actually working a case together. I was assigned the task of tracking Aaron down and Dwayne was the person who could help me most in my efforts.

Dwayne and I discussed at length the best way to set a trap. I took his suggestion and agreed to set up a stakeout around the clock. We were going to stake out the home of Aaron's brother, Kyle. We knew he would show up sooner or later, because his past record proved he loved his baby brother very much. In fact, he did nine months for beating a man almost to death who started an argument with his brother in a bar.

Kyle was a drug dealer, but we weren't there to bust him for that, since we had bigger shit to worry about. However, once we got our man, bringing his shady ass down would be inevitable. In fact, we were killing two birds with one stone by having a stakeout on him. We would get our killer, and we would have mad surveillance tapes to turn over to DEA agents on his brother.

Dwayne and I got all the necessary paperwork together and approved, arranged to have two other detectives assigned to the case as well, since it would be an around-the-clock operation, and put our plan into action.

Since it was our case, we opted to take the night shift, from 7 P.M. to 7 A.M., and let the other two work days. We didn't get permission to put live cameras in his place, because the equipment availability is limited and they didn't consider it a big enough case. Dwayne got hold of a telephone company uniform and had the landlord let him in one day while Kyle wasn't home to check his line. He placed several bugs throughout the place and in the two telephone receivers. He got out just in time. As soon as he got back to the van where I was waiting for him, Kyle pulled up in his Benz.

Our next task was to find a place to become our base of operations. A van parked outside his apartment building day and night would have stuck out like a sore thumb. After all, drug dealers are no dummies, or they would all get pinched with a quickness.

Kyle was not a big-time drug dealer, so he didn't have bodyguards and lookouts like most do. He preferred to keep his business on the down-low, having his clients come to his place to buy drugs instead of selling them on a street corner.

We decided to set up the base in a shabby hotel across the street. We told the hotel manager what the deal was, and he gave us a room with a bird's-eye view of Kyle's apartment on the third floor. From there we could take photos of some of the activities going on in the apartment. That turned out well during the day, when the other detectives were working. Kyle had a tendency to leave his shades open, and they were able to obtain quite a collection of pictures showing his clientele.

At night, Dwayne and I had to rely mostly on the listening devices. The first couple of weeks were frustrating—not one single Aaron sighting or phone call. Dwayne and I made the best of being stranded together in the cramped hotel room at night. We played cards, ate pizza, watched some television when we could get the stupid thing to work, and talked about everything from rap artists to religion.

Kyle was an interesting character, especially at night. He had a sex life that would put anyone to shame. Almost every night, a woman would show up at his place to give him the nightly fix he desired, and I don't mean drugs either. It made me feel a little uncomfortable to sit there in the room with Dwayne, listening to all the fuck noises coming from Kyle's apartment—mainly because I wanted to fuck Dwayne so bad.

Dwayne is so incredibly good-looking, it should be illegal to be that fine. He's about five-eleven and 185 pounds, light-skinned with black wavy hair and light brown eyes. One night he decided to do some pushups to loosen up because sitting there was tensing up his bones. He took off his shirt, got down on the floor, and started doing them. Watching the muscles contract in his back and ass while he went up and down made my pussy start throbbing and my nipples hard. To make matters worse, Kyle was banging the hell out some woman in his place, and her moans were making my feenin more escalated by the second.

When he got up, he looked at me, saw the perplexed look on my face, and asked me, "What's wrong?" I told him, "I'm fine, just a bit tired!" I excused myself to the bathroom. I didn't have to use it. Instead, I sat up on the edge of the sink, put one of my feet on the lid of the toilet seat, and started fingering my pussy with one hand and rubbing my nipples with the other.

I lost myself in the moans coming from the equipment in the other room and had to use all the strength I could fathom to prevent myself from moaning out loud. I was taking too long in the bathroom and realized it, so I start rubbing my clit really fast like a vibrator until I came all over the sink. I cleaned the sink and myself up and went back out to the room. Dwayne was looking at me with a weird expression, and I was praying he didn't know what I'd just done.

Two nights later, the sexual tension between us became too much to bear. Several times, I caught him glancing intently at my breasts and ass. Kyle was in his place, fucking a woman so hard, she was literally begging for him to stop. Then Dwayne's eyes met mine, and the shit was on.

Dwayne was sitting in a chair by the recording equipment. I walked over and stood in front of him so that my breasts were in his face. He gratefully took hold of them, squeezed them tightly, and began to bite gently on my nipples through the material of my sweater and bra.

I unbuttoned my sweater, removed it, and then straddled over him on the chair, letting his muscular thighs hold my legs up. We started tongue-kissing, softly at first, then deep, passionate kisses. I wrapped my arms around his shoulders as we both began to moan just like Kyle and the woman he had in his apartment.

He unfastened my bra, and I eased my arms down off his shoulders long enough for him to remove it and let it fall to the floor. I started grinding my pussy on his dick, and the zipper of his jeans was causing a friction against my clit, even though I had on panties underneath my pleated skirt.

Dwayne lifted me up, and I wrapped my legs around his back as he carried me over to the cheap iron bed. We started making out on the bed. He finished taking off all my clothes, and I helped him to get undressed as well.

We spent a few moments just exploring each other's bodies with our hands and tongues. His hands were soft and gentle for him to be such a strong man. I was soaking up every moment of it—the way he held me, the way he smelled, the way his skin felt against mine.

I got on top of him, reached for his jeans so I could get his handcuffs, and cuffed him to the bed. I'd left my cuffs at home by accident that night, something I'd never done before. Must have been a sign of sexual repression. As I was throwing his jeans back on the floor, I heard the keys to the cuffs fall out.

I started to climb off him to try to retrieve them, but he stopped me. "Don't worry about it, baby. We'll get them later."

I replied by letting him know, "I want you so bad!"

We started kissing again, and then I pushed up farther on the bed, grabbed onto the bars, and popped my breasts in his mouth one at a time. He was definitely what we women call a breast man, because he obviously enjoyed sucking them as much as I enjoyed having them sucked.

My pussy was dripping juice all over his stomach and belly button while he was sucking my breasts. I climbed off him for a second and turned around so I could sit on his face and suck on his dick at the same time.

We both sucked on each other, and it was the best oral sex experience I'd ever been lucky enough to be a part of. I noticed that things had gotten quiet in Kyle's apartment and figured they had fucked each other into a deep sleep.

After cumming in his mouth and sucking Dwayne until he came in mine, I slid down off his face, dragging my cum-drenched pussy across his chest and stomach before I sat on his dick.

His dick was so big, I could feel it throbbing inside my stomach and saw my belly button move in and out as his dick beat inside like a heart pumping blood. I grabbed a hold of his knees and started riding his dick like it was a wild bull.

He ground his hips on the bed and moved them up and down to meet the thrusts of my pussy. We were both moaning, but my moans could have put the woman in Kyle's apartment to shame. Dwayne came inside me seconds after I came all over his dick, my cum seeping down my inner thighs onto the bed sheets, now covered with sweat from our bodies.

I laid my back onto his chest, letting his now soft dick rest inside me. We were lying there, trying to regain our normal breathing patterns, when we heard the doorbell at Kyle's apartment ring. Dwayne whispered in my ear, "Probably some addict trying to cop some blow."

Normally, I would have agreed, but I had an uneasy feeling about that scenario for some reason. Maybe it was the fact we never heard Kyle ask who it was before he answered the door. All drug dealers ask who it is first because they never know if someone might be trying to take them out. Unless of course, he was expecting someone at 3 A.M. He obviously wasn't expecting a woman, since there was already one in his bed. My mind began to wonder about who else would be coming over so late.

Dwayne and I both hollered out, "Oh shit!" at the same time, when we heard Kyle say, "Aaron, 'sup, Bro? I was so worried about you until Julio saw me on the street today and told me you'd be coming by tonight!"

We were in a panic as we heard them exchange the usual hugs and such brothers do and listened to Kyle offer his older brother a beer. I jumped up and started crawling around on the floor naked, looking for the keys to the cuffs. Dwayne was helpless and squirming on the bed.

I screamed when my fingers found the keys and then accidentally pushed them through a heat grate in the floor. I jumped up and informed Dwayne the keys were gone. His response was, "What the fuck are we going to do now?"

I was already moving, throwing on the first pieces of clothing I could find. There was no time to be buttoning up sweaters and shit, so I threw on Dwayne's T-shirt that made me look like a three-year-old girl wearing her daddy's shirt as a nightgown. I threw my skirt back on and slid into my boots, grabbed my badge, police radio, and gun, and ran out the door, coochie free, with pussy juice and Dwayne's cum sticking to my thighs as I ran down the three flights of stairs to the lobby.

As I ran out the front door of the hotel, headed across the street, I called in for backup on the radio, letting them know the suspect was in his brother's apartment. I don't know what the hell I was thinking of, bursting in there like that with no backup in sight and no handcuffs at all. But I did it anyway.

There was no way I could kick down the door of Kyle's apartment, so I shot the lock out instead. Kyle came rushing up to me. I told him, "Back the fuck up, get your hands over your head, and sit on the couch!" He complied because something must have told him I meant business. I never said I was the police, but my badge was hanging around my neck on a long dog-tag chain.

The girl came running out the bedroom, screaming and hysterical. I got the feeling she was high as shit, because her dramatics were pathetic. I told her to put her hands up, sit on the couch next to her boyfriend, and shut the fuck up.

I didn't see Aaron within my area of vision, so I started to search the apartment for him with my hand on the trigger of my gun in case he tried to startle me. I knew he was going to try to take me out. He had no choice. I could hear the sirens of my backup approaching on the street below and the sobs of the pathetic bitch on the couch as I walked through the kitchen, into the dining area, and back out to the living room.

I reaffirmed my position to Kyle and his hoochie, telling them neither one better move or I would pop a cap in their ass. As I made my way into the master bedroom, I knelt down and looked under the bed, swung open the doors to the walk-in closet, and poked through the clothing, bending down to make sure there was no one standing behind them on either side.

Experience told me that only left two hiding places, the bath-. tub and the balcony. I decided to check the bathroom first. Considering how cold it was outside, it was the most logical choice. Any good cop must learn to think like the criminals she is trying to catch, or her arrest record will be downright horrible.

Once I saw the bathroom door was tightly shut, I knew his skank ass was in there. Most people never shut their bathroom door unless it's occupied. I stood to the side of the door, reached over, and turned the knob slowly. The knob was only halfway rotated when a shotgun blast took out half the wood paneling.

I heard the other police officers enter the apartment, yelling for Kyle and his woman to stay where they were while they analyzed the situation and got a chance to cuff them.

It was then or never, so I jumped out in front of the door and started shooting before his ass could stick another shell in the shotgun. The first one caught him in the shoulder, throwing him backward, but he didn't drop it, so I shot again. The second one hit him in the leg, exactly where I wanted, but he was such a big dude, and probably stronger than ever because of all the drugs in his system.

He managed to reload the gun, blood gushing out of the holes I put in him and all. He left me no choice. The third shot caught him dead center in his forehead. The impact was so strong it pushed him backward again, but this time he fell out of the bathroom window and landed on the street, three flights below.

I had never killed a man before, but honestly, I didn't feel bad about it. Aaron Redmond's wrath of terror on innocent female victims was over, and the world would be a safer place without him.

When I got back down to the street, there were police cars with lights flashing and spectators everywhere. The coroner's wagon had arrived, ready to scrape Aaron up off the concrete once the forensic team was done taking photos.

I saw the captain's car approaching, and that's when panic set in all over again. I had to get Dwayne uncuffed from the bed and down on the street before the captain could catch up to me and start asking questions. I ran up to a rookie and told him to give me his cuff keys. He complied without saying a word. I dashed up to the hotel room, got Dwayne uncuffed, gave him his shirt back, and threw on my sweater. We both dashed back down to the street just as we heard the captain's commanding voice, demanding to know where we were.

I took the liberty to explain the whole thing to him. Dwayne didn't utter a word and was clueless about how I planned to get us out of our predicament. I detailed how Dwayne had left the stakeout to go find an all-night drugstore because I was nursing a migraine and needed some aspirin. Upon his return, all hell had broken loose, and it was all over. The captain was suspicious and asked to see the aspirin. Luckily, I saw that coming too and reached into the pocket of my jean skirt, withdrawing a small unopened bottle of aspirin I bought on my way to the stakeout that evening. I was, indeed, nursing a migraine—at least, I had been before the hellified sex. That cleared it right up.

We got out of trouble by the skin of our teeth, and bottom line, the captain was just glad we got the bastard. The department gave us both medals. Dwayne and I are the star team of homicide detectives in the department, adding collar on top of collar onto our polished record.

Our love affair is still a secret, and for now, that suits us both just fine. Since we're permanent partners, we don't need to make up any excuses to see each other, and no one has figured us out. The mixture of police work and sex is a huge aphrodisiac. Life couldn't be better! I found both my career and my life partner in the same man. Who could possibly ask for more?

Masquerade

"Noelle, don't take it the wrong way, baby!"

"What other way is there to take it?" I reached over on the nightstand and retrieved a couple of facial tissues out of the dispenser. "You come over here and tell me you're dumping my ass, and I'm supposed to jump for joy?"

"No, nothing like that. I just hate to see you crying, so please stop." Pierce started caressing my right shoulder, as if that would help any. "Besides, I'm not dumping you. I just feel like we both need to see other people for a while so that we can explore other avenues."

"Explore other avenues?" My tears started to dry up, and the anger set in. "What the fuck do you mean? Other avenues?"

He jumped up from the bed and had the nerve to get a 'tude. "Look, Noelle, there's no reason for you to cuss at me. I mean, it's not like we're married, or no shit like that. You need to take a reality check."

"I just don't understand why you want to see other women."

"You want me to be honest with you, Noelle?"

"Honesty's always the best policy, so they say. Hell, yeah, I want to know the truth!"

"Okay, but I was trying to be nice about this." I couldn't freakin' believe that Pierce was doing this shit to me. After all I did to be with him, all the dinners I cooked for him, all the sacrifices I made, and his ass was kicking me to the curb. "I need a woman who is more——"

"More what?" My lips started trembling, and my nerves were wrecked. I was expecting him to say he wanted a woman with bigger titties or a bigger ass or a bigger bank account or some backass shit like that. Boy, was I wrong!

"I need a woman who's more freaky!"

"What the hell do you mean, more freaky?" That was the last fucking straw. I jumped up from the bed and got physical, taking the palm of my hand and shoving him in the chest. "You and I do a bunch of freaky shit!"

"We do? Like what?"

I felt a migraine coming on. "Well, I suppose if you have to ask, it must not be freaky enough."

"I guess not!" He headed out the bedroom and toward the front door of my apartment. "Look, Noelle, I'll give you a call in a couple of days. Cool?"

"You're really serious about this dating-other-people shit, aren't you?"

"Yes, I'm dead serious. I'm not saying I don't want to be with you, because I do. In fact, more than likely, I'll end up marrying you and having a house full of kids, but right now I need to get some things out of my system." *Damn him!* "I'll catch you later, boo."

He was out in the hallway waiting for the elevator when I peeked out my door. "Pierce, what about our date this Friday? The masquerade party at Trent's house?"

"I'm still going to go, and it's cool if you do too. I think we should go separately, though." With that, Pierce stepped into the elevator and was gone.

I was devastated, depressed, delirious, pissed the fuck off even. I cried myself to sleep that night, but by the time the sun came up the next morning, I was ready to pay his ass back in spades. If he wanted freaky, I would give his ass freaky.

I arrived at Trent's house about midnight. People in wild-ass costumes and masks were everywhere. I decided to wear a black leather cat outfit with a tail and snaps in the crotch, and no underwear underneath. It was strapless and had a push-up bra built in, so my 40DD breasts were looking succulent. I had a leather whip attached to my hip. I made sure Pierce wouldn't be able to recognize me by wearing a feathered mask like the ones they wear at Mardi Gras, a black wig cut in a cool-ass bob and white contact lenses that made me look like a straight-up freak. Freaky and sexy as all hell rolled into one.

Pierce was over in one of the dark corners, flirting with a couple of hoochies. I knew it was him, because he was dressed as a fireman. I had selected the costume a couple of weeks before, so he was easy to spot.

After downing a couple of Long Island iced teas and watching people dance and get intimate with each other in the designated dancing area, I decided to do what it was I came there to do and teach Pierce a lesson he would never forget.

I took a quick survey of the area and spotted the person I was looking for, Trent. He was dressed as the Phantom of the Opera, with a black tuxedo and cape on along with a white mask. Several of his friends were surrounding him and wishing him a happy birthday, since that was the whole purpose of the masquerade party from jump.

Pierce was one of the people crowded around Trent, and I kept my head down a little as I brushed by him. I cleared my throat and got ready to use the Jamaican accent I had practiced, walked up to Trent, and whispered in his ear. "Happy birthday to you, baby!"

He took me by the hand and looked me up and down, but didn't recognize me. He and I had only met a few times. He was a close friend of Pierce's from college. "Damn, do I know you, sexy lady?"

"Not yet, but you're about to get to know me." I reached down and started caressing his dick through his pants while Pierce and the rest of them hollered typical macho things out like, "Get that pussy, man," "Damn, man," and "She's hot for you, Trent."

"Really?" He started palming my ass and other people started looking on as well, including some of the women, who were instantly upset and jealous. "What did you have in mind?"

I pushed him down on a chair at one of the round tables covered with white linen tablecloths and then straddled myself over his legs, facing him. "Let me show you what I have in mind." I almost laughed because my Jamaican accent was the bomb.

I stuck my tongue deep inside his hungry and waiting mouth. He gladly returned the kisses, and I must admit, I knew right off the bat I was going to enjoy fucking the shit out of Trent's ass. I always thought he was fine anyway.

After we tongued the hell out of each other for about five more minutes, I got up and stood between his legs as I lowered the front of my leather suit, allowing my massive breasts to be viewed by everyone in the room. Miraculously, a silence befell the room, and the only sound that remained was the music. Ironically, it was "Do Me, Baby" by Prince. Everyone was in awe. I glanced around to look at Pierce, who was in a daze, before I decided to hold my left breast out for Trent to suckle on.

He eagerly took my hard nipple into his mouth and fed off it, slowly at first. Then he decided he wanted them both, grabbed a hold of each one, and rapidly moved his head and tongue back and forth from left to right. My pussy was getting so wet from all the excitement that I began to care less and less about who was watching. Besides, my identity was safe, and that was the beauty of it.

A waitress was walking past with a tray load of champagne flutes. I grabbed one and poured the champagne over my breasts so he could lick it all off.

The disc jockey cut off all the music so he could come and join the crowd of people watching the show. Needless to say, there wasn't a single person on the dance floor. The only sounds left then were his sucking noises and my moans.

I unsnapped the crotch of my cat suit and climbed up on the table, lay in front of him, and spread my legs. I put the whip around his neck and pulled him closer to me. I told him he had to be punished for being such a bad boy and that he had two choices. "Eat my pussy, or face the whip!"

Trent started laughing and looked around at his buddies, who started ranting and raving again and giving each other high fives. "Shit, I'm not afraid of the whip, but I prefer the pussy!"

With that, he drew the clit of my freshly shaved pussy into his mouth and started sucking on it. My pussy juices were really flowing as he spread my lips apart so he could lick up and down the inside of each one, lapping up every droplet of my nectar.

Once Trent made me cum two or three times, I got up from the table and got down on my knees so I could get his dick out of his pants. The white contact lenses almost popped out my eyes when I saw how big it was. His dick was twice the size of Pierce's. I realized there was a whole new world I had been missing out on by tying myself down to one man.

I took the tip of my tongue and slid it down the slit on the top of his dick, savoring the precum oozing out of it and admiring the way the veins were popping out as it pulsated. I gave his dick the royal treatment and proceeded to give it a wax job with my mouth. I could only fit about four inches of it in my throat, other than the head, because it was so thick and juicy.

I heard some sexually repressed sista yell out, "Oh no, girlfriend is not sucking his dick right in front of all these peeps?"

The hell if I wasn't! I sucked and sucked until my mouth was sore and he shot a hot load of cum down my throat, making a warm lining in my stomach. I sucked his dick soft and then kept at it until it was hard again.

Then I got up and climbed onto the table on my hands and knees, and it was all too obvious that I wanted him to hit it from the back. He grabbed a hold of my leather-covered ass cheeks and gently slid the head of his dick into my throbbing, wet pussy. I had to take a deep breath to brace myself for the rest of it, because I knew he was about to knock the bottom out of my pussy. That's exactly what he did!

Right there, in front of all his birthday guests, Trent fucked the hell out of me. I knew, at that moment, that he was the man for me and not Pierce. What started out as simple payback turned into pure, unadulterated lust, and I loved every minute of it. He fucked me so hard that tears started to run down my face from underneath my mask. Never has anyone fucked me so intensely, and I could barely stand it. It was a confusing mixture of pain and pleasure, and before it was all over and said and done, my ass was turned the fuck out, my mind was blown, and I was in love.

He tugged on the wig, trying to force my pussy back farther on his dick. For a moment, I thought my ass was busted. I got a hold of it just in time to prevent my light brown hair from being exposed. I took Trent's hands and put them on my breasts instead, so he could rub my nipples in between his thumbs and forefingers.

I sat all the way back on his dick and started riding it right there on top of the table, and both of us were panting and moaning. We fucked each other like beasts until we both exploded in unison and the tablecloth ended up covered with cum.

After he reluctantly took his dick out, I jumped up from the table and pushed my way through the crowd, my 40DD breasts still uncovered and bouncing up and down. Trent tried to run after me, but Pierce and the rest of his buddies were too busy bombarding him with comments, slaps on the back, and congrats for fucking the shit out of me in front of the whole crew.

I made it outside and took in some of the fresh, night air. I searched, through tear-drenched eyes, for the Toyota Camry I had rented so no one would see me driving my actual car. When I was pulling off, I saw Trent run outside and stop in the driveway, catching only a glimpse of my taillights.

I went home that night and fell asleep, dreaming about Trent. I woke up the next morning and took a long, hot shower. While I was in there, I fucked myself with the wooden handle of my back brush until I came all over the fiberglass surface of the bathtub.

For an entire week, I wouldn't answer phone calls from Pierce, who kept leaving messages asking why I never made it to the party because he was waiting for me. Lying ass! Finally, he got fed up and showed up at my door, banging and demanding to be let in.

"What are you doing here, Pierce?" After I opened the door

just a little bit, he forced it the rest of the way open so he could barge in.

"What the hell do you think I'm doing here?" He was mad and obviously stressed. "Why haven't you been answering any of my calls, Noelle?"

"I've been busy, and besides, you were the one who wanted to cease and desist for a while so you could get your freak on with other women." I had endured more than enough of his bullshit.

He looked at me and pulled me down on the couch beside him. "Noelle, I made a mistake. I miss you, and I was a fool. I made the mistake of thinking the grass was greener on the other side, but you're the only one for me. I don't want to see anyone else. It's all about you and me, boo."

It was all I could do not to laugh in his fucking face. Instead, I just looked at him with a perplexed look on my face. "Let me get this straight. You think you can come in here and lay down rules and regulations, and once I accept them, you have the audacity to try to take it all back?"

"I love you, and I miss being with you. I thought I wanted some sex fiend, but all I really need is you. Your innocence is what's so truly special about you."

That's when I burst out in laughter. "Oh, really?" I paused before I continued, "Well, I hate to be the bearer of bad news, but I think there's something you should know."

Pierce got up and went in the kitchen to get a beer from the fridge, pretending that my last statement never came out my mouth. "Speaking of sex fiends, you should have seen what happened at the masquerade party. It was off the hook!"

I smirked. "What happened?"

"This girl showed up, someone none of us had ever seen

before, and fucked Trent right there in front of every damn body. She was a straight-up freak!"

"Sounds like your kind of woman. You said you wanted freaky sex, right?" I didn't know how much longer I could maintain my composure, because it was mad funny.

"For the last time, I was wrong about that. Sure, she was sexy and out there, but I'm ready to settle down, have a couple of rug rats, and buy a white house with a picket fence."

He was serious, and I almost had second thoughts about what I was about to do. However, the shit he did to me was unforgivable, and I could no longer look at him in the same way. "Well, Pierce, I like things the way they are."

"Whaaa—what do you mean by that?" He was flustered.

"I think seeing other people is a good thing. In fact, I think it's a wonderful idea, and I've already taken your words to heart."

Pierce jumped up in my face with his typical male, double-standard ass. "Are you saying you're already seeing someone else?"

"Not exactly, but I do have someone in mind." It was time to drive the knife in. "In fact, I fucked him about a week ago, and I loved the way he fucked me. He tore my little ass up and fucked me without mercy. He had a big-ass dick too."

I thought he was going to punch me for a second, but instead he just sat down on the coffee table and put his head in his hands. I went into the bathroom as I added, "In fact, you loved the way he fucked me too."

I heard him shout from the other room, "What the fuck are you talking about, Noelle?" I didn't answer him. Instead, I just came back in the living room wearing the black wig and white contact lenses. He leaped to his feet. "What the fuck? It was you?"

I giggled and crossed my arms in front of me while I leaned against the wall. "Yes, it was me. Truth be known, all this time you were saying I wasn't freaky enough for you, but it's the other way around. You're not anywhere near freaky enough for me!"

He balled his hand into a fist, looked at me with his lips trembling for a couple of minutes while the whole sordid madness of the situation sunk in, and then left slamming the door behind him.

I've never seen Pierce again. The friendship between him and Trent ended the day Pierce found out I was moving into Trent's mansion with him. I went back and claimed the man I really wanted. Trent was shocked at first to discover I was the woman who had turned his ass out, but he had been feenin for me the whole time, so it was all good.

Let this be a valuable lesson to all you men out there who don't know a good thing until it's gone. Never judge a book by its cover, and never underestimate the power of a woman, or else you might just find yourself by yourself.

Wanna Watch?

It was late at night on a Saturday, and we both had such a boring day. We'd hardly said a word to each other. I was beginning to wonder if you were getting bored with me. The sex was great, at least I thought so, but there was something missing. As I sat there watching you read the newspaper on the couch, a brilliant idea popped into my head. I went into the bedroom to make a quick phone call.

When I came out, you asked me why I was grinning, and I said, "No reason." I asked if you wanted to take a quick shower with me. You declined, mentioning that you were waiting for a boxing special to come on HBO you wanted to check out. Reluctantly, I took one without you. I was gonna try to seduce you into some quick lovemaking in the shower, but you just seemed totally withdrawn. Doubt was growing in my mind about whether my plans for the evening were appropriate. It was too late for me to call her back and tell her not to come. I just crossed my fingers that it would all work out for the best.

Once I got out of the shower, I slipped into a black lace nightie with no panties. I knew I wouldn't need them in a few minutes, whether you decided to touch me or not. By the time I came back out into the living room, your boxing special was on. Before I could sit down beside you, the doorbell rang. You asked, "Who could that be this time of night?" and I replied, "Just a good friend of mine I asked to come over."

You turned around to look at the door while I went to answer it. You were surprised to see a long-legged, deep chocolate, beautiful female come into the door in an extremely short, tight red dress. I introduced my friend to you, "Honey, this is my roommate from college, Karlin. Karlin, this is my boo!"

She extended her hand and shook yours, but took you totally off guard by bending over and kissing you on the lips lightly, flickering the tip of her tongue in your mouth. I sat down in the middle of the floor, turned off the television, and explained to you, "Boxing will have to wait, baby. I have another show for you to watch!"

Karlin giggled while she joined me on the bearskin rug, setting the leather duffel bag she brought with her down beside us. Your eyes lit up with wonder, and you were speechless; you had no clue as to what we were up to, until I said, "Honey, you know how you always say you wouldn't mind seeing me with another woman?" You nodded, still speechless. I replied, "Well, tonight's your night."

A wide grin appeared on your face, and for the first time, I got the feeling that my little plan might perk you up after all. Karlin lowered the straps on her dress, exposing her bare 38DDs with hard firm nipples already standing at attention. Then she reached over and caressed my breasts through the black lace of my nightie. Karlin had always been a dominatrix. I knew from past experiences, from the many times she had taken control of me in our college dorm room, that this was to be her show, and I was to just go with it.

I could feel my nipples become hardened as she rubbed the material against them. Then she leaned over, and the kiss began. You watched as our soft, thick, lipstick-covered lips met and we flicked our tongues out at each other before finally engaging in a deep, passionate French kiss.

We stopped kissing for a moment so that Karlin could pull my nightie up over my head and off, leaving me completely in the raw. Then she pushed me all the way down on the rug so that I was lying flat on my back. She stood up and pushed the red dress, already around her waist, down over her thighs onto the floor.

Then she sat down and straddled over me, our pussy hairs rubbing up against each other, and we began to kiss again. Karlin grabbed both my breasts, one in each hand, and rubbed my nipples with her thumbs. This brought back some sweet memories, and my pussy began to get very wet. But mostly, I was pleased because I knew that this was pleasing you. I could tell by the look of excitement on your face and the way that you were sitting on the edge of the couch like a predator ready to attack.

Karlin and I both moaned with delight as she began to suck on my nipples, still holding a solid grip on both my breasts. Karlin reached over into her leather bag, removed a can of amaretto-flavored whipped cream, and squeezed it all over my breasts. She made a trail going down the middle of my stomach over my belly button and spread my legs open so that she could squeeze some onto my pussy lips as well.

Then she began to lap all the whipped cream up from my body, making long strokes with her thick tongue, beginning with the undersides of my succulent breasts. I lost myself in the ecstasy and closed my eyes, pretending that it was your tongue devouring me instead of hers. When she had licked it all up except for the whipped cream on my pussy, I turned my head to face you and stared deep into your soul while Karlin buried her head between my thighs.

My moans became louder when she began to do what she does all too well. Karlin had always told me she loved eating my pussy. Judging by the way she was eating me out that night, it was nothing but the truth. She used to come over to my bed in the middle of the night, remove my panties, and go to town. She knew I had a weakness for having my pussy eaten and that I didn't care much the gender of the person doing the eating. In fact, there was this other girl named Sandy, a friend of Karlin's from high school, who used to come over to our dorm room and eat me out too.

Of course, you never knew any of this. In fact, the few times you'd mentioned seeing me with another woman, I made it seem like it was totally out of the question. But I wanted to do something special that night for you and frankly, I kind of missed the good old times. I knew that you were a happy camper, and so was I. Karlin was dayum sure pleased. When I called her, she couldn't wait to get over there and get some.

When she finished eating my pussy, she told me to turn around and get on all fours. Of course, I complied. She made a trail of whipped cream down the crack of my ass and then proceeded to lick it all out, sticking her thick tongue into my asshole and taking a quick survey of its warmth. I looked in your direction. You were taking your dick out and beginning to caress it softly. It was so hard, and I remember thinking that I wanted to feel you inside of me so bad.

But Karlin wasn't done yet, and the show was not over so I knew I would have to wait. She reached back over into her bag and removed the star of the show, a strap-on ten-inch penis, and put it on. She slowly pushed the dick, then attached to her hips, into my juicy pussy from behind. It was on fire. Karlin fucked me royally with the strap-on. The whole time I watched you masturbate and precum just started cascading down the inside of my thighs. Karlin pulled me by the hair, making me bring my pussy back farther onto the fake dick. She reached around with her other hand and fondled my breasts. I rubbed my clit and helped to guide the strap-on in and out.

It was amazing, because it seemed like all three of us exploded in unison. Karlin screamed out at the same time I did, and cum squirted out of my pussy onto the bearskin rug. I think the sight of me squirting cum, which always turns your ass out, made you explode. I saw the cum erupt out of your juicy dick within seconds, and I wanted some. I told Karlin to take the strap-on out and crawled over between your legs where you sat on the couch and lapped all the cum up I could find. Karlin crawled over behind me and ate my pussy from behind as I began to wax your dick with my mouth. You were so delicious, boo.

The whole night was delicious, and we finished it off with a bang. After seeing Karlin to the door and giving her kisses on her cheeks, you and I retired to the bedroom and fucked like minks till the sun came up. You were in rare form that night, baby. I've never regretted sharing that experience with you.

If you ever feel bored again and want Karlin to come over, maybe even Sandy too, just whisper three words in my ear, baby: "I wanna watch!"

Nymph

My name is Page, and I'm a nymphomaniac, a sexual thrill-seeker, a sexual renegade. I love playing with fire, living a life full of drama and excitement, defying all the good girl rules, approaching situations that are both sexy and perilous. I'm a sexual rebel, and to me, danger itself is the most tremendous sexual stimulant of all.

One night I was at a club, and this sorry excuse for a man asked me was I pure. I asked him, "Do you mean pure as in pure chewing satisfaction?" He was dumbfounded, so I added, "Unless you want to suck on this pussy tonight, get the fuck!"

Like most men, he was intimidated by the sexual prowess I exude. Men like him disgust me. They brag about how they're all that in bed and can make a woman scream out their name when half the time they have trouble even finding the clit. As for the G spot, forget about it. They couldn't find a woman's G spot if she handed him written instructions and a map.

Fortunately for me, there are plenty of mad fuckers around too. A mad fucker is a man who doesn't talk about turning a sista out. He just does it. A mad fucker is a man whose cum

tastes so damn good, it makes a sista feel drunk. A mad fucker
is someone who fucks a sista so hard, the next day her pussy
and nipples are sore, she has a helluva stomachache, and she
has trouble sitting down. That's how you know you've been
the victim of a mad fucker drive-by.

Sex to a nymphomaniac is like doughnuts to a police officer. We both gotta have it. My body is so accustomed to cumming, if I don't have at least three orgasms a day, I feel sick.
Sometimes when there's no man around, which is extremely
rare because I have more male bitches than the electric company has switches, I make myself cum through the art of masturbation.

Masturbation is damn sure an art too. Everyone can't do
that shit like a master. Those of us who have surpassed the
amateurs masturbate so well, sometimes it seems like we're
actually fucking. I often wonder why people feel it's more
kosher and acceptable to touch the private parts of someone
else than their own. Silly as shit, if you ask me. If you don't
want to play with your own coochie-coo, why should a man?

I play my whole body like it's a trivia game. What's the
strongest part of a woman's body? Her tongue. What are the
most sensitive parts of a woman's body? Her tits and clit.
Where does a woman like a man to insert a finger during sex?
In her ass. What's a woman's favorite sexual position? Doggy-
style. What parts of a woman's body should be sucked and
licked on during foreplay? All of them bad boys.

When it comes to sucking dick, move over, 'cause there's a
new sheriff in town. I can just picture a big juicy dick in front
of my face right now. Slobbering all over it, making those
slurping sounds, teasing it around the tip just before I deep-
throat the whole thing, bouncing my head up and down as I
catch a good rhythm, licking and gently sucking on the nut-

sack, swallowing every last drop of cum. Ummm, damn, makes my pussy ache just thinking about it.

There have been several mad fuckers in my life, starting way back in high school with Ryan. I remember one Thanksgiving, he invited me over his parents' house for dinner. After dinner was over, everyone except the two of us went downstairs to the family room to watch a football game.

Ryan and I were supposed to be cleaning off the table and washing the dishes, but we got sidetracked. Ryan took me off guard by forcing me up onto the dining room table and sitting in the chair between my legs. He pushed my panties to the side and starting fucking me with a roasted turkey leg. After he fucked me with it, he ate it down to the bone.

Ordinarily, the notion of being screwed with a greasy-ass turkey leg would be unappealing to me, but the fact his family was just a split-level away cheering for their respective football teams to win turned my ass on. That was the first sign I was kind of out there.

Then I started a scrapbook in high school where I kept everything from nude photos of myself and some of my menz to a male pubic hair collection. I even had a collection of used condoms with the guys' names written beside them in the book. My friends thought I was a true freak, and they were right.

There were other signs as well, omens so to speak, of what I would be like as I got older. I used to wear teddies under jackets to school with no shirt and flash the boys. My sex education teacher made me go to the principal's office for bringing a small vial of Ryan's sperm to class as a visual aid for my project on the reproductive system.

I was so desperate to go to a sold-out Prince concert one time that I bet these two guys I could sit on their dicks without making a noise in exchange for a pair of tickets. I couldn't sit on their dicks without making that dick-slapping-against-the-pussy-walls noise, but I fucked them both big-time and they gave up the tickets anyway.

Yeah, I was a bit out there in high school, but that's what growing up is all about. My senior year in high school was the year I discovered watching others having sex was just as big, if not bigger, a turn-on as doing the nasty myself. I'm quite the voyeur.

Camcorders were not popular back in the day. When I couldn't actually witness the act, I would ask my gurls to audio-tape their sexual escapades for me so I could cop a listen. My gurls were wild also, but nowhere near as off da hook as me.

Four of us had a female singing group. We called ourselves Rough, Ready, Sexy, and Steady. We used to prance around in my gurl Winnie's living room after school in lingerie, singing everything from Teena Marie to Vanity 6.

When I got to college, my sexual rebellion really took off. Freshman year, I joined the sweetheart court for one of the fraternities on campus. Once again, another year brought with it yet another revelation. My freshman year, I discovered I like trains, and I don't mean Amtrak. The only thing better than one good dick is ten good dicks. The more the merrier!

I used to have men wait in my gurl Cherise's dorm room, down the hall from mine until it was their turn. One day I had so many men waiting to hit this, some had to wait out in the hall. Hell, I even had my manager from the fast-food restaurant, a married man, up in that bitch. It's all good, though. Often times, married dick is the best dick of all.

Don't turn your nose up at me because I fuck other women's husbands. I never took vows with and promised to love, honor, and respect no damn body. I can tell you this much. I'm the woman your mother warned you about. Don't let me in your house, because if he's fine, I *will* take your man. If I borrow a pair of shoes, your best bet is to make me throw them bad boys out the window of my car at 50 mph, 'cause if you let me in, I'm leaving with more than some 9 West pumps. And don't let your man have some of that turn-your-ass-out-Alabama-black-snake-make-a-pussy-scream-out-his-daddy's-name-dick. Forget about it! I'm going to fuck his ass every day, married or not. Well, at least I'm honest. Most women will just go behind your back and do it. I'm telling you my plans straight up.

Am I a freak? Hell, yeah! Do I care what you think about me? Hell, no! You can kiss my black ass. As long as there's a breath in my body and I can spread my legs, I'm gonna get some dick.

My favorite mad fucker of all time was Sutton. Sutton was this dude I met at the house party of all mutha-fuckin' house parties. A friend of mine, Faye, was house-sitting for a wealthy couple in the upper-crust part of town. The house was the bomb. It had eight bedrooms, a circular living room, and a full staff of servants. It also had both indoor and outdoor swimming pools.

There were a good hundred people at the bash Faye threw, the food was slamming, and the bars were stocked with enough liquor to fuck everyone up. I had on a black hoochie dress covering up my black thong bikini. Yes, I did say hoochie dress. *Hoochie* happens to be my middle name.

Anyway, I was in the basement level, chillin' with some of the peeps around the indoor pool. The pool had a water-level brick bar going along one entire side of it. There was also a sitting area with a leather sectional sofa and bearskin rug in front of a huge fireplace with a roaring fire.

I was sitting on the sofa, tore the hell up, listening to the kicking-ass music coming from the speaker system wired into the walls. Some girl was trying to talk me into letting her eat me out, and to be honest, I was about ready to take a walk on the wild side. I hear a woman can eat pussy just as good, if not better, than a man. Sutton walked up behind us and eaves- dropped on our conversation.

He stated his objection. "Ladies, no need for all that. It would be my pleasure to devour both of you!"

"That's what I'm talking about!" I was quick to reply because he was definitely my type of I-don't-give-a-flying- fuck-what-you-think man. "I get to go first, though. Bet?"

The other girl got mad. Apparently, she was strictly about the nana and didn't want a man doing shit for her. She got up and walked away, cussing under her breath. Didn't faze me one bit, since that meant more tongue action for me.

After thoroughly checking Sutton out from the top of his slick, bald head to his bulge to his satiny smooth skin, I was ready to get busy. He was about six feet even, built and F-I-O-N-E. The bald head just did my ass in, though, 'cause that's my weakness. He was wearing a pair of swimming trunks and nothing else, which suited me just fine.

I was ready for him to dig right in and start eating me like the fabulous and delicious feast I am. Instead, he took me off guard. "Let's take a swim!" With that, he left me on the sofa, walked away, and jumped into the pool. The way he squeezed his nose and yelled out before he jumped in reminded me of little boys jumping off a wooden pier at a lake.

I decided what the hell. Following a good dick around is a small price to pay for hellified sex. So I seductively got up from the couch and pulled my dress up over my head as I switched toward the pool. My little show was not only for Sutton's benefit but also for the other men in the room to wit- ness. For a hoochie like me, every move I make is carefully planned out to be sexy, and my entire life is a masquerade.

I continued my little show by sitting on the edge of the

pool with my revealing thong bikini on and splashing the water around with my perfectly manicured toes. I used my hand to fling my hair back over my shoulder, and all eyes were on me 'cause I got it like that.

Sutton was over by the pool bar. I got all the way in the pool and swam across it with the grace of a swan. He was ordering a drink from whoever was standing in as bartender at that moment. The guy behind the bar appeared to be drunker than everyone else put together. Sutton ordered a rum and Coke and asked me what I wanted. I told the truth: "I want you!"

Our eyes met, and he started blushing. I turned toward the bar and asked for a frozen strawberry daiquiri. I made sure to ask for an orange slice and cherry, so I could show off my oral skills, and boy, did I. While Sutton was watching, I took the cherry, arched my neck back, and slowly dipped it into my mouth, sticking my long, pink tongue out to meet it. Then I chewed it seductively, just the way I perfected it when I practiced at home on a regular basis. I followed the cherry up with the big finale, the orange slice. I took the orange slice and put it in my mouth, letting the rind fill out the entire outline of my lips, and then sucked on it and whispered, "Yummy!"

It was time for my pitch. "I wonder if anything on you tastes as yummy." My eyes were locked on his dick like a missile locked on an enemy fighter jet.

He was still blushing. "Well, there's only one way to find out!"

I kept my head down, but flashed my eyes up at his. "Ummm, do tell!"

Sutton took me by the hand. We carried our drinks along the ledge on the wall of the pool until we got to one of the corners. I pressed my back into the contour of the corner, sat my drink on the tiled floor surrounding the pool, and propped my elbows on the edge of the pool so my breasts would look even more enticing than they already are.

He put his hands around my waist after setting his drink down also. "Now, what's all this shit you've been talking, missy? I bet you're all talk and no action, just like all the rest."

I took one of my hands, placed it in the water, and started rubbing his dick through his swimming trunks. "Try me!"

The pool had at least twenty people in it and another dozen or so standing around, who all ended up getting an added treat when Sutton and I turned the house party into a live sex show.

As our kisses began, Sutton picked me up, and I locked my lengthy legs around his waist. He wasted no time untying the skimpy top of my bikini, removing it, and letting it float away on top of the chlorinated water. I leaned my shoulders back as his head moved down to discover the sweetness of my dark, hard pearls. While he was sucking my nipples, I noticed the same girl who had offered to eat me out standing on the other side of the pool, glaring at us. Thank goodness looks can't kill, or I would be one dead hoochie.

After a few moments of him feeding off my breasts, pouring some of the frozen daiquiri on my nipples and sucking it off, I unwrapped my legs and stood down in the pool. I gave Sutton a peck on the lips and then disappeared underneath the water, pulling his swimming trunks down as I went. He kicked his trunks completely off, and they too ended up floating on the water. I took his dick in my mouth underwater and started sucking on it. When I took it the entire way in and started deep-throating it, the echo of the water intensified his moans.

I stayed down there as long as I could without taking in too much water with my nose and then popped my head back up above the surface. I wasn't surprised to see everyone was paying avid attention. More people had joined the crowd from upstairs and the pool outside. I could understand the thrill; I love to watch other people getting their freak on myself.

Sutton told me to turn around, so I did, and put my hands on the edge of the pool while he ripped my thongs off and threw them on the tile. He started caressing my rotund ass cheeks and pressing his dick up in between them. Then he pulled my ass out toward him some more, knelt down a little in the water so the head of his dick could find my pussy lips, and pushed it up in me.

I reached my right hand up over my shoulder and started rubbing his bald head while he fucked me slowly underneath the water. He picked up a steady pace, reached around, and started pinching my nipples. I loved that shit!

People were saying things like, "Damnnnnnnnn!" Look at this shit!" and "You go, girl!" Then there were the sexually repressed and threatened women who were urging their men to leave or go to another room so they couldn't watch. As usual, I didn't give a fuck about any of them, 'cause I was getting mine.

The sensation of being fucked underwater made me cum within minutes, but Sutton kept working his dick in me until my moans grew so loud, I almost scared myself. About ten or fifteen minutes later, he finally came all over my water-covered ass.

We spent the next few minutes caressing each other all over and asking some of the pertinent questions we should've been asking before we fucked, like name, marital status, involvement situation, etc. After getting all that out the way, we realized neither of us had any balls and chains, so it was all good.

Sutton suggested we get out of the pool and go sit by the fire. As we walked over to the seating area, men were giving him high fives and slaps on the back like crazy. Most of the women were staring at me, but my friend Faye, the one giving the party, was laughing her ass off. "Page, you're just too wild, Sis!"

I just looked at her, curled my lips into a smile, and kept on going. Sutton and I sat down on the bearskin rug by the fire, water droplets still covering us both, since we hadn't bothered to dry off with towels. I started rubbing his dick up and down the shaft, hoping it would get hard again.

After some well-spent effort, it did, and he fucked me again on the rug in front of everybody. He took my ass the second time around. People are a trip. They always talk about the things they would never ever do in a million years, but are gung-ho when it comes to watching it.

Sutton and I dated for a few months, but he was in the military and was sent overseas, so that was the end of it. We had the time of our lives while it lasted, and I miss him terribly. However, life goes on, and so did my sexual escapades. You can't keep a sexual diva like myself down.

I only have one piece of advice. If you have a good man with a good heart and, most importantly, a good dick, don't let other women anywhere near him. One of these days, you might fuck around and let a nymph like me in the front door. Scary thought, huh? I'm only one of many, so you better watch your back!

Kissin' Cousins

I've always *loved* sex. The look on a man's face when he cums. The way his entire body shivers and loses control. The way his knees tremble and almost buckle under him. I don't know what it is, but there's something so stimulating about it that just drives me wild.

I don't have time for the love and relationship part, though. My career keeps me much too occupied for that. So whenever I can get a break in my busy work schedule, I check out a couple of the local nightclubs, if that's what you want to call them. I prefer to call them juke joints, 'cause I live right smack in the middle of the country, and the men that frequent the clubs around here are what one might call country bumpkins. There are no ambulances here, just *bamalances*. But hey, it's all good, 'cause the majority of them know how to fuck big-time for small-town homies.

I live in the heart of Alabama, and trust me, it's true what they say about the Alabama black snakes. They love to devour things, if you get my meaning. I've been here for two years, moving into town to work at the local perfume factory as a chemical engineer. I came straight from my college dormitory in Texas after graduation. It's a cool little town. The kids keep out of trouble, they have fish fries, hot dog and chicken dinner sales at the local churches, and three or four little parades a year down Main Street. We even have a little bandstand in the town square. Looks like something out of a Southern romance novel.

One night about a month ago, I was mad bored after getting home from a late night at the plant. I had worked overtime try- ing to get this new line of rosewater together. I got home about 11 P.M. It was too early to crash, and there wasn't a dayum thing on cable. Since it was a Saturday night, I decided to throw on a skimpy little outfit and hit this hole in the wall called Toasties. A local black police officer and his wife own it. They're cool peeps, and the place is all right. You pay a $3.00 cover charge and get all the free beer you can guzzle down. There are a dozen or so tables scattered around the little place. The entire club is no larger than most people's living rooms. Like I said, a juke joint. I'm sure some of you from the country can relate to what I'm saying.

So there I was, chillin' in a black crop top with a little glitter pattern going on and some black skintight shorts. Yeah, I was looking kind of hoochie that night, but don't knock shit you've never tried. Whenever I went there, I saw basically the same dayum people, and I never really fit in. Let's just say you can tell I'm not from around these parts. It wasn't surprising that pickin's were slim as it pertained to possible dick action. Most of the attractive men in the country get snapped up and dragged to the altar by the time they turn twenty-one. But you can luck out and find some good prospects every now and then.

None of my usual dick action was in the house that night, so I knew I would have to improvise. The DJ, who still had a Jheri curl in the Year of Our Lord 1999, was playing "Flashlight," and the pimp daddies were shaking their asses on the floor with their hot mommas. It was a trip. Then I spotted them come in the door. The taller of the two I'd seen in there before a couple of times but never talked to. The shorter one I didn't recognize. They both looked like rough riders, so I targeted my marks. Hell, two dicks are always better than one.

I was standing against the wall over by the ladies' lounge, which is really a bathroom so small that you can barely get your ass in there and close the door. Plus, the door doesn't lock, so you have to maneuver and shit by squatting and holding the door shut at the same time so another woman can't open the door, exposing your ass to the entire joint. When they walked past me, the shorter one winked at me, I smiled at him, and gave him the look. You know, the look where you tell a man how much you want to fuck the shit out of him without having to utter a word. That one look was all it took.

I'm gonna cut to the chase. It turns out that their names are William, the tall one, and Tom, the shorter one, and they're first cousins. Tom, who's about five-foot-nine, light skin with curly brown hair and hazel eyes, was visiting his cousin, William, who's about six-two, caramel, with a nice fade and deep brown bedroom eyes, from out of town. Tom's from Maryland and was down for the weekend.

The three of us sat around the juke joint for an hour or so, chitchatting and dancing whenever the DJ decided to take a walk on the wild side and step into the '90s with some hip-hop. We were all drinking beer out the ass and lost count on how many we guzzled down. It was hot as all hell in there. Peeps really started crowding in there about midnight, until we were cramped in there like a can of sardines.

We were chillin' at the table we had managed to scramble for over in a dark corner, watching and ogling at several couples slow-dragging off some Marvin Gaye. By that time, we were all feeling good and horny. I was sitting between the two of them. Tom leaned over and yelled in my ear. I could hear him over all the music, "Is your pussy sweet?" I looked him in the eyes and asked him, "Do you wanna find out?"

He took me totally off guard by reaching underneath the tablecloth and pulling my legs open. He looked me in the eyes and said, "Yeah, let me find out right now!" He managed to get a finger into the side of my shorts, which wasn't easy considering how tight they were, and fingered my pussy with it. Then he took his finger out and licked it dry. I was in shock, but turned on at the same time. Tom yelled in my ear, "Ummm, you are sweet! But I want to suck on the whole thing! Can I?"

I said, "Sure!" He started fingering me again and sucking on my earlobe. About that time, William, who had been watching the action on the dance floor, turned his attention toward us and noticed what was going on. He saw Tom's hand between my legs and then saw him pull his finger out and suck on it again. William and Tom looked at each other for a brief second. I guess they must've had a secret body language thing going on, because William decided to take his turn without even asking. He fingered me and tasted me too.

This went on for a good ten, fifteen minutes. We were getting out of hand and beginning to draw attention. They were both sucking on my ears, one on each side, and fondling my breasts and my pussy and all that. We decided to bounce up out of there.

I left my car at the juke joint and rode with them, sitting in the backseat with Tom while William drove us back to his apartment. Tom and I tongue-kissed, and he sucked my breasts on the way there. My nipples could have cut diamonds, they were so hard. By the time we pulled up to William's crib, I had Tom's dick down my throat. We stayed in the car until I was finished sucking him off and he came down my throat.

We went inside William's apartment, which is laid out nicely. He has a cozy little one-bedroom about ten minutes from my place. Of course, in a small town, no one and nothing is more than fifteen minutes away. It's just as easy to drive around town and pay your water, electric, phone, and cable bills as it is to mail them.

William took me to bed first. I guess he won that honor by default, since it was his place, and since Tom already got a jump start with the blow job in the car. There was no need for a bunch of words. We all knew the dilly and why I was there. Besides, like I said before, I have no time for the love and relationship part. I prefer to get straight down to fucking. So we did.

William was a pretty good lover, as good as a man can be when he's drunk. When he kissed me, I noticed that his tongue texture was rough, like he'd burned it recently or something. Everything happened kind of fast, going from the kisses to the nipple sucking to him eating me out for a few. He didn't ask me to suck his dick. He opted to go ahead and stick it in. His fucking technique was okay, but he came way too quickly. I was thinking to myself, "Dayum, yet another two-minute brother!"

Tom, on the other hand, was a great lover. William got up and went in the living room while Tom came in the bedroom, already butt-naked, and worked his way backward from his cousin, spreading my legs wide open without uttering a word and proceeding to suck my pussy good, and for a long time, too. Then he feasted on my nipples, one at a time, sucking on them like a newborn baby. He kissed me with the taste of my pussy on his mouth. He was a much better kisser than his cousin. His tongue was soft and thick, and I enjoyed it very much.

Tom did the daddy longstroke on my pussy, grinding his dick into me nice and slow. He lasted much longer. He was far from a two-minute brother, and he hit it from all sides: the front, the back, and with me lying on my side. But, he really tore my pussy up when he fucked me doggy-style. He grabbed my ass cheeks with a kung fu grip and tore it up just the way I like it. That shit makes me cum so hard. Ummmm, if I was gonna ever take on a long-term lover, Tom would've been the one. Unfortunately, I knew that was out the fucking question, since he was only here for the weekend. I decided to just enjoy him while he was here.

Tom and I fucked and sucked on each other for hours. William's sorry ass must've gone out in the living room and passed out on the couch, drunk. He didn't reappear until almost sunrise. Like most men, he woke up with a hard-on and came back for some more.

I decided it was time for the grand finale and told them I wanted them to both fuck me at the same time. Why have two dicks if you're not going to use them both simultaneously? I straddled over William's hips, sat down on his dick, and began to ride it, squeezing my pussy muscles on it as I went up and down on it slowly. Tom started fingering my ass. I could feel a little cum trickling down the inside of my thighs.

He stuck two fingers in my ass and then pushed my back down so my stomach was lying flat on William's chest and I began to kiss him. I could feel the head of Tom's dick rubbing up against my asshole, and then he slowly started to put it in. The anticipation was killing me, I wanted a dick in my ass so bad. I didn't have to wait much longer, 'cause he stuck that bad boy up in my ass and went to work on it. William must have got his second wind, because his dick stayed hard a long time that go-round. I guess most men are like that, the second nut taking longer to achieve than the first. All I can say is that I had both their dicks in me long enough for my cum to be all over the fucking place. That's one thing I love about being a multiorgasmic woman. The cum never ends, and it's so physically gratifying.

We all fell asleep in the bed together for a few hours. After we woke up, we took a shower together and ate each other for breakfast. First they put me on the kitchen table and took turns eating me out, pouring honey and syrup on my pussy and ass. It was wild. I had them both stand in front of me and alternated between sucking their dicks, holding onto both of them at the same time and going from dick to dick until I had a hellava rhythm working. I got bold and decided to put both the heads into my mouth at once. I suckled on them bad boys with a vengeance. My mouth was sore as shit, but it was worth it when they both came in my mouth at the same time.

William took me back to the juke joint to get my car and then asked for my phone number. I told him I'd take his instead, knowing good and dayum well my ass would never call him. Now, if it was Tom's number, that would have been a totally different story. My little escapade ended right there. I know it's inevitable that I'll run into William again at the club or on the street or in a store. That's how small towns are. But, as far as I'm concerned, our friendship, if you can call it that, began and ended that same night. Easy come, easy go!

The Voyeur

Six months, that's how long I watched him. Six whole months. Ever since my sister gave me a telescope for my birthday, I had been watching him from across the avenue. I have been living in my apartment for three years. Until six months ago, I never knew he existed.

We both live on the ninth floor of our respective buildings. I have no idea how long he has lived in his building. That's not surprising, since I don't even know his name. None of that matters much because he and I can never be together. At least, not in a *real* relationship. My husband would never allow it.

Yes, I am married, and have been for five years. Leonard and I moved here to Chicago from New York City when his brokerage firm relocated him. I am a branch manager at a bank. We are very well off, and he takes great care of me, spoils me even.

Which is why the surprise party he gave me for my thirtieth birthday wasn't much of a surprise at all. However, I wasn't expecting my baby sister, Brianna, to fly in from college in Connecticut. I was overwhelmed that Leonard was thoughtful enough to purchase her plane ticket.

So there we were, surrounded by about forty friends, feasting on the buffet prepared by the caterer my husband hired for the event and sipping on champagne out of fine crystal goblets, when my adventure started.

I was opening my presents, and most of them were way too extravagant to ever actually use. I came to a long box wrapped in gold paper with a huge red bow. After reading the card, I realized it was from Brianna. I opened it and was tickled pink to discover a large telescope inside. I gave her a huge embrace and kiss on the cheek. The gift was very special to me, not only because it was from my sister, but because I had wanted a telescope ever since I was a little girl. As I grew older, I felt it was kind of silly to go out and purchase one. I was thrilled and utterly delighted to receive one as a gift.

One of Leonard's associates from the firm set the telescope up by the balcony doors while the party was still going on. Several of us took turns looking up at the stars.

All the guests finally cleared out about two. The caterer and his staff cleaned up and cleared out about half an hour later. Brianna went straight to bed in the guest bedroom, still suffering from a bit of jet lag. Leonard carried me to our bedroom, where he made love to me on crisp white sheets covered with rose petals.

After all the excitement and the lovemaking, I should have been exhausted, but I couldn't fall asleep for anything. I left Leonard fast asleep and decided to finish a bottle of opened Moët and look at the stars some more through my favorite new possession. It was almost five.

I am not sure what drew my attention to his bedroom window. Maybe it was the fact not many people had lights on in their apartments at that time of the morning. However, it was more likely the fact that he was directly across from me, fucking the hell out this sista.

I know I should have pointed the telescope elsewhere or, better yet, gone back in the bedroom and fallen asleep in my husband's arms. I couldn't do that, because I was enthralled by the way he was fucking her.

At first, I couldn't see his face because it was buried in between her breasts. I remember thinking that she had the biggest breasts I had ever seen. She had to be sporting at least a DDD bra, putting my little B-cup tits to shame.

As for him, he had the most scrumptious ass. I zoomed in on his ass so I could see the muscles contracting while he pumped his dick in and out her pussy. My own pussy was so wet. I started fingering it with one hand while I used the other one to keep the telescope steady.

When he came, so did I. It looked like he was having convulsions. I was so turned on. Cum exploded from me, down the center of my thighs, and onto the carpet. I hurried to the hallway bathroom to get a soapy towel to blot it up with. I looked back through the telescope when I was done. They were both lying there, fast asleep.

I was halfway disappointed and then ashamed. What had I done? I felt like such a peeping tom. I went back to bed and fell into a deep sleep, rehashing what I had just witnessed in my dreams.

Ashamed or not, I started watching him every chance I got, day or night. Anytime when Leonard wasn't home. I was totally mesmerized by him, because he was so intriguing. It wasn't that he was so much fine as he was sexy. Sexiness is the way a man carries himself, the energy and charisma that exudes from him. He was about five-foot-nine, light-skinned, with dark brown eyes and wavy black hair. He had a stocky build.

Roscoe, on the other hand, has always been beautiful to me. That is the pet name I gave his dick. It was long, thick and smooth. I watched Roscoe tear up some pussy during those six months. I even watched him tear up some ass from time to time. I watched Roscoe being sucked and caressed and licked all over. That Roscoe had some serious staying power. He never seemed to lie down for long.

Roscoe's owner was heavily dating two women, the one with the big tits and another woman who was more on the petite side, like myself. I watched him parade them in and out of his place on a regular basis. He was a typical bachelor.

My desire for him grew stronger as each day went by, my pussy juices flowing for a man who knew absolutely nothing about me. I withdrew from Leonard sexually a little bit. Not because he did anything wrong, but because I craved for this stranger in the worst way. This continued for six whole months, and then fate intervened.

I stayed late at the bank one night for a meeting. I was about to make the right turn into the underground garage of my building when I saw him approaching from the opposite direction in a black Lexus coupe. He turned into the garage of his building across the street. In that one split second, any fear and apprehension I had disappeared, and body heat took over. I cut across three lanes of traffic, almost getting sideswiped by a truck, and entered into his garage. My front wheels hit the speed bump at the entrance too fast and made me bounce up out of my seat.

After finding a visitor's spot, I jumped out of my car and walked hastily through the parking lot, looking for his car. I found it empty, three rows over. I anxiously walked toward the elevator and got there just as the doors were closing. I thought to myself that it was a sign to take my ass home, but while my mind was telling me no, my pussy was telling me yes. I pushed the button for the elevator and waited for it to come back down, looking up and watching the lights for the individual floors go on and off as if that would make it get there any faster.

When I got off the elevator on the ninth floor, I heard a door shut and headed in the direction from whence it came. I managed to figure out which door was his quite easily. I had watched his ass enough. But once I discovered he lived in apartment #913, I was a nervous wreck all of a sudden. I heard some jazz music come on from inside and leaned against the door, breathing heavy and rubbing my fingertips up and down the cool exterior. I was startled by some voices coming down the hall from the direction of the elevator. I started walking up and down the hallway, pretending like I was trying to locate a particular apartment. There was an older couple carrying their groceries in and chatting about their day.

They went into their apartment about six doors down and across the hall from his. At that point, I knew that I was being totally ridiculous. There I stood, a happily married woman, lurking outside a stranger's apartment. I decided to get the hell out of there, go home, cook dinner, and fuck the living daylights out of my husband. I pushed the button for the elevator, got on it when it arrived, and pushed the button for the garage level. But as the doors were closing, I reached my hand out to block them from shutting completely and stood there dazed and confused.

I wanted him, I really did. It was then or never; in a million years, I wouldn't have the nerve to do that shit again. I marched straight down the hallway to his door and knocked. The music was still on, so I knocked harder, practically banging on the door. I heard the music being turned down and a man's voice saying, "Who's there?"

I froze. That was my first encounter with his voice, and I realized I was really doing something crazy. Yet it was sexy and uninhibited and erotic, and I needed some real excitement in my life.

When he opened the door, he was wearing nothing but a robe, and he was wet. Obviously, he had just gotten out of the shower. I must have been out in the hallway longer than I thought if he had time to take a shower. There I was, standing five-two with a bronze complexion and long, jet-black hair in a white blouse, navy skirt, and navy leather shoes.

Before he could ask who I was or what I wanted, I put my index finger up to his lips and stepped into his living room. I moved my finger down from his lips, over his chin, down his chest and stomach to where his robe was tied and yanked it open, exposing Roscoe.

I dropped to my knees, took his nuts in my hand, and kissed the base of his dick. I couldn't believe I was doing that shit, not me, but it felt so good. I took the head of his dick into my mouth. It was so warm, and I enjoyed taking him to the point of no return. I sucked some mad dick that night and sucked it good. His knees weakened, causing him to fall to the floor. I never missed a beat. I kept holding onto Roscoe and sucking for dear life. He was still on the floor when he exploded into my mouth. I swallowed every drop, lapping up any I may have missed the first go-round off his thighs.

I pushed my skirt up around my waist and straddled his body. I told him to rip my panties off, which he did, leaving only my thigh-high stockings and garter belt on my bottom. I let Roscoe slide into my wet pussy. I began to squeeze my pussy muscles onto him and dug my fingernails into his bare chest. We both moaned loudly, and I came for the first time.

Then I told him I wanted him to hit it from the back. I got up and bent over the back of his sofa. He got up from the floor and lifted my ass up so he could get to the pussy, making my feet dangle about five inches from the floor. There I was, bent over his sofa, letting Roscoe tear my pussy up from behind. He started fingering my ass, and I came again.

I guess he could tell that I was a three-input woman by my reaction to the fingers in my ass. So he did what came naturally, pulled Roscoe out my pussy, and slowly let him enter my ass. He fucked my ass royally and came so hard in it, I was on fire.

As I went to leave, he asked for my name, and I told him, "You don't need to know that!" Then he asked if he would ever see me again, and I didn't respond. I left my ripped panties there in the middle of his living room floor and left.

I went home, packed up my telescope, and put it in the hall closet on the top shelf. When Leonard asked me why I had taken it down, I told him that the thrill was gone, just like a kid who gets sick of a particular video game after a while. The truth of the matter was, I realized what was done was done, and that it could never happen again. So I have moved on with my life, and as far as I am concerned, both he and Roscoe ceased to exist that night.

Sex Me Down Village

When my friends first invited me to go to the village for the weekend, I said, "Hellz, naw!" Frankly, I thought all of them were full of shit and lying their asses off. No way could such a place actually exist, but they held fast to their story, insisting it was real.

They told me they wanted to get my mind off my recent divorce, which became final a few days before the invitation was extended. I never took them seriously until Joan, the sister I had been rooming with since Paul and I separated, showed me our plane tickets to the Caribbean.

Even then, I figured they were pulling my leg about the village and were really taking me to some resort hotel on the beach. I told them I would go. I couldn't turn them down once they bought my ticket and all. I packed some shorts, tees, a couple of tight dresses, and my thong bikini and told my job I wouldn't be in that Friday or the following Monday.

Joan and I met our other two friends, Leslie and Rhonda, at the boarding gate for the plane. I tried my best to get them to tell me where we were *really* going, but they all told the same old story. I had to give them mad props. At least they were consistent.

The plane trip over was great. We were served a nice dinner and watched a great movie about two American tourists who fall in love in London. I didn't ask any other questions on the plane. I knew the truth would have to come out once we landed and headed to our lodging.

I wasn't ready for the truth! The truth was they had all been dead serious from the get-go. We deboarded the plane and got onto a bus that was waiting to pick us up along with about seven other African-Americans who were on the same plane. The sign on the side of the bus was decorated with palm trees and straw huts under an island sun and read "Sex Me Down Village."

I told Joan, Leslie, and Rhonda they were out of their fucking minds. They all laughed and told me I would love it, and it was the bomb. I didn't have any questions on the plane, but I had fifty million of them bad boys while the bus made its way down several long winding dirt roads to the village. I wanted to know what would happen there, had they been there before, was it safe, were we staying there the whole weekend or going someplace else the next day, etc., etc. They told me to calm down and go with the flow. Joan assured me I wouldn't have to do anything that made me feel uncomfortable. I told them I knew that shit already. If I was not down for it, it wasn't happening.

When we arrived at the village, I knew straight off the bat the shit was off da hook. Nothing but a bunch of naked-ass African-Americans on the beach. Some were just chillin', others were swimming, water skiing and riding jet skis. Most of the rest were knocking boots. Yes, knocking boots as in fucking. I couldn't freakin' believe my eyes.

Everyone got off the bus. I was dead last because I was halfway afraid. I followed my friends into the lobby of the plush hotel. The place was nice as hell—it looked like a palace inside. We got checked into our individual bungalows and made plans to meet up in an hour after we all had time to grab a quick shower and settle in.

I put on my thong bikini and sarong and met them in the lobby, where we were led to a conference room. That's where we met our activities director, Julius, who was a straight-up, nasty-ass freak. I almost fell in love with him, though. He was right up my alley.

While he was going over the itinerary for the weekend, I realized I could really get into the whole thing. Having married young, I never got a chance to truly explore my horizons so to speak. If there was ever a place to explore your horizons, Sex Me Down Village was it.

We had dinner that night on the beach, and it was a trip, a cross between a Hawaiian luau and a black family reunion picnic. They had everything from pig pickings to bid whisk and spades games going. There was even a group of naked peeps playing bingo at one of the tables.

Was I naked? *Hellz, naw!* My friends and I all still had our clothes on, except Rhonda. Rhonda is like that every day, though. She will let her ass hang out in the breeze twenty-four/seven if someone is willing to look at it. After the cookout, most people retreated inside to the ballroom. A few stayed outside and fucked. Those of us who were in the ballroom engaged in various planned activities. Julius was there, with his fine ass, coordinating the whole thing.

The night consisted of several contests with gold, bronze, and silver medals going to those who won, placed, and showed. They even handed out programs for the shit! First on the agenda was the dance contest. Both men and women could participate, but there was one catch. You had to take it all off or have it all off already. Six winners were selected, three male and three female. Contestants were judged on the basis of body structure, dancing ability, and the capability of controlling their private parts. The women had to make their breasts take flight and did everything from making them bounce up and down to gyrating so they jiggled around in circles. The men had to make their dicks do the Bankhead Bounce. It was off da hook.

Next came the beer-guzzling contest, with a twist. The women who participated had to guzzle down the beer with a dick in their mouth at the same time. As you might imagine, men were falling over each other trying to volunteer. There were eight contestants. Each one selected the man she wanted to suck off. So there they were, with a beer bottle sticking out one corner of their mouth and a dick sticking out the other. The woman who could intake the greatest amount of beer with a mouth full of dick was declared the winner. The official Sex Me Down Village photographers took snapshots the vacationers could take home as mementos.

Other contests of the evening included the pussy-burger-eating contest, the pussy-shaving contest, and the ass-fucking contest. The ass-fucking contest was the highlight of the evening. The grand prize of a free weekend at the village went to the woman who could take the most inches of dick up her ass and the man who did the honors. My friends and I all sat there in astonishment, not even wanting to take bathroom breaks in case we missed something interesting. Even Rhonda sat her ass down, though. She's out there, but not quite that far.

That didn't stop everyone except me from picking up a man that night and taking him to a bungalow to fuck him. All of us were mad horny, but I alone maintained—only because I couldn't get a crack at Julius. He disappeared before I caught up to him. I went back to my bungalow and got my own shit off.

The next morning, Julius was up bright and early, hosting breakfast for the fuckers. The girls were all sitting up under the men they fucked the night before, so I grabbed a seat at an empty table by a window with an oceanside view. I was sitting there, picking at a grapefruit half topped with an artificial sweetener and watching the waves crash against the shore, when fine-ass Julius approached me.

"How come you look so lonely, baby?"

He looked soooooo good. Tall, dark, handsome, and hung like a mutha-fuckin' bear. I had never seen him naked, but dayum near it. I can spot a big dick, even through clothes. "I'm fine. Just a little tired after last night."

He sat down across from me. "Well, I'm just making sure. It's my duty to make your vacation here as enjoyable as possible, and you're too lovely a lady to be sitting here all alone."

"Thanks for the compliment." Our eyes met, and my left leg started doing the female thing that happens when a sister gets horny. It started moving back and forth, causing a light friction on my pussy. Men are so stupid; most of them never figure out that when a woman is moving a leg from side to side while sitting down, it means she is itching for some dick.

Julius was a native of the Caribbean and looked very exotic, with a deep bronze complexion tanned permanently from the island sun, medium brown huge eyes, and a smile that was so sexy. He had the whitest, cleanest, straightest teeth, and I just wanted to run my tongue over them.

He and I sat there by the window, chatting and getting to know each other, for the rest of the breakfast social hour. Then he invited me to go with him on a glass-bottomed boat in the afternoon. He was taking a group of people out and wanted me to tag along and keep him company. Since it was a free day, meaning there were no set scheduled activities for the entire village like there had been with the cookout and contests the night before, I told him I would be honored.

Besides, my friends were doing their own thing, so it wasn't like they would miss me. I got the feeling they were all dick-whipped, and I wouldn't be seeing much of them for the rest of the weekend anyway. That was fine with me. I would see enough of their asses back in Detroit.

I put on one of my skimpy sundresses and met Julius down by the shore. The boat ride was awesome—the boat ride of all boat rides. The captain described all the various sea life we were seeing through the glass bottom of the boat. It was beautiful and all the coral reefs and tropical fish were so . . . sexually arousing. In fact, the sea life was so arousing and sensual, everyone on the boat ended up butt-naked except for the captain. Yes, even I shed my clothes. I couldn't take five more minutes of not slapping skins with Julius. He fucked me right there in the center of the boat, with my back against the cool glass bottom. It was so wild! Everyone was watching, but like a woman in a delivery room in the throes of labor, I didn't give a flying fuck who was looking at my kitty-kat.

We fucked in the missionary position at first, and then we changed places so I could ride his dick. It was awesome. While I was riding his dick, I could look down at all the fish surrounding his physique. He stuck one finger in my ass, and then the shit was on for real, 'cause that always turns me out.

People started cheering us on and everything. Then most of them got busy themselves, fucking all over the glass bottom and the benches along the wall. Julius finished me off by fucking me from behind, moving a finger in and out my ass with one hand and slapping my ass with the other one. His balls were slamming up against the backside of my thighs, and when he came, he shot it all over my ass cheeks. I came all over the glass bottom of the boat. I know once we all left the boat after it docked, the captain had one hell of a time getting all the cum up. On the other hand, he was probably used to it and kept a heavy-duty mop handy.

I rushed to find the girls and tell them what had happened. Joan was in her bungalow, getting a massage from her weekend lover, some dude from Lexington, Kentucky. Rhonda and Leslie were both deeply involved in various activities on the beach. I told them all what I did on the boat with Julius. Of course, they all called me a liar, like I did them when they first told me about the village. They refused to give credence to my story, saying they knew I would never do anything like that. Joan told me she figured I might get some dick over the weekend, but couldn't digest the idea of me fucking in front of a bunch of people. You see, the problem was I had surpassed the freaky nature of all my friends combined, and their asses were jealous.

Fuck it, though! I showed their asses later that night in the ballroom when I participated in just about every contest they had with Julius as my partner. He was ineligible to win any prizes, but I wouldn't do shit with any of the other men. I won the gold medal in the dick-sucking contest, which went to the women who could make a man cum in her mouth, following it by sucking on a lemon and taking a shot of tequila, in the least amount of time.

I won the silver in the dance contest, only because the sister who beat me out was sporting 40DDDs at the very least. The ass-fucking contest was all mine, though. I knew that from the start. I took Julius's entire dick in and loved every second of it too. I won the free weekend, and Julius won my undying devotion to his dick.

My girls were speechless from seeing me up there, in front of the world, doing such vile and nasty things. They had never pegged me to be a sexual diva, and truth be known, neither did I.

I left the village with a newfound sexual freedom and a big-ass grin on my face. As the bus driver took us back to the airport to get on the plane, instead of me asking a bunch of questions, everyone was asking me how this and that felt, including some people on the bus I didn't even know. Apparently, they'd seen me in action.

Back in Detroit, I recovered from my divorce quickly and have been dating my ass off, doing all the things I missed out on by marrying so young. I have yet to use my voucher for the free weekend, but I fully intend to when I can make the time. When I get there, Julius better be ready, willing, and able. I'm sure he is 'bout it 'bout it. If by chance, some other hoochie is trying to claim him, I'll just have to push the bitch to the curb.

Dream Merchant

*"Love is the mutual gratification of the body and the mind!" but—
—lying here on the couch while this man sucks on my clit like a
pit bull with lockjaw, I am not too sure about all that.*

There are times when I love what I do to make
ends meet, and then there are times, such as this one, when I
would rather be scrubbing floors and cleaning toilets. I'm
sorry though. I was just never cut out to work a nine-to-five,
so I do what I gotta do.

To make a long, drawn-out story short, I'm a dream merchant. Most people say "call girl," but I think dream merchant
sounds more professional. I mean, what I do isn't sleazy. It's
not like I stand on da corner flagging down cars in thigh-high
patent leather boots and daisy dukes. Hell, naw, this sister has
class. In fact, I have more class than most of the women whose
husbands and boyfriends I'm boning.

They come see me when the little uppity misses start
fronting on the dick, taking shortcuts and shit because they're
under the false impression their man is pussy-whipped and

wrapped around their little finger. Chile, please! They need to get real!

Conventional sex is all right, but straight-up nasty, raunchy fucking is where it's at, and most women can't deal with the notion. They think their man will view them as a slut if they do certain things or wonder why they know so much about fucking. It's true that men are the cause of a lot of it. They want the women they marry and settle down with to be virginal and innocent, yet they want a beast in the bedroom. Men don't want to ingest the fact their woman has been with several other men before them, so they make her feel like she better cover up the real sexual goddess within herself. Then they turn around and seek out a freaky-deaky sister like me to do the things for them their woman won't.

Personally, I wish all my sisters could be as uninhibited and as sexually free as I am. They're missing out on so much pleasure. On the other hand, if all women were like me, there would be no demand for my services, so it all pans out. I don't play either, because I always get the benjamins.

In fact, I went to a nightclub once with a girlfriend, and this brother was all up in my face, staring at my tits, darting his eyes back and forth between them like they were a hypnotist's pendulum. I grabbed him by the chin, redirected his eyes to my face, and said, "Read my lips. You want to look at me? That's two drinks!" Guess what? He hooked my girl and me up with drinks for the rest of the night. All I had to do was suck him off real quick in the men's room. While most women would turn their nose up at that, a little dick in the mouth ain't never hurt no one. Dicks are cleaner than mouths, anyway. Read a medical book.

I've read plenty of books, and I'm a certified sexologist, an expert in carnal knowledge, so to speak. My clients love me, and their women hate me but subconsciously wanna be just like me. It's truly a shame I have to pick up the slack for the sisters, but that's the way the cookie crumbles. I know what evil lurks in male minds, and I use it to bring them pleasure. In return, they please me by dishing out the cash. I give them their dreams, and they give me mine. Like I said, I'm a dream merchant.

Take Burton, for example. He prides himself on being a happily married man, and for the most part he is. He's been married for eight years and has three children. His wife stays at home and keeps it clean and cozy. She wipes the snot off the kids' noses and all of that. She really loves him, and he adores her, but . . . she can't fuck AT ALL!

That's where I come in. I fuck him just the way he likes it. I do it all, from head to toe, from front to back, 'cause I got it like that. He pays me $300 a visit, one to two times a week. If you think that sounds steep, fuck you! I work hard for the money. Some people spend their money on crack addiction, and others spend it on pussy addiction. Same difference.

Burton likes several kinky things his wife won't do or let him do. He loves to toss my salad, and I love to have it tossed, with Italian dressing at that. Fat-free dressing, though, since Burton could stand to lose a few inches around the middle. I love the way he has me lie on my stomach and then props some pillows under my stomach so my ass will protrude up in the air. He always starts at the bottom and goes up. It's his favorite routine, I guess. Kind of like the way women get used to wiping from front to back with toilet paper. Anyway, I didn't mean to get off track.

He pours the dressing down the crack of my ass, takes his fingers and rubs the oily substance all over my round ass cheeks, and takes the tip of his tongue and licks it off one cheek at a time. He gives my whole ass a tongue bath, and then he starts working on the crack. He licks it from bottom to top and then works his way back down to the center until he finds, oh my, how many licks does it take to get to the middle of an anus pop?

Let me say this. The man has mad skillz. Skillz on top of mutha-fucking skillz. He's so good at eating ass, they need to name him the Grand Dragon of the Ass-Eating Knights of America. Dayum, my ass is starting to pulsate right now just thinking about it.

Burton also likes to suck toes. He told me he tried to suck his wife's toes once, and she thought it was disgusting. See, that's why she's in the position she's in now; having a husband come home to her with my ass on his breath. Don't frown up at that, because just like all women, my shit don't stank. I love to have my toes sucked. It tickles. Especially when he soaks my feet and then gives me a foot massage first. Then he sucks on each toe and takes his time. Drawing the whole thing into his mouth, suckling on it, and then slowly pulling it out. Dayum, Burton and his oral fixation turn my ass on.

Now, you know any man so gifted with his mouth eats the nana half to death. Chile, you ever seen them shows where big-ass, husky men have pie-eating contests? Well, there you go, 'cause Burton flows just like that. He eats and eats, and he does a good job, unlike this pit bull gnawing on my shit now. Sometimes he likes to put whipped cream, fat-free of course, and honey, which is naturally fat-free, on my pussy before he dines. I bought this baby bib I put on him so he doesn't mess up his clothes. Sometimes when he's sucking my ta-tas, I put a baby bonnet on him too. It's too cute.

Norman is a nice gentleman too. He's not married, but seriously involved with some socialite who thinks her pussy is the bomb but ain't hitting on nothing at all. Now, Norman also has an oral fixation, but the opposite of Burton's. Norman wants me to lick all over him. He loves to have his dick sucked day in and day out, and sucking dick happens to be my specialty.

He likes me to suck his dick with warm tea in my mouth, which can be kind of tricky if you don't know what da hell you are doing. He likes me to suck it with ice in my mouth too. Norman has this thing for extreme temperatures. He even went so far as letting me pour hot candle wax on his dick once. He's crazy, 'cause I would never let a man pour hot candle wax on this here pussy. That shit is just out of the dayum question.

Norman also likes me to bathe him. I run him a hot bath with honey and lemon and kneel beside the tub nude while I wash everything from his hair to his ass. He likes me to do it gently, like he is a newborn baby. I use a soft sponge and caress every inch of him, letting the warm water trickle all over his skin.

Norman's my favorite client because he's the most gentle. He's gentle with me, and I'm gentle with him. I only charge him $100, since I like him. If I were to settle down, and that's a big-ass if, I would want it to be with a man like him. Dayum shame his woman doesn't realize what a good man she has. Sometimes he comes over and I just suck his dick for hours on end. He doesn't even want to stick it in all the time. He just loves to feel my mouth and hands work their magic.

Now, as far as this *thing* between my legs at the moment, I hate him. He's a fucking beast. I tolerate him because he's dumb enough to pay out his ass for my services. His name is Luke, and he's such a fucking idiot. He pays me $500 a pop. Dumb ass! It hurts sometimes when he fucks me because he's so rough. He's into bondage, whips, chains, dildos, butt plugs, all that. But the worst thing about him is the way he bites me.

He told me once that his teeth are so sharp because he used to chew on tin cans when he was a child. I'm telling you, chile, his teeth are razors. He bites me everywhere from my neck to my breasts to my pussy to my ass, and I can't stand it. In fact, after he finishes doing his dirt to me tonight, I'm thinking of telling him never to come by here again. It's just not worth it.

One time he took me to the basement of my building, down by the furnace, and tied me to the ceiling pipes butt-naked. For a few minutes there I was scared shitless after he stuck some sort of metal tube in the furnace until it got red hot and threatened to brand me with it. He put it down after he made me beg him not to do it and then just spanked me with a hand paddle instead. Then he fucked me from behind while I struggled to get my hands loose. That's when I knew this mutha-fucka was crazy.

I guess that's just a part of the business—taking the good with the bad. I know I can't do this forever, since there will come a time men won't want me cause of floppy tits and a sagging ass. I've been making some investments here and there, and hopefully, a few years from now, I can quit and do something legitimate. Still not working a nine-to-five though. Fuck all that!

I will keep my head up, though. There's no danger of developing eyestrain from looking on the bright side of things. So men, bring me your dreams, and I'll make them all come true. If you need some help locating me, let your fingers do the walking. I'm listed in the yellow pages. Just look for the Dream Merchant.

The Pussy Bandit

"I was always told to eat everything on my plate.
Well, the bed is my plate.
Ladies, may I fellate?"
——The Pussy Bandit

No one knows his name or what he really looks like. In the middle of the night, he sneaks into his select choice of the evening's dorm room, ready to strike. He feasts on his meal and then leaves as quietly as he came. He bequeaths a single long-stemmed rose on the pillow of yet another woman who'll never be the same. The small New England university for women I attend is his hunting ground. Every student is his potential prey. No one ever complains, though. In fact, most women want him to stay.

We sit in our dorm rooms at night, giggling and wondering who'll be next. We always make sure our coochies are clean in case it's our turn to pass his taste test. It's like jury duty. You never know when you'll be called. Many of us lie awake at night listening for footsteps in the hall. Some call him crazy, others call him fine. I used to just hope and pray he would hurry up and get to mine.

You see, there are not many eligible black men in our small New England town. Often we find a few good men and have to pass them all around. Lots of women at the school wait their turn, saying, "Dammit! Hurry up and suck on this, you Pussy Bandit!"

I first heard of the Pussy Bandit my freshman year. I thought he was imaginary, an old wives' tale, something for the freshman students to worry about, laugh about, joke about. It wasn't until I was returning home late one evening from a midnight movie that I gave any credence to his existence. My roommate freshman year, Kelly, and I saw a man in black clothing climbing out the second-floor window of an upperclassman dorm. His face was covered with the kind of mask ninjas wear. He jumped from the window and landed on his feet behind a bush. He raced off into night, and to say the least, we were horrified. We rushed to the front door of the small dormitory and banged on it as loud as we could, almost knocking a glass pane out with our fists.

A girl on the bottom floor came out of her room with a short nightie on and opened the door for us. We both started yelling at her simultaneously, telling her what we had just witnessed and running down the hall toward the stairwell. She chased after us as we bounded up the stairs, rushing to the aid of what we just knew was a victim of some sort on the second floor. All sorts of bad things were rushing through my mind. Rape, robbery, even murder.

When we reached the second floor, I couldn't help but notice the upperclassman who had opened the door was very calm while she followed behind us. She appeared to be giggling when she said, "Oh, calm down! It was just him!"

Kelly took the time out to ask her who she meant by *him*

while I walked the hall, looking for the door that matched the window we saw him leap out of. I found it and started banging on it. A woman's voice came through the door saying, "Just a second!"

She opened her door with a smile on her face, saying, "I've just been had by the Pussy Bandit!"

Kelly looked as if she might faint, and I said, "What the fuck?"

The upperclassman that opened the front door for us hollered out, "You go, gurl!" She pushed her way inside the other girl's room, sat down on the dresser, and asked, "Was he all I have heard?"

Kelly and I went in too, sat down on the bed, and didn't utter a word. We wanted to hear what happened as much as the other girl.

The girl, who was named Mandy, started telling the tale of how the Bandit had crept into her window and eaten her out like all hell. She was so graphic and excited about all the details, I could have sworn she looked like she was under a spell.

After that night, I was no more good. Having my pussy eaten is like winning the grand prize on a game show. Just about every other day, I would hear about a girl who was eaten in this dorm or that dorm. I knew my chances were slim, since all freshmen have roommates. I spent the remainder of my freshman year taking long walks in the courtyard late at night, hoping he would change his pattern and suck on me under the moonlight. *Nada!*

I went to summer school just so I could stay around campus, figuring my chances would be better, since most women had gone home. Boy, was I wrong!

He seemed to hit every coochie-coo on campus but mine. Kelly finally got eaten, afterward telling me she told him, "It's about dayum time!"

Sophomore year came and went faster than the speed of

light. I had my own dorm room then, and a lot of sleepless nights. I swore to myself that I wouldn't say a thing if he would just suck on my bones like a chicken wing. Still, *nada!*

I went home that summer 'cause I had a work-study job. I worried about whom was getting eaten while I was gone. Geesh, my clit was so hard.

Junior year rolled around, and on my face there was always a frown. I started trying to calculate how much pussy there could possibly be in such a small town. I knew I would be much more healthy, wealthy, and wise if I could just get his lips between my dayum thighs. Still, *nada!*

It was halfway through my senior year when he finally got to me. It's time for the real deal, so fuck all this poetry!

It was winter break, and most of the students had already left for the holidays. I was one of the few ones left. I decided to stay and complete a term paper one of my English lit professors was sweating me for.

I worked on the paper until about 4 A.M. and finally had to lie down. I couldn't keep my eyes open another second without propping them open with toothpicks.

I had been asleep about thirty minutes when I was awakened by the smell of his cologne. When I opened my eyes, I realized there was a slight breeze coming in from the open window he used to come in. I never locked my window. I didn't want him to waste any time prying it open, if and when he ever got around to me.

I knew who he was right away. He was dressed very similar to the way he was the night Kelly and I saw him years before. He had on black jeans, boots, and a turtleneck. His face and head were covered with a ninja hood and mask. The only things visible were his eyes. They looked so serene and sensitive in the light of my desk lamp, the one and only light on in the room.

I spoke, even though I had sworn to myself I wouldn't. "Are you really the Pussy Bandit?"

He put his finger up to my lips, and I could smell the scent of aftershave lotion on his mocha-colored hand. All he said was "Shhhhhhhhhhhhh!"

He reached into his rear jean pocket and pulled out two black silk scarves and a black blindfold. I eagerly raised my hands above my head so he could tie my wrists to the headboard posts of my bed. All the years I had heard about him made me feel comfortable around him, like an old family friend who showed up unexpectantly for Christmas dinner. Ironically, it was almost something like that.

He covered my eyes with the blindfold, making sure I wouldn't be able to see his face once he removed his mask. He obviously couldn't eat my pussy through the mask, so the blindfold was no surprise. I had heard the details from enough women to know what the deal was.

I could feel his soft hands on my skin as he gently pulled my black lace panties off. The only other thing I had on was a big T-shirt with an athletic brand label on the front.

Before I knew it, he began to dine on his meal. I knew immediately he was all the things I had heard and more. He gave my pussy a tongue-lashing it will never forget. I have had my pussy eaten a lot, mostly by men who had no fucking idea what they were doing.

Years of practice had given the Pussy Bandit the gift of a silver tongue and the ability to lick a woman's belly button from the inside. His tongue was thick, juicy, long, and very, very hot.

He spread my legs open as far as they would go and then dove right in like a professional swimmer diving into an Olympic pool. He got straight tens across the board.

For those people who don't know the award-winning qualities of a good pussy eater, allow me to enlighten you. First of all, a good pussy eater never, and I do mean *never,* gnaws on the clit. It's true that clits do get hard, almost like miniature dicks. However, the clit is extremely sensitive and can't tolerate too much direct stimulation.

So, all you men out there bragging to your buddies about how your woman tries to pull away from you while you're eating the nana because it feels so good need to wake the fuck up and recognize. Half of the time, women are trying to pull away 'cause the shit hurts.

Secondly, the mark of a good pussy eater is the ability to get up on the Big G. You know, the G spot. If they can hit that with some smooth tongue action, all hell will most definitely break loose.

Last, but sure as shit not least, is the ability to interject toys and other things into the total pussy-eating experience. Like I said, the Pussy Bandit got tens all across the board.

He hit my G spot with his tongue, and I thought milk was gonna spurt out my tits, even though I wasn't even producing any milk. Instead, so much cum came shooting out of my pussy that I was alarmed. I thought he had ruptured some hidden cum bank inside my coochie-coo or something.

I was squirming and trying to pull away, but not 'cause it hurt. The experience was nothing short of splendid. It was such a sensual experience, moans escaped my vocal chords and nothing at all came out. I just bit my bottom lip and decided to grin and bear it.

He got up from the bed and I heard him walking toward my private bathroom. I had no idea, nor did I care, what he was doing. I figured he had to take a leak, but he came back without doing that. Instead, I felt him lift my hips up and place a towel underneath my ass. I was mad wet and assumed he didn't want me to soak my bed with cum too much.

As it turned out, he placed the towel there and then poured something cold all over my pussy. I felt something sting me on my clit and then recognized the smell of mint-flavored mouthwash as it hit my nose. He set his sights back on my pussy and began suckling on it again, tracing his tongue through the baby-fine hair on its lips. The mixture of the stinging feeling of the mouthwash and his powerful tongue made me cum again, even harder than the first time.

He loosened the scarves around my wrists, and I was praying he was only doing it to change positions or something. I hoped he would let me sit on his face for a bit, but *nada!*

I yelled out, "Wait! Don't go!" I struggled to finish removing the scarves. I got them loose, jumped up off the bed, ripping the blindfold off in the process, and ran to the window. I got there just in time to see him hit the freshly mowed grass and run off into the night.

I had waited four years for him to pay me a visit, itching for the opportunity to brag about him just like all the others. I didn't, though. I decided to keep the overwhelming experience between the two of us. Years from now, I'll open up my college scrapbook to the page that holds a single wilted red rose—the rose the Pussy Bandit bequeathed on my pillow the night he showed me what a true pussy-eating was all about.

Alpha Phi Fuckem—
The Convention

"Ooops, I'm sorry, Miss!" We both reached for the lettuce tongs on the supermarket salad-bar island at the same time. "Ladies first!"

"No, you go right ahead. I insist." I was checking his ass out, and he was too damn fine.

He smiled at me, and I wanted to take a ride on his black pony. "You sure?"

"Yes, you were here first."

He started getting his iceberg lettuce, and I kept getting my peep on. He was about six-one, 200 pounds of solid muscle with chocolaty smooth skin and was sporting the roundest, firmest butt I had ever seen.

"Can I ask you a question?" He looked at me, probably thinking I was going to ask him the time of day or something normal. He couldn't have been further off base. The convention had snuck the hell up on me, and time was of the essence for me to find a playmate for the upcoming weekend. "Are you married?"

He blushed. "No, I'm not. You?"

"No." We stood there smiling at each other, but there was no salad-fixing going on. "Engaged? Shacking up?"

"No. None of the above."

It was time to go for it. Patricia already had her partner for the weekend, as did all the other sorors in the D.C. chapter. I had been so busy pulling long hours in the courtroom that I hadn't had a chance to go dick hunting. "I see. I was just wondering what you're doing this weekend."

He started blushing even harder. I got the impression he was used to being the hunter and not the hunted. "I'm supposed to go over to one of my boys' houses to watch the fight on pay-per-view, but that's about it."

"You can never tell with those fights. Sometimes they only last a couple of minutes."

We were flirting, no damn doubt about it, but I didn't want a man for a relationship. I had one of those already. However, taking him to the convention was out of the damn question. He knew my name and everything about me, and that's against the rules. The sacred vows of Alpha Phi Fuckem must never be broken. *Never!*

"You're so right about that! The last fight I saw only lasted a few seconds. If you blinked, you missed it."

"Hmmm, I see. Well, the fight might only last a few seconds, but I can ride your dick all night long."

He almost dropped the salad container he was holding onto the floor but caught it as it ricocheted off the edge of the counter. He cleared his throat and gave me the most perplexed look. "Is that right?"

"Damn skippy." I didn't have time for all the bullshit. Either he was going to be the one or he wasn't, so I got straight to the point. "Listen up, boo. It's like this."

He was grinning like a wino that just found a bottle of unopened Mad Dog 20/20 in a garbage can. "Yes?"

"My sorors and I are having our national convention in Atlantic City this weekend, and I was wondering if you're up for a fuckfest?"

"Excuse me?" He started choking. On what, I have no idea. "Did you say fuckfest?"

"Uh-huh. Fuckfest!"

He cleared his throat, wondering how he ended up having such a blessed day. "What sorority are you in? AKA? Delta? Sig—"

"Nope, none of that." I was hoping he wouldn't pass the hell out when I told him the truth. The brother's nerves seemed a bit on edge, but I like them timid sometimes. "The name of my sorority is Alpha Phi Fuckem."

That did his ass in. "Oh, come off it. This is a joke, right?"

"No, not at all." He started looking around as if he thought I was working for *Candid Camera* and trying to play a trick on his ass. "I'm for real. I want you to accompany me to Atlantic City this weekend and knock some boots."

"DAMN!" He had that look they all have—the one they get when they realize that we're not bullshitting and just want some dick carte blanche without the attachments.

"Look, are you down or what?"

"Hold up, baby. You never even told me your name. I'm—"

I put my finger to his lips. "You're my cumdaddy, and you can just call me Soror Ride Dick."

Well, by the time the last crouton hit the top of my blue cheese dressing, it was a done deal. I told my cumdaddy to meet me along with the rest of the crew behind Iverson Mall the next evening at 6 P.M. sharp to get on the bus for Atlantic City. The sorors and I opted not to fly or drive different cars and decided to charter a bus instead. We wanted to get a bit freaky on the way up there, and boy, did we!

The D.C. chapter now has thirty members instead of just twenty-four. It was a real tight squeeze on the bus with all the sorors and their playmates on board, but the more, the merrier. Some sorors sat on laps, with or without the man's dick whipped out and inserted, and Soror Lick 'Em Low, a new inductee who has a thing for sucking on balls, got her freak on in the tiny lavatory of the bus.

The bus driver, Ralph, was the happiest man alive on the way up and almost wrecked, between trying to see what we were doing and glancing at the porno tapes we were playing on the tiny television screens throughout the bus. Soror Voyeur was responsible for providing the videos. She has quite the collection, so it was mad interesting.

We all got fucked up on the way up, and I literally got fucked too. My cumdaddy shed all his inhibitions, flipped my ass over one of the plush seats, and banged me slowly from behind while I sipped on a Bartles & Jaymes. Patricia's playmate was a male stripper she picked up at some thug club. I could tell she was going to have problems with his ass all weekend. He was smoking so much weed that he had trouble keeping a hard-on while she was sucking his dick on the bus.

When we got to Atlantic City about 10 P.M., most of the other chapters had already arrived and settled in at the casino hotel. NYC, L.A., and Atlanta were strongly representing. Those three chapters seem to grow by leaps and bounds every year and have at least fifty members each. Detroit is up to about fifteen members now, and Chicago has about twenty. The Miami sorors had yet to arrive, but their plane was due in before midnight. They are about a dozen members strong.

The biggest surprise came out of left-fucking-field when we

met the members of our new chapters from Nashville, Tennessee, and Atlantic City. The two chapters worked together to plan and host this year's convention, and to say the new sorors are a bit out there is a serious understatement. They're fucking wild, and you know that's deep if I am saying it.

They had all the room keys already, so none of the men could get our real names from the registration desk. In fact, we were all registered under aliases anyway, so it wouldn't have mattered much. I still had to admire the lengths of discretion the new sorors went to. What was even more appreciated were the toys they strategically placed in all the hotel rooms. Instead of breath mints on the pillows, there were dildos, edible panties, and a pair of shiny new handcuffs on each bed to enhance the weekend's activities.

In the bathrooms, along with the shampoo, soap, and toothpaste provided by the hotel, were baskets full of scented body oils, liquid latex, butt plugs, and anal beads. They also had a bottle of champagne chillin' in every soror's room. It was the bomb, and I knew the weekend would be the shit.

The main activity of the night didn't start until 1 A.M., so cumdaddy and I made good use of time by taking a hot shower and doing the flying 69 in the warm stream of water. He turned me upside down and ate out my pussy while I sucked his dick. The water hitting up against my clit and his tongue action made me cum at least three times before we hit the bed and destroyed all the effort the hotel maid had put into making it up neatly. For about an hour, I did what I do all too well and rode the hell out his dick.

We were exhausted but woke up a little when we took another quick shower to get dressed for casino night. At 1 A.M., the happenings began in a private casino of the hotel. As soon as everyone hit the door, all the clothes had to come off. We enjoyed a night of playing blackjack, poker, roulette, and craps in the nude. By prearrangement with the hotel, all the cocktail waitresses and dealers were nude too—just a big-ass room full of butt-naked people, and it was all good.

Instead of cashing in chips for money, you had to cash in your chips for sexual favors from the person of your choice. That's when the shit got real interesting, 'cause the sorority ended up having the biggest orgy in its history that night. People were fucking anywhere they could find a spot. I fucked three men at the same time on top of the green velvet cloth on a craps table while my cumdaddy fed his dick to two of the new sorors from the Nashville chapter. They were all on him, and I thought they were about to come to blows over it, because they were both being so damn greedy with the dick. Can't say I blame them, though, 'cause the brotha did have some good-ass dick.

I enjoyed myself immensely. A dick in the hand, one in the mouth, and one in my pussy beats two in the bush any damn day. By the time 6 A.M. rolled around and the sunlight began to stream in through the skylights of the private casino, we were all ass-out, dicks and tits and ass everywhere.

We were served brunch in our respective hotel rooms about noon and then set out at 3 P.M. to head to a private spa. There, the hosting sorors had us all pampered with full-body massages, and different people enjoyed sexing each other down in various hot tubs, saunas, and massage rooms.

Cumdaddy and I had a great time making love on a massage table with the ceiling fan going full speed overhead. Both of our bodies were still silky smooth and tingling from the body masks we were given. I'm sure you can probably guess who was on top. They don't call me Soror Ride Dick for nothing.

At 8 P.M. Saturday evening, we got down to business, and it was the only time any of us were fully clothed the whole weekend. We had our banquet in a ballroom at the hotel, all dressed in formal wear. The men all had on tuxedos, and the sorors were all decked out in the latest fashions. I wore a skintight black sleeveless gown with a split going all the way up the back and no panties. What can I say? I have this thing about walking around coochie-free, and so I did. In fact, my cumdaddy and I played a little game to see how tight my pussy muscles really were and how much control I have over them. He put a pair of Ben Wa balls in my pussy before we left the room and bet me I couldn't walk around all night with no panties on and keep them from falling out.

The keynote speaker was from the old school of sorors. We call her Soror Love Lace because she wears something made of lace 90 percent of the time. She's actually an investment banker, and she went over the investment strategies and agenda for the national chapter's combined assets. The evening was informative and enlightening as we dined on lobsters, scalloped potatoes, and string beans almondine.

After the banquet was over, most of the sorors went clubbing at another hotel a little way down the boardwalk. Since I won the bet and kept the balls in place all night, I collected on it and made cumdaddy suck on my pussy under the moonlight on the beach for a good hour before we joined the others.

We turned that mother-fucking club out too. They were expecting us to be stuck-up and snobbish because of the way we were dressed. Instead, we ended up scaring half of the sexually repressed customers away and putting on one hell of a show for the ones who stuck it out. The Nashville sorors got up on the stage and started freaking all over one another and ripping each other's expensive gowns off while the rest of us cheered them on.

After they were all in their birthday suits, they had a dance competition and a sexy body contest. The winner was awarded a twelve-inch dildo in a black velvet box, and the runner-up received a gold-plated vibrator with an anal sleeve. The sorors from Nashville are my type of peeps. I was digging it.

We finished the evening off by having a Soul Train line in the nude. There were mad dicks doing the Bankhead Bounce coming down the aisle, and I was admiring every one of them. We had a beautiful dick contest, and I was proud when my cumdaddy took the honors and received a golden dick trophy. I bet he's still showing that shit off to his friends now.

We all went back to our rooms about 2 A.M. and did whatever was clever. I spent the last few hours with my cumdaddy, getting to know him better in three ways: mentally, physically, and orally. It's a damn shame we can never keep any of the bomb-ass dick we run across. Sometimes I wish the rules were different, but a vow is a vow is a vow, and I will never break it.

The majority of us were so fucked out that we slept most of the way home on the bus. When we got back to Iverson Mall, I almost got emotional when it was time to say goodbye. Patricia had to practically drag my ass to the car. I maintained my composure in the end, waved farewell to cumdaddy, and went home to my man. When he asked me how the antitrust law seminar in Richmond, Virginia, went that weekend, I simply replied, "Awesome!" It damn sure was. Soror Ride Dick, over and out!

A Personal Reflection from Zane

"Nothing could have prepared me for the outpouring of support and appreciation I have received from my loyal readership. I can only say that I am glad that people find my work interesting and that it can keep their attention. It feels great to have men tell me that my stories are the first thing they have read in years other than professional manuals and sports magazines. It feels great to have women tell me that they are glad someone else in this world has the same thoughts, wants, and desires that they do. As far as I am concerned, the time for the female sexual revolution has arrived. We have embarked on the new millennium, and the days of women fighting for the right to vote and the right to work have come and gone. Women make more money, own more businesses, and are more independent than we used to be. Shouldn't we be entitled to sexual freedom as well? If we can free our bodies, then we can also free our minds!"